Dragon's Mark

Chronicles of Alcabaza Book 1

Morgan Lee Clasper

Published by Morgan Lee Clasper. For any inquiries, please contact:

morgan@morganclasperauthor.com

or visit: https://www.morganclasperauthor.com/

Cover Design by Fabrice Bertolotto

Illustrations by Marina Baskakova

Edited by Darcy Werkman at The Bearded Book Editor

Proofread by Darcy Werkman

ISBN: 978-0-473-58348-4

Books also by Morgan Lee Clasper

The Frostwing Quadrilogy

Frostwing: Dragonbond

Frostwing: Firebreath

Frostwing: Permafrost

Frostwing: Reaver's War

The Chronicles of Alcabaza

Dragon's Mark

Raider's Oath

Nomad's Ruin

Alchemist's Order

Contents

Isiah

ISIAH STUMBLED ON THE LOOSE SCREE. The blaring sun beat against his shoulders, and a dry wind stirred his clothes and filled his nostrils with dust. His throat, dry and scratchy, felt swollen shut. He raised a hand to his forehead and surveyed the horizon.

Rooftops. Amid a sea of dusty brown dirt and copper-red rocks, he almost missed the squat buildings with their flat roofs and mudbrick walls.

Willing his aching limbs to move faster, he hastened toward them. A handful of scraggly trees stooped around the buildings. Isiah hoped they weren't another mirage.

His clothes clung to his skin, slick with sweat. He knew that somewhere far behind him, a series of hoofprints led back the way he had come. *I should have known they'd rob me*, he thought. Isiah ignored the pounding in his skull. He pushed a mop of dark hair out of his eyes and felt the hard lump that had formed on his head. The guides had promised to take him into the Badlands, but they'd stolen his gear and left him for dead.

The houses grew closer—painfully slow. Shielding his eyes, Isiah looked at the twin suns far above. One shone a brilliant blue-white, hurting his eyes to look at. Its smaller sibling hung off to the side, burning with a dim, smouldering red.

Isiah adjusted his clothes. Thin layers of linen and cloth were supposed to draw the heat and moisture away from his body—but beneath the midday sun, nothing could help him. He peeled the material away from his shoulders, wincing at the pain in his skin. Clusters of angry red blisters seemed to stare back at him.

Redoubling his pace, Isiah staggered the last few hundred feet and made it to the houses. They huddled around a shallow pool of brownish water, giving life to trees and a mass of thorny bushes. As he arrived, talking met his ears.

A handful of people stood around the houses, alongside mules and pack animals laden with supplies. Long, colourful robes masked their features and protected them from the searing heat. An old woman, stooped with age, sat on a doorstep and haggled with them. Some of the people turned as Isiah approached.

"What have we got here?" one asked. A short beard poked out from his hood. "You look half-dead, boy. Didn't anyone ever tell you about travelling alone?"

Some of the others snickered. Isiah forced his parched mouth to speak. "Do you have water?"

The man pulled a waterskin from the side of his mule and tossed it to him. "Normally I'd charge you. Charity doesn't get you far out this way."

Isiah caught it with fumbling hands and raised it to his lips. The lukewarm water took the pain out of his dried throat. His burning skin urged him to pour the water over his shoulders, but he forced the thought away. *Not here.*

As Isiah finished the waterskin, the others went back to haggling. They exchanged sacks of supplies, passing gold coins between dust-coated hands.

Isiah reached down and slipped his boot off, revealing a pouch of coins. He sighed. His former guides hadn't taken everything. As the strength returned to his limbs, he hobbled over to the rest of the group. "How much for the waterskin?" he asked.

The man named his price, and Isiah handed over a couple of coins. They shone with the insignia of a crown—a stark contrast to the hammer-beaten disks the merchants in front of him used.

"Anything else?" the merchant asked.

Isiah ran his eyes over the mule. A couple of larger creatures stood further off, their hulking shoulders adorned with leathery scales. Large humps on their backs formed saddles and places to hang harnesses. They grazed on the bushes with beaked mouths.

"Not for sale." The merchant's voice distracted Isiah.

"Oh—" he stammered. "I was just looking, is all." He spotted a cloak with a hood draped over the man's mule. "But I'll take that too." He tossed a couple of coins at the merchant and the man handed him the cloak.

The old woman caught Isiah's attention. She leaned against the wall of her house, waving a walking stick in the direction of the merchants.

"You know we don't get much trade in these parts," she scolded. "You're trying to take advantage of us with these prices."

"It's the same for everyone, lady," one of the merchants replied. "It's not our fault you live in such a forsaken part of the border. We can barely take this route without losing any mules."

The woman slumped onto the step, muttering. Faded garments covered her shoulders, their edges caked with dust. Isiah clutched his money pouch.

He approached the woman. She eyed him suspiciously. "What are you trying to sell me now?"

"Nothing," Isiah replied. He cracked open the pouch and pulled out a few coins. "It sounded like you needed help."

The woman's gaze went from him to the money. She darted out a hand and grabbed it, as if afraid he'd change his mind at any moment. A faint smile tugged at the corner of her mouth.

"Take this," she said. She produced a small knife. "I don't want no handouts." She pressed the hilt into Isiah's hands. "My son used to have it, before he disappeared in the Badlands."

The worn wooden grip fit neatly in Isiah's palm. A faded blade gleamed in the sunlight, with an amber-coloured gemstone embedded in its hilt. Isiah tucked it into his belt.

"Awful lot of coins from Paradon you've got there," one of the merchants cut in. He narrowed his eyes. "What were you doing wandering around on your own earlier?"

"I got lost," Isiah said quickly. He wiped his sweaty palms. "My group's probably looking for me now." He took a step back.

"So close to the border?" the merchant cocked his head. "It's not like a nomad to come this way." He lowered his voice. "But it *is* like an outsider."

Isiah tucked his money pouch away. "What's wrong with having some coins from Paradon?"

The merchant raised his hands. "Nothing, nothing . . . as long as you're not one of them, that is. We get plenty of their kind crossing over and meddling where they aren't welcome."

Isiah's skin itched, tugging at his mind. The salt in his sweat caused his blisters to sting. "Of course not." He put on his new cloak and turned to leave. "Thanks for the water. I've got to go and find my friends now."

Before the merchants could question him further, he hurried away, losing himself in the mass of jagged rocks and spires that littered the terrain. He was sure he could feel their eyes on his back as he went. Isiah pulled up his hood to shield himself from the sun's glare.

Keep it together, he scolded himself. *You've come too far to give up now.*

* * *

Months prior . . .

Isiah darted through the palace hall, keeping to the shadows of the giant pillars that supported the arched ceiling. To his right, towering windows gave a sprawling view of the gardens and courtyards below.

It's not fair, he thought. Nobody was telling him what was going on. His father had been locked away in his chamber for weeks. *He's sick*, Ward had told him, but the man had refused to say anything more on the matter. And nobody had told him when his Ceremony was going to be—

Isiah jumped as a shape flashed past outside. The blast of a dragon's wings swirled through open windows and made the curtains flutter. He ran to the window and pressed his forehead against it. He made out a shining, serpentine form gliding away, its leathery wings suspending it on the air currents. If Isiah squinted, he could make out the armour-clad soldier atop the beast's shoulders.

Beyond the palace windows, the city of Paradon formed a maze of streets and jumbled buildings, bordered by lush green forest and farmland. A few more dragons, belonging to the palace guards, wheeled above.

Tearing his attention away from them, Isiah hurried along the hall. He reached the door at the far end and pressed his ear against it. Voices wafted through. Isiah made out the voice of Ward, his dragon-trainer.

"I'm warning you. He's too young. Nobles aren't supposed to face a dragon until they've reached their eighteenth year."

"His father insisted," another voice replied. Isiah recognized it as one of the other nobles. "And the nobles won't have it any other way. His father doesn't know if he'll make it to Isiah's eighteenth year, and he'll be damned if he misses such an important event."

"And I'm sure he'll be damned if his only son is cast out of Paradon," Ward replied. His voice climbed in volume for a second, before he calmed himself. "You know as well as I do what fate awaits people who fail the Ceremony."

Isiah's pulse quickened. He tried to make sense of what the men were saying. He crouched and pressed his eye against the keyhole. The noble stood out of view, but Ward paced back and forth. A coat of armour, the same shimmering blue-purple as dragon scales, hung from his broad shoulders. A necklace of dragon teeth, shed by growing hatchlings, adorned his neck.

"What if we're rushing into things too quickly? Isiah has a way with the hatchlings, but facing a full-grown dragon is no easy feat."

"If he's incapable of bonding, then why do you go to such lengths to train him?" the noble replied. "The nobility *must* be able to bond. If he can't, what will the commoners think?"

Ward's pacing grew faster. "It's not a matter of *if* he can do it, it's a matter of *when*."

"His father made it perfectly clear when that will be," the noble snapped. "Remember your place, dragon-trainer. If Isiah isn't ready for the Ceremony, perhaps you should spend more time training him."

"Don't lecture me," Ward shot back. "Perhaps his father would recover, if you weren't treating him like he had the plague. You claim you have the courage to bond with dragons, yet you're terrified of your own countrymen."

The noble huffed. Footsteps sounded as he marched away. Ward shook his head and walked to the door. Isiah backed away and searched for somewhere to hide.

The door swung open and Ward spotted him. He frowned. "What are you doing here?"

"I—" Isiah started.

Ward cracked a smile. "I know eavesdropping when I see it," he said. "But you have a right to know. The nobles are acting too paranoid."

"Will my father be alright?" Isiah asked. He suppressed the unease gnawing at his gut.

"He'll be fine," Ward replied. He smiled, but his eyes showed no emotion. "I saw him myself this morning. He'll be back on his feet in no time."

They stood in awkward silence for a moment. Isiah's gaze drifted to the window, where he'd seen the dragon fly past. "Was it true?" he asked. "What you were saying about the Ceremony?"

"I was worried they're rushing it." Ward put a hand on Isiah's shoulder. "That's all. You'll do fine."

"But what if it doesn't work?" Isiah said. He wrung his hands. He'd seen what happened when dragons rejected people in the Ceremony. "What if you have to banish me?"

"We won't." Ward marched along the hall. Isiah hurried after him. "You've got a way with the hatchlings. The big ones are no different. You'll go into that Ceremony, face that dragon, and show it who's boss."

The nausea in Isiah's gut failed to subside. He'd only ever seen the adult dragons from afar, when they were already tamed. The Royal Guards used them to protect Paradon from the Raiders and thieves in the Badlands.

"Bonding is a symbol of nobility," Ward continued. "Right from the days our ancestors first tamed the dragons. It's in our blood." Ward paused and turned to face him. "Once you show that dragon what you're made of, you'll be next in line for your father's place among the nobles."

Outside, wingbeats sounded as another Royal Guard departed on his dragon. The iridescent creature cut through the air, its tail whipping behind it as its massive wings lifted it into the heavens. The leathery membranes ran down its sides, snaking to the tip of its tail and flaring out over its hind legs like a cloak.

Isiah nodded to himself. "You're right." He willed himself to believe it.

"That's the spirit." Ward clapped Isiah on the back. "I was your age when I bonded with a dragon myself. If you follow my advice, you won't have a thing to worry about."

Isiah turned away from the window and followed Ward deeper into the palace. As he went, he tried to silence the nagging voice inside his head. If he failed, he'd be Marked.

And once Marked, the dragons would stop at nothing to hunt him down.

Badlands

ISIAH TOOK ANOTHER SWIG FROM HIS WATERSKIN. The last few drops swished about inside. He lowered his hood and dumped the last of it on his neck. Insects buzzed in the branches of skeletal trees nearby, their deafening chorus feeling alien compared to the birdsong he was used to.

Ahead, a mass of spires and buttes towered into the sky, rising above the surrounding boulders like an army of soldiers. Isiah hastened toward them and let their cool shadows wash away the Badland heat.

Loose dirt and sand piled around the base of rock formations. Bushes grew in the shade they afforded, providing homes to small lizards. Isiah pulled his collar over his nose to keep the dust off his face. It rode on the breaths of wind that crept across the rocky landscape, stinging his eyes and getting into his clothes.

Isiah tried to take his mind off his aching body by organizing his thoughts. His guides had deserted him, but he had enough supplies to help him survive for a few days. His new cloak helped protect him from the worst of the twin suns' glare, letting the inner layers of clothing draw the moisture from his itching skin.

He resisted the urge to scratch it. He knew it would only make the sensation worse. Isiah scoured the landscape for another pool, not caring how murky or unclean it might be.

A faint trickle echoed from somewhere ahead. He hurried toward the source and his eyes came to rest on a tiny stream, bounding down the rocks and settling in a depression in the land. Isiah crouched and refilled his waterskin, then pulled off his cloak. He winced as the material peeled away from his blisters.

Cupping the water in his hands, he splashed it over his shoulders. It helped sap some of the heat and redness away. Isiah prodded the area tentatively. Some of his skin was lumpy, like the melted wax of a candle.

That's why I'm here. Isiah finished washing his wounds, then pulled his cloak back on. The material still clung to his skin—but at least this time it was cool. He staggered to his feet and pressed deeper into the arid landscape.

He lost himself in the rocky maze. Hoodoos sat as lumpy piles of stacked boulders, overshadowed by tall cliffs and crumbling spires that were riddled with hidden caves and hollows. Somewhere distant, a hawk gave off a lone cry that echoed above the eerie silence.

Isiah put his head down and focused on placing one foot in front of another. He kept his ears pricked for any sign of life. Away from the sun, his damp clothes chilled his injured skin. He knew that come nightfall, the temperature would drop to near-freezing in the open.

I've got to find people, he thought. There were settlements deeper in the Badlands. He could find a place to stay when he got there—then he could begin looking for his cure.

11

Spires loomed overhead like the pillars in the palace back home. They seemed to uphold the vaulted heavens, chiselled by the elements into wavy layered patterns of orange and yellow. Isiah reached out and ran his fingers over the surface. The sun scorched their pinnacles far above, but the rock in the gulley felt cool to the touch.

The hawk called again—panicked. Isiah paused. A rush of wing-beats sounded above. Far too big to be a bird.

Isiah dropped to the ground as a shape flashed overhead. Icy fear flared in his chest. He scanned the gulley for someplace to hide. Cliffs penned him in, sheer and unscalable, but a cluster of boulders lay nearby where they had fallen from a cliff face and shattered into chunks. He made a beeline for it.

The wingbeats grew louder. The earth seemed to tremble as something big landed above. Isiah already knew what it was.

He reached the boulders and threw himself behind them. A startled lizard hissed a warning. He ignored it and peered over the boulder's rim.

A long, frilled tail hung from a ledge. It swished lazily back and forth, the rest of the creature concealed inside the cave it had landed in. Dust rained from the spire as it took a step, making the ground shudder and rocks clatter to the earth.

Isiah quelled his pounding heartbeat and abandoned the boulder, darting to another rock formation. He ran doubled over, hoping his clothes would camouflage him against the reddish-brown rock.

With every step, he kept his eyes fixed on the cave mouth. If it turned around . . .

His skin began to burn. A familiar pain, like red-hot needles piercing his skin, crept over him. Isiah gritted his teeth and kept moving. He could almost feel it calling out, betraying his presence.

Isiah froze as the dragon's head appeared at the mouth of the cave.

He pressed himself against the rock wall, hoping it wouldn't notice him against the rocky backdrop. A hiss, like escaping steam, made his skin crawl. The dragon swivelled its head and its eyes came to rest on him.

Isiah bolted. An ear-splitting roar echoed behind him. He sprinted along the passageway, his cloak flapping madly behind him. He risked a glance over his shoulder.

The dragon unfurled its massive wings and launched itself into the gulley. The tips of its wingspan brushed against the cliffs on either side. Its head lowered and its beady eyes fixed on him. An orange light brewed deep inside its chest.

Isiah reached the end of the gulley. He took a sharp turn into a mass of hoodoos as an eruption of liquid fire struck where he had been seconds earlier. He choked back a scream and scrambled through a patch of bushes.

A stinging pain gripped his legs as the thorns snagged his clothes. Isiah tore himself free and kept running. The dragon whipped past, making dust swirl in the air, before tilting its wings and circling around. Fire brewed inside its chest a second time.

Isiah stumbled. His heart flew into his throat as he hit the ground and a shockwave coursed through his knees. The dragon grew closer by the second, bearing down on him. Isiah shoved his back against a hoodoo as a fireball hit the ground.

The rock behind him cracked and hissed under the heat. Flames licked around it, threatening to catch his clothes alight. Isiah squeezed his eyes shut as the dragon blasted overhead. It climbed in altitude to avoid a cliff, then pivoted in mid-air.

Isiah forced himself to his feet and kept moving, sliding over boulders and shoving his way through bushes. A few acacia trees stole the dragon from view for a second, but he knew they would offer him no protection. His skin prickled, calling out his location. Isiah scrambled aside as the dragon landed.

Branches snapped and groaned as trees collapsed. Isiah spotted a narrow crevice caught between two cliffs, forming a tunnel. He made a dash for it. The dragon's cries stabbed at his eardrums. He crawled into the crevice just as its jaws closed around empty air.

Dust and sand billowed in Isiah's face, filling his nostrils and stinging his eyes. Sharp rocks scratched his palms and pressed into his already aching knees as he scrambled forward. The tunnel soon became tall enough to stand in. He limped to safety as a stream of fire enveloped the entrance. The dragon's frustrated roars echoed behind him.

Isiah kept his eyes focused on the tunnel exit ahead. It grew wider as the rocks parted to reveal a strip of daylight snaking along the ceiling. He reached the other side and collapsed against a bank of loose earth, lungs heaving. Dust filled his hair. Thorns filled his cloak. He winced at the trickle of blood oozing from his palm.

Isiah let his head fall back and closed his eyes. The burning in his skin subsided as the dragon lost interest and flew away. After waiting a minute to make sure it wouldn't return, he climbed out of the tunnel.

Then something leapt on him from behind.

Nomads

ISIAH HIT THE GROUND. A STAB OF PAIN went through his ribs as the air escaped him. He squirmed and thrashed against the weight that pinned him.

"I've got him!" a voice yelled.

"Let's get a look at him then," another ordered.

Hands grabbed Isiah's arms. The weight on his body lifted and they dragged Isiah to his feet. He sucked in a wheezing breath and squinted against the sunlight at his captors.

"False alarm," one of them said. "He's no soldier."

The hands released him and Isiah stumbled away. A group of men and women, clad in long robes, watched him from a ledge above the tunnel.

"What do you think you're doing, wandering around on your own?" one of them said. His hair, bleached white-blonde from the sun, contrasted his tanned skin. "Keep doing that and you'll be a dead man."

Isiah calmed his heaving breaths. "I—I thought there weren't any dragons in the Badlands."

"There aren't," the man replied. "Not normally, at least. Sometimes they stray too far from their territory and end up here in search of easy pickings."

Isiah dusted himself off. "Why did you grab me?"

"I thought you might have been a Royal Guard." He extended a hand. "Name's Reuben."

Isiah shook it weakly. "Isiah."

As the adrenaline faded, he got a chance to inspect the group. There were eight of them, a mix of men and women. They had with them a couple of the large scaly beasts he'd seen with the merchants. "Are—are you merchants?" he asked.

Reuben spat at the ground. "Merchants are nothing more than foul-tempered thieves and liars. We're nomads," he said. "We've got no base of operations, nor any trade routes. We're not interested in profit. We go where the Badlands takes us."

One of the beasts tossed its head as a nomad tugged on its reins. Reuben beckoned the others and started off.

"Where are you going?" Isiah asked.

"Away," he replied. "Before that dragon swings by again."

Despite himself, Isiah's legs spurred him into motion after them. "Can I come with you?"

Reuben snorted. "Haven't you got a group or something?"

Isiah shook his head.

"No wonder you nearly died," Reuben said. "Being alone is a fool's gamble. You might as well face that dragon and save yourself from a slower and more unfortunate death."

Isiah's insides churned. He cast a wary look in the direction he had come from.

"We're going to Alcabaza," Reuben said. "It's only a couple of days from here."

"Alcabaza," Isiah repeated. The name brought back memories—ones from what felt like a lifetime ago, deep in the palace archives...

"You good?" Reuben asked.

Isiah realized he hadn't answered. "Yes—I'll go with you, I mean."

The nomad resumed his march. "Then we'll set off immediately."

* * *

Bags and harnesses rattled as the nomads and their beasts trudged through the terrain. The twin suns dipped lower in the sky, letting the temperatures fall and giving Isiah relief from the relentless heat.

Reuben led the group, taking them to a dusty road that snaked across the Badlands. The spires and cliffs where the dragon lived faded into the distance behind them. Ahead, the land slanted into a flat plain, broken by lone buttes and weather-beaten rock formations.

Isiah had to half-run to keep up with Reuben's gait. The nomads moved quickly, well-adjusted to the Badland heat. Isiah forced his tired body to fall into stride with their leader.

"Why did you think I was a Royal Guard?" Isiah asked him.

"They love to encroach on our lands," he replied. "And they attack anyone they can find. You have to be careful out here. You can never be too sure."

Isiah looked away before Reuben saw his expression. His burns itched again, but he didn't dare do anything about it. He still felt it calling out his location, acting as a beacon to any nearby dragons . . .

He stumbled and bumped into one of the scaly pack creatures. It bellowed a warning at him. Isiah staggered away and raised his hands.

Reuben laughed. "Don't mind them. They're temperamental."

The creature lost interest in Isiah and returned to its steady trek. Stout, muscular legs supported its lumpy body. The tall hump on its shoulders made its armoured head look comically small, while its rear section dropped to a short tail.

"They say these beasts are related to the dragons," Reuben said. His gruff tone lightened. "If you can believe it, that is. They're like reptiles, but warm-blooded and built like mammals. In any case, they're sturdy creatures—and the perfect food for their bigger cousins."

"Dragons prey on them?" Isiah asked.

Reuben nodded. "When they get the chance." He paused. "But you should know this already. What stone did you crawl out from under?"

Isiah racked his brains. "The Tablelands," he lied. "Near the border."

"Border-folk, ey?" Reuben replied. "Your kind aren't the brightest. I almost pity you. Do you have any idea what could have happened to you out here? Dragons are the least of your problems. You could have been found by cave trolls, or a pack of gorgons."

Isiah frowned. "Gorgons?"

"Yeah. Nasty things, those." Reuben patted the beast beside him. "They prey on these too. They hunt in packs, like wolves, ambushing us and using their massive jaws to rip us to shreds."

19

Isiah's face paled.

"They like to hide in dark and cool places," Reuben continued. "They're not fans of the midday sun. They hunt at night, mostly. I've seen too many nomads pitch tents in the wrong spot and end up being mauled."

"Are there any out here?" Isiah asked.

"The Badlands are crawling with them." His hand dropped to his waist and he pulled back his cloak to reveal a curved scabbard. "But with the right weapons, we can see them off."

Isiah's hand went to his own knife. It felt tiny in comparison.

"You always know them because of their jaws," Reuben said. "Their canines are longer than knives, and their mouths can stretch wide enough to close around a man's torso."

"Come on, Rueben," one of the other nomads called. "You'll scare the boy to death."

"It's better than walking in blissful ignorance to his doom," Reuben said. "Still, we're not too far from Alcabaza, so we won't have to worry about gorgons or dragons for a while yet."

The mention of Alcabaza reminded Isiah of his mission. "What it's like there?"

"It's a city," Reuben replied. "They help protect the Badlands from Paradon and their dragons. We stop there to refill our supplies."

"You don't like Paradon either?" Isiah asked tentatively. He already knew the answer.

"After how their Royal Guards treat us?" Reuben kicked the ground. "They fly around on their dragons and attack anything that moves. I've heard stories of merchants finding downed Royal Guards and stoning them to death."

Isiah's gut churned. "You can shoot down their dragons?"

Reuben shrugged. "*We* can't. At least, not with our arrows and crossbows. But the Raiders, on the other hand." He let out a low whistle. "I don't like them much more than soldiers, but their eagles guard the skies for us."

They fell into silence. The road continued ahead, past a shallow stream bordered with bushes and squat trees. The nomads paused to top up their waterskins and let their beasts drink.

Isiah kept half an eye on the skies for any sign of the dragon. The familiar pain in his skin had subsided, but he was reminded of it every time he moved and his clothes brushed against it. He hung on the edge of the group, trying not to let his unease betray him.

But at least they hate dragons, he thought. As long as he was with them, he'd be safer.

Because all the while he was Marked, the dragons would never forget about him.

Tessa

TESSA GRIPPED HER EAGLE'S NECK AND SCOURED the rocky plains below. The wind rushed in her ears as the mighty bird powered himself through the clear air with rhythmic wingbeats. Around her, other eagles flew, Raiders atop their shoulders.

Her eagle's feathers rustled as his head darted about. Beady dark eyes scanned the earth. Tessa adjusted her seat on the harness around his middle. Her hair, the same colour as the bird's deep plumage, trailed behind her.

"See anything?" Lazaro yelled, cupping a hand around his mouth. The wind almost stole his voice away.

"Not yet," Tessa replied.

Her older brother gave her a thumbs-up, then his eagle drifted away. The Raiders spread out, flying in formation over the Badlands. Tessa scanned the ravines and mesas for reflective scales—or any sign of the wild dragon they were hunting.

A fire welled in her chest. "How dare the Royal Guards stalk our territory," she said when Lazaro drifted next to her. "Who do they think they are?"

"It might be a wild one," Lazaro replied. He raised a hand to his forehead. Short-cropped hair covered his scalp, and his nose slanted at an angle from a scuffle years prior. Far from the flowing robes of merchants and nomads, their clothes hung close to their bodies so they didn't interfere with flying.

Far below, a tiny cluster of figures walked silhouetted against the terrain. A couple of hulking beasts marched alongside them. Tessa ran her eyes over the group.

"See any eagles down there?" Lazaro asked.

She shook her head. "Just nomads. Do we ask them if they saw anything?"

Lazaro scoffed. "We don't need their help."

The Raiders passed over and continued their flight. As they soared over a deep ravine, a handful of shapes scattered—gorgons, Tessa realized. Her eagle's eyes locked onto them.

"Not now, Vyrro," Tessa told him. "We're not here to cull them."

Vyrro's golden beak gleamed, hooked and sharper than any sabre. His wingspan stretched wide, each one longer than she was tall. The bird tore his attention away from the fleeing gorgons, then gave off a shrill call.

"What is it?" she asked.

She followed the bird's gaze. A couple of dark shapes marked the horizon. Her eyes narrowed.

24

"Too big to be eagles," she spat.

The Raiders drifted closer, until they could make out the leathery wings and snaking tails of dragons.

"Looks like Royal Guards," one of the other Raiders sneered. A jacket clad in scaly armour covered her chest, and her silky dark braids trailed behind her.

"Right you are, Darla," Lazaro said. He leaned forward in the harness, trying to get a better look. A sabre dangled at his side, its blade hidden inside an elaborate sheath. "And on our side of the border, too."

"They're not the ones we're supposed to hunt," Darla replied. "We don't have the numbers to get into a fight with Royal Guards."

Lazaro clenched his jaw. "We'll swing by and give them a warning. They're nothing but a cowardly patrol."

The Raiders fell into a closer formation. Tessa counted all half-dozen of them—nowhere near enough to face the two dragons. Her face twisted into a snarl as she glared at them. Despite her fury, a spark of panic flared in her chest. Tessa quelled it.

"We should get reinforcements," she said. "Then we can drive them out."

One of the other Raiders—Antony—shook his head. "It's not worth it," he replied. "Remember what we're here for."

As they approached, the dragons and their riders veered away. A surge of power swelled in Tessa's chest. "See? Cowards."

"Then let's get to it," Lazaro replied. "We'll have ourselves a dead dragon soon enough."

Marked

As the twin suns dipped low on the horizon, the shadows lengthened and the nomads came to a stop. They pitched tents off the side of the road, hidden among a mass of boulders and trees near another shallow stream.

Isiah rubbed his arms. His breath formed a cloud of mist. The nomads stacked dead branches into a pile and began a fire. Thin curls of flame drove away the deepening shadows.

Reuben sat on a flat rock, his sabre across his lap. He ran a stone over the blade. The soft scraping sound rose above the chirp of insects. Beyond, silence stretched across the Badlands.

The nomad's pack animals wandered to graze on some bushes. A few ropes secured their thick necks to tree trunks. Isiah tightened his cloak and tried to ignore the itch under his skin.

"Did you see those eagles earlier?" Reuben asked.

Isiah nodded.

"Raiders. I reckon they're on the hunt for something. Maybe the dragon that chased you."

Isiah drew his knees to his chest. He kept half an ear out for the sound of its beating wings.

"Relax," Reuben said. "You really *are* inexperienced. Timid, too. That attitude won't help you here."

The nomads gathered around the fire. They strung a few pots over the curling flames, boiling food and talking among themselves in hushed voices. In the shadows, one of their creatures grunted.

"What are the Raiders like?" Isiah asked.

Reuben snorted. "Elitist. They think that unless you have one of those birds of theirs, you aren't worth their time. We don't mix."

Isiah remembered the sight of them, soaring high above. Half a dozen, he'd counted.

A familiar itch brought him back from his daydreaming. He excused himself from the group and wandered to where he'd seen the stream. It lay outside the ring of firelight, babbling over rocks in the darkness.

Isiah knelt and peeled back his clothes. He touched his burns and found them red-hot. Cupping his hands in the stream, he began washing them for the hundredth time.

The nomads talked and laughed somewhere behind him. Something small scurried about in the darkness on the other side of the bank. The lukewarm water trickled down his back, taking the worst of the itch out of his blisters. The constant rub of his clothes had left the skin red and sore.

Footsteps crunched somewhere behind him. Isiah jumped to his feet and fumbled with his cloak. He spun around to see Reuben.

The nomad furrowed his brow. "What are you doing?"

"Nothing—" Isiah started.

Reuben narrowed his eyes. "Let me see."

"It's just a sunburn," he said quickly. His eyes darted downstream, already planning his escape.

"That doesn't look like a sunburn." Reuben made a grab for the cloak. It slipped to reveal his red, wax-like skin.

"You're Marked," Reuben said slowly.

Isiah froze, waiting for what would happen next. The nomad's eyes washed over his wounds.

"So that's why the dragon was so eager to kill you," Reuben said.

Isiah took a step back. "You're not angry?"

Reuben cast a look back at the nomad camp. He dropped his voice. "You'd best cover up before anyone else sees you."

Isiah did as he was told.

"The others might not be so understanding," Reuben said, "but I know what a Mark means. Paradon cast you out, didn't they?"

Isiah nodded.

"Cursed to wander the wild," he continued. "Enemy to the dragons, and hated by everyone this side of the border."

"But I'm not part of Paradon anymore," Isiah said.

Reuben shrugged. "Doesn't matter to most of us." He raised his hands. "I've got nothing against you, boy, but there are more than a few nomads who would kill for a chance to take their revenge on Paradon— whether you're with them or not."

"What do you mean?" Isiah asked.

"We've lost friends to Royal Guards," Reuben said. "Family, too. And if you're a magnet for dragons, that's one more reason to kill you and throw you in a ditch somewhere to save our own skins." Reuben turned. "Come on."

Isiah hesitated for a moment. Part of him urged him to run in case Reuben sold him out. But he took a deep breath and rejoined the group. Reuben said nothing to the others, and as the other nomads drifted off to sleep, he remained awake, sharpening his sabre.

"I knew you weren't from these parts, but I didn't think you were Marked," Reuben said. "You're too young."

Isiah swallowed. "The nobles pushed my Ceremony forward."

"And it didn't work out, I take it. What drove you to come here?" Reuben asked. "Thought you'd be safer than staying in Paradon with all their dragons roaming the skies?"

Isiah hesitated. He checked the other nomads were still asleep. "You promise not to tell anyone?"

Reuben gave him a nod.

"I want to cure myself." Isiah felt like an idiot saying it. Nobody had ever cured a Mark before. "There's an oasis out here. I saw a parchment in the palace archives. It's got some kind of magic, hasn't it?"

"I've heard of it," Reuben said slowly. "But nobody has ever found it. *Hidden* would be an understatement. Even the Raiders gave up trying."

"I found a map," Isiah replied. "It pointed to this part of the Badlands. I came here to look for it."

Reuben shrugged. "I don't know what old tales you've been reading, lad, but I've never seen it."

29

"I *need* to find it," Isiah said. "Once I'm cured, the dragons will leave me alone, and the nobles will let me back into Paradon."

Reuben raised an eyebrow. "Why do you want to return? They threw you out." He spat into the fire. "Shows how much they care about you."

"They *had* to banish me," Isiah said quickly. "They didn't want to, though. They can't let someone who's Marked live in the palace. There are too many dragons there."

"We've got plenty of lowlifes in these parts," Reuben said. "But to exile your own flesh and blood? That's a special kind of low."

"They still care," Isiah insisted. He willed himself to believe it. "And once I go back, I'll prove it. They'll *have* to accept me."

Reuben raised his hands. "If you say so. I'll tell you this, though. It'll be no easy task."

"I know it exists," Isiah replied. "And when I reach Alcabaza, I'll start looking."

"As long as you don't let anyone know about your Mark," Reuben warned. "You know what we think of your kind." He stood and marched to the edge of the camp, then took a seat and rested his sabre on his lap.

"What are you doing?" Isiah asked.

"Keeping watch for any unwelcome visitors." He twisted around. "You should sleep. We depart at first light."

Isiah took a seat by the fire and curled up against a rock. The stone emanated a faint heat, warmed by the previous day's sun. He watched their campfire flicker, feeling the last of his energy sap from his weakened body.

The oasis does exist, he thought. *I know it.*

He just had to find it before somebody else did.

* * *

Months prior . . .

Drums sounded. Trumpets blared. The din of the crowd echoed through the arena, penetrating the thick doors and swirling around Isiah's head. He stood in a wide room at the far end of the arena. Two Royal Guards, seated on their opal-coloured dragons, guarded the way ahead.

Isiah wrung his hands. He gripped a long spear—his only protection against the beast inside. Many of the other young nobles had already bonded, but he was the youngest of them all.

"Do you remember your training?" Ward asked. He stood near the gates, hands on his hips.

Isiah nodded—but deep down, he wanted to call the entire thing off. He knew he wasn't ready. He couldn't . . .

"It's a simple task," Ward said, interrupting his thoughts. "The dragon is already used to people. That spear of yours is nothing more than for show, to re-enact the achievements of our greatest heroes."

Isiah gulped. Chains rattled inside the arena. The crowd grew louder. He knew the dragon was almost in position.

"They have three kinds of fire," Ward continued. "Their regular fire, the very same one we use for our hearths and forgeries—then their magical fire, passed down from our two suns."

31

Isiah forced himself to focus on Ward's words. He'd heard all the stories countless times before.

"The fire they use to bond won't harm you," Ward said. A grin spread across his face. "It forms a connection with you, unifying the two of you as a single force. All you have to do is think. They do the rest."

The drums rumbled, building in volume. The Royal Guards, seated on their dragons, leaned over and grasped the chains that would open the doors. Ward had to shout over the noise.

"Then there's the bad kind—the one that will leave you Marked if they reject you." Ward paused. "But you don't need to worry about that."

Isiah's stomach knotted until he was sure he was going to vomit. A horn blast sounded and the Royal Guards yanked on the chains. The doors groaned and swung open. Light flooded in, forcing Isiah to squint.

"Now go and become a noble!" Ward gave Isiah a shove and he stumbled into the arena.

A chorus of cheering went up from the crowd. It echoed in Isiah's eardrums, commanding his senses and making every thought a struggle. He raised a hand to shield himself from the sunlight far above.

The arena sprawled ahead of him, a wide mound of sand with a dome covering it. Wrought metal bars formed a giant cage, with netting in between to protect the crowd from dragon fire. Banners hung around the rim of the arena. The brilliant blue-white sun hovered overhead, its dark cousin nowhere to be seen.

Isiah forced his legs to carry him into the arena. The feeling of so many eyes fixed on him made his heart spasm. Spectators lined the seats, and further away, nobles sat in their own arena skyboxes. His father's seat sat empty, but the nobles still shied away from it as if it was contagious.

Isiah didn't have much time to think. From the far side of the arena, chains grumbled as a door began to lift.

Isiah clutched his spear as a serpentine head slithered from the shadows. It surveyed the crowd with wary eyes. Each footstep seemed to make the ground tremble. Against it, Isiah's spear felt like nothing more than a toothpick.

"Remember what Ward told you," Isiah said to himself. He had to be strong.

The dragon slithered into the light. Isiah took a tentative step forward. The crowd urged him on, their voices climbing into a single deafening chorus.

The dragon noticed him. Isiah's heart dropped into the pit of his stomach as it lumbered over. It skidded to a halt in the centre of the arena, head raised and neck poised to strike.

Isiah forced himself to suck in a deep breath. Light-headedness threatened to make him pass out. He lowered his spear in the direction of the dragon and began circling it. As he went, a nagging voice tugged at his mind. *You're not ready. Ward was right.*

Isiah shoved it away. Sweat made the shaft of the spear slick and slippery. A deep rumble emanated from the dragon's chest. Twin plumes of steam and mucus erupted from its nostrils.

Isiah shrank away, then collected himself. The constant din of the crowd made him want to scream. *The dragon won't accept you.*

Light swirled inside the dragon's chest. It made a mock lunge at him. Four rows of razor teeth flashed in the sunlight—two lining each jaw. Above, the sun began to inch over the rim of the arena.

Isiah jabbed his spear in the dragon's direction. He willed himself to speak. "I'm here to bond." His voice came out more like a squeak. "I'm strong enough to face you."

The dragon lunged again. Its head swayed like a serpent about to strike. Isiah stumbled aside. His eyes widened as he tripped. The spear nearly flew from his grip as his back connected with the ground. The crowd shouted with renewed vigour.

Isiah scrambled to his feet, his lungs fighting for breath. The light inside the dragon's chest materialized—first orange, then a deep black-ish red. Isiah's blood ran cold. He screamed and jumped aside as a spray of dark flames erupted from the dragon's jaws.

He wasn't fast enough. The stream caught him across the shoulder and raced across his clothes. White-hot pain buried itself in his skin. He crumpled to his knees.

The crowd's cheering turned into screams. Horns blasted a warning and Royal Guards flooded the arena. Isiah frantically beat at the flames. The pain spread to his chest and upper back. Royal Guards ran to his side and doused him with water. The dragon bellowed and wheeled away as the Royal Guards jabbed their spears in its direction.

"Get him out of here!" one yelled. "Take him to a medic."

Hands yanked Isiah to his feet. He writhed under the searing pain. He didn't hear his own screams. The Royal Guards picked him up and carried him out of the arena, his feet trailing on the ground. His skin began to go numb as the fire smouldered inside him, eating away at his nerves, melting his flesh . . .

Isiah's head dropped forward and darkness consumed him.

Raiders

REUBEN PRODDED ISIAH WITH HIS FOOT. "Wake up. It's time to go."

Isiah groaned and rolled over. His body still ached from the previous day and his escape from the dragon. As Reuben left to tend to one of their beasts, Isiah shifted himself into a sitting position.

The first rays of sunlight peered over the horizon. Droplets of water had settled on the rocks and plants overnight, reminding Isiah of his parched mouth. He unscrewed his waterskin and took a swig.

"It's only a day's journey to Alcabaza," Reuben said. The other nomads adjusted their sabres and tightened their flowing cloaks. "We'll make good time before the day gets hot."

Isiah pulled himself to his feet, wincing at the stiffness in his knees. A night spent on the hard earth left his back aching and tender. He patted his pockets. "Did you search me?"

"Hey, we're giving you free passage." Reuben gave him a wry smile. "Not that you had anything to pay us with."

Isiah felt about with his foot. The familiar pouch of coins pressed against his toes. The nomad hadn't looked hard enough.

Reuben passed him a bowl of cold broth. "Eat up. You'll need energy."

Isiah took it. The substance slipped down his throat, ice-cold and bitter. He wiped the tears out of his eyes.

Reuben grinned. "You get used to it. The plants here aren't known for their taste."

The nomads finished prepping their supplies and headed out. Isiah fell into stride with Reuben. As the white sun crawled above the line of horizon, they entered a rolling land of wide mesas and flat-topped mountains. Layers of painted rock formed their sides, red and orange giving way to white and even a deep purple.

Reuben dropped his voice. "It might not be like the forests and grasslands where you're from, but the Badlands has a beauty of its own if you know where to look."

Isiah craned his neck to survey the sight. His gaze fell to a gulley, where sun-bleached bones littered the ground. A gaping skull lay open, filled with four rows of razor teeth.

"What's that?" he asked. He already knew the answer.

"See for yourself."

Isiah cautiously wandered over, then cursed his skittishness. *It's dead. It can't hurt you.*

The dragon's bones filled the gulley, scattered by predators and picked clean. Reuben stooped and picked up a weathered tooth.

"They shed their teeth, don't they?" Reuben asked, turning it over.

Isiah nodded. "The back ones grow and push the front ones out."

Eyeless sockets glared up at them. Isiah's skin crawled. He tried to ignore the familiar burn of his Mark.

"Eagles aren't strong enough to fight a dragon alone," Reuben said. "They hunt in packs and harass it to death. Once they exhaust it, they knock it from the sky. The gorgons do the rest."

Isiah tore his eyes away from the skeleton. Standing so close to the dragon's remains made his palms sweat. "Then let's go before we find any."

They kept travelling until midmorning. The temperature returned to its usual intensity, evaporating the last traces of dew and bearing down on the nomads as if trying to crush them with its rays.

As they passed through a narrow trough between two mesas, the ground began to tremble. Panic flared inside Isiah's gut.

"The dragon—" he started.

"Earthquake," Reuben said, cutting him off.

Isiah fought for balance as the earth shook. Dust and loose stones rained from the mesas, clattering around them. One of the nomad's scaly beasts lumbered aside in fright as a large boulder hit the ground and broke into fragments.

"Damn miners," Reuben swore. "We get enough earthquakes as it is."

"What are they doing?" Isiah asked.

"Their explosives upset the fault lines," Reuben said. "They don't care if the entire Badlands comes down on their heads, if only they get their gold."

After a minute, the shaking subsided. Reuben dusted himself off and beckoned the others. "Come on. It's just a minor quake. Nothing to worry about."

Isiah redoubled his pace. They cleared the mesas and its unstable cliffs and pressed on into new terrain. A flash caught his attention in the skies above.

"There are more eagles." He thrust his finger in their direction.

"And not wild ones, neither," Reuben replied. He raised his hand and brought the nomads to a stop as the Raiders circled above.

"What do they want?" Isiah asked.

Reuben narrowed his eyes. "That's what we're about to find out."

The eagles wheeled in the sky, before coming to land one at a time. Isiah counted six—the same ones he'd sighted before.

The lead eagle settled on a boulder and folded its wings. Isiah fought the urge to shrink away. Its head darted back and forth, surveying the group with beady black eyes. The bird sat like a totem pole, twice the height of Reuben.

The nomad raised a hand to his forehead to squint up at them. "What brings you here, Raider?"

The eagle fluffed its wings and a man dismounted. Around him, the other Raiders climbed off their eagles. Straps and harnesses wrapped around the man's middle, pinning his robes flat. His cropped hair matched the murky yellow-brown dust beneath his feet.

"We were searching for something," he replied. "Nomads like you love to slink around and spy where you're not welcome, so we thought we'd ask."

"Since when did a Raider need a nomad's help?" Reuben said. "I thought you only needed your eagles."

A snicker went around the nomad group.

The Raider's face twisted into a snarl. "Unless you'd like us to abandon you to death by dragon, you'd better help us." He paused. "Some merchants reported there's a dragon lurking in the Badlands somewhere around here. We wondered if you'd seen it."

Isiah's gaze drifted past the man to the other Raiders. A girl stood next to one of the giant birds, surveying the group with a hard expression. Her long dark hair fell about her shoulders, and a sabre hung at her side.

"It's nice of you to care about us," Reuben said. "Since when did your kind still hunt dragons? Haven't you got more ruins to loot?"

The man's nose crinkled. "Don't insult us, nomad."

"Careful," Reuben replied. "I hope you aren't about to break the Raider's Oath."

"You know the Raider's Oath doesn't extend to your kind."

One of the others put a hand on the Raider's shoulder. "Lazaro."

Lazaro's expression dropped. He relaxed his shoulders. "Did you see the dragon?"

Reuben gestured back the way they had come. "Early yesterday, among a mass of spires close to the border."

"We've already searched there," the girl started.

"Maybe you didn't search hard enough," Reuben replied. He caught sight of Lazaro's face, and his tone softened. "It's easy to miss. It must be lurking in a cave someplace."

"It is," Isiah blurted out. Lazaro's attention shifted to him. "I mean—"

40

"We know where to look," Lazaro said. "And I'll be dead before I take directions from a nomad."

He turned and climbed atop his eagle. The other Raiders rejoined theirs and the mighty birds launched themselves into the sky. Isiah ducked as they soared overhead. As the dust settled, he watched the birds climb higher and higher into the heavens.

Reuben dusted his hands off. "That went well."

The nomads spurred into motion. Isiah tore his eyes away from the birds. "What did you mean about the Raider's Oath?"

"It's an Oath they take," Reuben said. "It stops them from fighting one another. Otherwise, every time they found a ruin there'd be a bloodbath." Seeing Isiah's expression, he continued, "The Raiders look for treasure. Old crypts, burial sites, buried temples, the likes. They're competitive. They'd be at war constantly if they didn't have some kind of agreement among themselves."

Isiah mulled it over. He lowered his voice so the other nomads didn't hear him. "Do you think the oasis might be hidden in a ruin?"

"Maybe," Reuben said. "But Raiders are no friends of ours. We nomads mean nothing to them."

Isiah twisted around to get another glimpse of the Raiders. They disappeared behind a mesa.

"We'll leave them to their business." Reuben's voice distracted him. "Like I told you, part of their job is to fight off dragons. *Our* job, however, is to reach Alcabaza."

The nomads quickened their pace, leaving Isiah struggling to catch up. As he settled into their steady march, his mind buzzed with visions of the Raiders and their massive birds.

And the buried ruins that might hold his cure.

Thousand Cuts

THE WIND RAN THROUGH TESSA'S HAIR AS VYRRO climbed in altitude. The mesas and the nomad group faded into the distance.

"Ungrateful lot," Lazaro said. "We should leave them to the dragons."

"And let the dragons get away with hunting here?" Tessa replied. "Next we'll let the Royal Guards invade."

At the thought of the nomads, her mind went back to the boy she'd seen. There was something odd about him, something she couldn't place.

Inexperienced, she thought. He'd looked half-dead. *He must be new on the trail.*

"I'll summon the others," Antony said, distracting her. "Darla, you up?"

Darla gave him a salute, and the pair veered away. Tessa flew on for a few minutes in silence. She silently prepared herself for the task ahead.

"Do you remember what to do?" Lazaro asked.

Tessa nodded. "Dragons are nothing." She narrowed her eyes at the distant spires that the nomad had pointed them to.

"Don't get full of yourself," Lazaro said. "This isn't like seeing off Royal Guards. Wild ones are dangerous."

Tessa tightened her grip on Vyrro's reins. "I can look after myself."

They neared the spires. As they did, Antony and the other Raider groups appeared on the horizon to their left. Tessa's pulse quickened at the sight of two dozen eagles flying in formation. The groups merged and Lazaro directed them to a wide, winding river nearby.

Tessa urged Vyrro forward. The eagle dropped to the Badlands and soared over the river. Around her, the other eagles did the same. Vyrro stretched out his wings and glided over the water's surface. He then lowered his feet and kicked up a spray. Water droplets formed a mist in the air, settling over his feathers and Tessa's clothes.

Tessa wiped a hand across her eyes as Vyrro climbed back into the air currents. Streams of water dripped from the eagle's dark plumage.

"I don't see how this will help us," Tessa called.

"The water will help keep you from catching alight," Lazaro replied. "I've heard enough stories of eagles being hit by fireballs and burning alive—their riders burning with them."

Tessa shuddered.

"My advice is *don't get hit*," Lazaro said.

The eagles ascended into the heavens and wheeled around to face the spires. Tessa calmed her shaking hands. She pulled up her hood so Lazaro couldn't see her expression.

Get it together, she told herself. *You're a Raider.*

The eagles soared over the first of the spires. She scanned the gulleys and ravines between them, searching for any sign of the elusive dragon. With every beat of Vyrro's wings, her pulse grew faster.

Then Lazaro's eagle let out a shriek.

A shimmering flash caught Tessa's eye as a dragon erupted from its cave. Its ear-splitting roar sent a stab of pain through her head.

Vyrro lurched to the side as a fireball ripped past. The eagles scattered, splitting off and weaving among one another. A few arrows arced through the air as the Raiders fired their bows. The arrows struck the beast and bounced harmlessly off.

The dragon climbed in altitude. It dwarfed the eagles, three times their size. Lazaro and Darla wheeled around and attacked it from behind, scratching at its back and then pulling away to evade its snapping jaws.

Tessa regained her composure. She took a deep breath, then dug her heels into Vyrro and directed him to attack. The eagle obeyed, dropping like an arrow past the dragon's outstretched wing. Vyrro flexed his claws and dug them into its leathery skin.

The dragon roared in fury and wheeled through the sky. Fire spewed from its jaws. It caught an eagle with a fireball and a plume of steam billowed from its plumage. The Raiders circled the dragon, darting in to attack and veering away before it could retaliate. One eagle swung upside down and clawed at the dragon's underbelly.

45

"Keep going!" a Raider yelled. "We're wearing it down!"

The dragon launched another fireball. Tessa yanked on Vyrro's reins and he flipped onto his side to avoid it. The flames curled past his underbelly.

She unsheathed her sabre and aimed a thrust at the dragon. The blade found its mark in a gap between the dragon's scales. Her arm was almost yanked from its socket as they rushed past and their momentum pulled the sabre free. More fire streaked the sky—weaker than last time.

"It's running out of energy," Tessa called.

The dragon broke away from the eagles and dropped into the shelter of the spires. The Raiders regrouped and went after it. Tessa ducked as an eagle whipped past inches from her head. Vyrro wove through the twisted rock formations, dodging cliffs as he kept the fleeing dragon in his sights.

Loose rocks crumbled as the dragon landed on a ledge and skidded to a halt. It whipped around with a bellow of warning, its back against a rockface. The Raiders circled, waiting for their opportunity to swoop in and attack.

"Death by a thousand cuts," Lazaro roared. "This'll teach dragons to enter our lands."

The eagles flew closer. The dragon snarled a warning. It snapped at the air. Four rows of razor teeth glistened with saliva. Some of the Raiders landed and dismounted, sabres and spears at the ready.

Vyrro landed atop a hoodoo and folded his wings. Tessa slid off. The dragon coiled, neck poised to strike. Its sides heaved with exertion, red trickles of blood welling from a dozen wounds. Raiders brandished their sabres and loaded crossbows.

"Let's finish this," Tessa said. Fire filled her chest, making her puff up and daring her to join in the fight. The dragon lunged in her direction. She stumbled away and almost dropped her sabre. She scolded her skittishness.

"Hold it," a voice ordered. A Raider marched past her. Patches of reflective scale armour hung across his shoulders and thighs, and the harsh sunlight reflected off his bald, tanned skull. The corner of his mouth twisted into a cruel smile. "I've got a better idea."

The dragon shrank away as the Raider raised a new weapon—an amber-coloured crystal, fastened to a long pole. It emitted a smouldering red light, burning with the same intensity as their second sun. The Raider shoved to the front of the crowd and jabbed the weapon in the dragon's direction. It shied away from the light, hissing a warning.

The Raider nodded in satisfaction and puffed out his chest. "Get the ropes," he called.

"What do you think you're doing, Enrik?" Lazaro marched forward. "You know what we came here to do."

"Calm yourself, Lazaro," Enrik replied with a sly smile. "You lead your Raiders, and I'll lead mine."

Tessa stumbled and almost fell as Enrik's group of Raiders pushed past her. Several carried thick coils of rope and netting slung over their shoulders.

"Watch it," Lazaro snapped. He turned to Enrik. "We're here to kill it." He motioned to the dragon. "We can't risk letting it live."

47

Enrik kept his eyes fixed on the dragon. "You're short-sighted, Lazaro. Your hatred blinds you."

"It's going to get away," Tessa cut in. "This is our chance—before it recovers."

"Quiet, girl," Enrik replied. He smirked. "The Raiders are talking."

Lazaro clenched his jaw. "Leave her out of this."

"She's welcome to kill the dragon herself," Enrik said, ignoring him. He nodded to her sabre. "Go on. Drive that blade into its throat—if you have the nerve."

Tessa tightened her grip on her sabre. She met the dragon's gaze. The air trembled as it rumbled a warning. Tessa's grip faltered.

"Get to work, boys," Enrik called. He waved the crystal. "This'll keep it docile long enough to do what we need to do."

The Raiders threw their ropes at the dragon. It tried to writhe away, but the Raiders looped a coil around its jaws and pinned down its wings.

Lazaro looked to the others. "You can't be serious! How can you stand here and let this happen?"

"Because they trust my judgement," Enrik replied.

Several Raiders moved to push Lazaro and Tessa away. Lazaro swatted their hands. "Don't touch me," he snapped.

"Fly back to Alcabaza," Enrik said. "Leave us to our work. This dragon will be more useful to us alive."

Alcabaza

"NOT MUCH FURTHER NOW," REUBEN CALLED.

Isiah dug his boots into the ground and scrambled up the trail to the top of the mesa. Loose sheets of crumbling stone broke underfoot, forcing him to tread carefully. He wiped the sweat off his forehead as he tried to keep pace with the nomads.

Rolling low mesas and plains sprawled around them, forming impassable walls and low valleys clogged with thorny bushes and beds of rippling grass. The nomads clambered to the top of the mesa, leading their pack animals behind. Isiah kept to their shadows, trying to avoid the twin suns' glare.

A rock came loose under his foot and he collapsed to one knee. Isiah gritted his teeth and pulled himself up, then jogged to Reuben's side.

"See that?" Reuben asked.

Isiah turned his attention to the land ahead. The mesa's rough, staircase-like surface descended to a flat plain. Tall grass and maize waved in the breeze, colouring the ground a dull, washed-out green. Further off, a wide river snaked past, its surface a murky brown.

Beyond the mesa, looming proudly over the fields and crops, stood a mountain. Its square, lopsided top broke the sky as if someone had cut off its peak. Its sheer walls dropped to the plain below, standing like a lone soldier against the relentless elements.

Isiah let out a low whistle. "Do we get to rest there?"

Reuben unhooked a bag from one of their beasts. He fished around in it and drew out a spyglass. "See for yourself."

Isiah took it and pressed it to his eye. The mountainside appeared, blurry at first, but he adjusted the spyglass and the slopes came into view. Isiah's breath caught in his throat.

A city clung to the side of the mountain, built on a series of flat terraces. A mass of wooden beams rose from the ground below, supporting the city's lower levels like scaffolding against a building. Higher up, near the mountain's peak, the jumble of squat buildings gave way to circular platforms and wide awnings coloured in vibrant red and purple.

"The Raiders land their eagles there," Reuben said. He plucked the spyglass from Isiah's grip. "Let's go. You'll see it up close soon enough."

With renewed vigour, Isiah took off down the uneven path. They descended the side of the mesa and reached the plain below. The terrain changed from hard rock to soft mud and sand, letting a thick sea of grass dominate the land. Seedpods swayed gently in a breath of wind, brushing against Isiah's chest as he passed.

"The water table supports it," Reuben said. "The city draws its water from wells in the earth, and what's left runs off and feeds the plain." He led the nomads onto a narrow trail. "It's the only arable land for miles."

Isiah hopped onto the trail and hastened toward the mountain. It dwarfed them, rising above the mesas and buttes to form a lonely beacon. As they drew closer, Isiah made out the jumble of buildings covering its side.

"Why did they build it here?" he asked.

"To make the most of the land," Reuben said. "They can't farm it if it's covered in houses. And," he added, "it protects them from the likes of Paradon and their armies."

Isiah's face fell as he became aware of his situation. He tightened his cloak, half-expecting somebody to see his burns through the material.

"Keep your head down," Reuben said. He lowered his voice. "And not just because of your Mark. This city belongs to the Raiders."

Isiah remembered their tense encounter—but it quickly faded from his mind as they reached the base of the city. Thick logs formed a crisscrossing network of beams, built against the mountain's side. Ropes squealed and machinery grumbled as elevators were raised and lowered. Isiah and Reuben fell in with other groups of nomads and merchants as one of the elevators slowly descended towards them.

"All aboard!" a voice yelled. The elevator formed a wide platform with low wooden walls. One of the walls dropped to the ground to form a ramp, letting the nomads and their animals climb on. Ropes squealed in protest as Reuben and his two beasts climbed on.

Other elevators thudded as they hit the ground. Merchants drove their mules on with long sticks. One of the animals tossed its head in protest as a merchant whacked it. Isiah caught another merchant ushering a group of people clad in rags. Chains rattled, linking their wrists together as they huddled together like a herd of cattle.

Reuben leaned in. "Labourers. Don't stare too long, or the merchants might try to kidnap you and make you one of them."

One of the merchants wielded a stout stick. He barked orders at the group, driving them onto the elevator.

"What happened to them?" Isiah asked.

Reuben shrugged. "Captured from the border, or maybe their debts caught up to them. We don't ask questions here."

Isiah steadied himself against the elevator wall as the other merchants and nomads piled on, squishing against him and making it difficult to breathe. The musty aroma of mules and unwashed bodies made tears prick in his eyes. He eyed the mass of pulleys and winches warily. The voice from earlier gave the all-clear and the elevator lurched into motion.

Machinery rumbled to life. The elevator shuddered and swung as it rose toward the city above. A network of walkways, staircases and platforms rolled past, forming the underbelly of the city. Workers scurried back and forth as they managed the elevators and kept them running smoothly. Isiah spotted a handful of long pipes running between rickety wooden platforms.

"They've built an entire system," Reuben said. "They pipe water from the plain below, and the labourers have cut tunnels in the mountainside to carry it around."

53

The elevator reached the top and jolted to a halt. The other wall swung down, and Isiah fought to keep from falling out. Impatient merchants shoved past him and streamed onto the ramp beyond. Reuben grabbed his arm and guided them along with the flow.

"Doesn't anybody ever fall off the elevators?" Isiah asked.

Reuben shrugged. "Occasionally."

The ramp led up from the city's dark underbelly and onto the first of the terraced levels. The wood beneath Isiah's feet changed to worn stone slabs, cut into the mountainside. He raised a hand and squinted against the sun's sudden brightness.

Reuben ushered Isiah forward. "Watch your pockets," he warned. "It's a city of thieves, here."

They travelled deeper into the city, past jumbles of squat buildings with dusty walls and peeling plaster. Houses filled every available space, hugging the mountainside and teetering on the edge of the terrace. Children ran through the cramped streets, dodging merchant stalls and ducking under colourful awnings. Isiah's head spun as he tried to take it all in.

Yelling voices and the grunts of animals filled the air, and the wind carried the noxious aroma of spices mixed with dirt and grime. Awnings cast triangular patches of shade over the city, concealing narrow alleyways. Some of the houses were piled atop one another like toy blocks, overlooking the crowds with small windows and thick wooden shutters. Isiah's gaze dropped to the beggars slumped at the side of the road.

"It makes you wonder whether being a labourer is better," Reuben said, noticing Isiah staring. "At least they get a steady source of food."

"Who runs this place?" Isiah asked.

Reuben shrugged. "Raiders. As long as their Oath holds them together, they figure things out among themselves. There's no king, nor any guards or soldiers." He wrapped his fingers around his sabre. "It's every man for himself."

Isiah craned his neck. Three terraces were built into the mountainside, each one bursting with houses. Some leaned precariously over the edge, supported by wooden beams jutting from the stone.

"Most of the Raiders live near the top," Reuben said. "Their eagle roosts are there."

Isiah spotted a couple of eagles in the sky above. They approached the top of the mountain and disappeared behind one of the many landing pads. Reuben gave him a push. "Enough staring."

The nomads stuck together as they navigated the bustling street. Merchants hollered their prices and haggled with customers. Crowds of children massed around anyone who looked wealthy—hiding pickpockets, Isiah guessed.

They reached the far side of the terrace. Staircases led to the next level of the city, a mix of carved stone and shaky wooden structures that creaked whenever someone walked on them. Doorways and windows were carved into the mountain itself, with awnings hanging over and streams of travellers coming in and out.

"Taverns are big business," Reuben explained. "People come and go all the time. Nothing is permanent here, save for the mountain we're walking on."

Some of the nomads broke away to secure their beasts with a group of others. Reuben produced a pouch of coins and ducked through the doorway. Isiah went after him.

The tavern's cool shadows washed over him. The acrid aroma of pipe smoke made his nose crinkle. A few merchants sat around tables, long pipes gripped between brown teeth. A hazy mist of smoke pooled against the ceiling and seeped through the open windows.

Reuben jostled his way to the counter and dumped the pouch on it. He haggled with the tavernkeeper for a minute, before breaking away.

"I bought you a room," he told Isiah. "Until you figure out where it is you're headed."

"Oh," Isiah started, "you didn't need to." He started to reach for his pouch of coins. "I can pay."

Reuben shook his head. "You've grown on me, boy." He laughed. "Consider it payback for us ambushing you."

As the nomads bought a round of drinks, Reuben led Isiah down a rough-cut passageway to their rooms. A stout door swung open to reveal a cramped space with a single bed and no windows.

"It's not pretty," Reuben said. He tapped the heavy door. "But it keeps the thieves away."

Isiah wandered into the space. A threadbare rug covered a smooth stone floor, and an oil lantern stood on a squat table.

Away from the smoke and filth of the tavern, he could breathe more easily.

"Tell me," Reuben asked, "just where *are* you headed next?"

Isiah hesitated. "I don't know." He'd been so focused on reaching the city, he hadn't stopped to think what he'd do once he got there.

"If you plan on asking around and learning more about the oasis, I'd suggest going to a bazaar," Reuben replied. "There are plenty of sellers there. Maps, artefacts, the works. Some might have an idea of where to start looking."

Isiah nodded to himself. Part of him urged him to go immediately, but the ache in his body made him think twice.

"I'll leave you to it," Reuben said. "You know where to find me."

He tossed Isiah the key. Isiah tucked it into his belt. "Thanks for your help."

Reuben waved him away. "All I did was let you tag along. If you do find that oasis, though," he added, "be sure to come tell me."

He shut the door and left Isiah alone with his thoughts.

The Bazaar

ISIAH STUMBLED ALONG THE CROWDED STREET. People pushed and shoved past him, knocking him about like a raging current. He stumbled into a donkey and then reeled away before it bit him.

He went over his mission. *Find the bazaar.* On the street, everything looked the same.

A gap in the houses to his right revealed a thin strip of the plain beyond. Isiah's legs went weak at the sight of how high up they were.

Shaking his head, he redoubled his attention on finding whatever bazaar Reuben had told him about. Sand filled the gaps in the bricks beneath his feet, and dust flew into his face as passers-by disturbed it. People aired their clothes on clotheslines strung over their flat rooftops.

A group of beggars were slumped in the shade of a building. Some rattled cups at passers-by. All ignored them. An old man peered out between strands of greying hair. The harsh sun had left his skin leathery and dark. Isiah shifted his weight.

He fished about in his boot for one of his coins, then dropped it in the beggar's cup. The man inspected it and his smile dropped.

"A Paradon coin?" he said. "It's because of Paradon that I'm homeless!" He spat on Isiah. "We don't want this filthy currency here."

Isiah hurried away as the beggar threw the coin after him. Embarrassment burned in his cheeks. He looked around to make sure nobody had seen him.

The houses parted ahead, forming a covered side street with an arched roof and thick sandstone pillars. Nomads streamed through it, carrying jugs and leading animals laden with goods. Pairs of merchants carried long rugs suspended between them. Isiah's embarrassment melted.

He hastened toward it and found the bazaar. Merchant stalls lined the walls of the long structure, with brightly coloured awnings above their heads and piles of merchandise lying everywhere. Isiah joined the crowd and pushed his way inside.

Incense and spices made him cough. The noise of the crowd swirled around his ears, making it hard to think. Rugs and tapestries hung suspended from the beams crisscrossing the ceiling. Children crouched in the narrow space above, dangling their feet over the edge. The sun failed to penetrate the arched rooftop, shrouding the bazaar in cool shadows.

Isiah ran his eyes over the stalls. The blend of sights and sounds made his head spin. One merchant sold ceramic jugs, another displayed racks of jewellery. The steady clip-clop of a donkey's hooves echoed out as a merchant bought it and led it away.

Isiah racked his brains for where to begin. *Ask around*, he told himself. *Someone has to have heard about the oasis.*

A commotion went up from further in the bazaar. Isiah spotted a group of Raiders pushing their way through the crowd. A few young nomads loitered around the stalls, jeering at the Raiders as they passed. One spat at the man in the lead. The Raider's face darkened. He shot out a hand and caught the boy's collar.

"If you've got a problem, say it to my face," he said. His teeth were yellowed from pipe smoke. "You should remember who runs this place."

The nomad boy wrested himself free. He was only a few years older than Isiah. "You're a blight on the face of the Badlands, and your cities are lawless slums."

The Raider gave him a shove. "Remember your place, boy. Our Oath doesn't extend to the likes of you."

The other nomads crowded around, leaning against pillars and whispering among themselves. The nomad boy the Raider had threatened cracked a smile. "Did you ever find the nomads who stole your eagles that time?" He patted his stomach. "The butchers cooked 'em well."

A laugh went around the nomad group. Several of the Raiders sneered back. Their leader rolled up his sleeves.

"I'll drag you to the border and feed you to the Royal Guards," he snapped.

"The dragons will get you first," the nomad replied.

Isiah's gaze drifted away from the Raider and his group. A second group sat further off, talking among each other in hushed voices. Isiah recognized them as the ones he and Reuben had encountered in the Badlands.

"This is our city," the Raider spat. "If not for us, you wouldn't even have a city to call home."

"We call nowhere home," the nomad replied. "Least of all this dump of yours."

Their shoving match escalated. One of the Raiders threw a fist.

Merchants scattered as a scuffle broke out. People covered their heads and ran for cover. Lazaro and his friends laughed as the two groups threw fists at each other. Jugs fell and shattered as the Raider pushed the nomad boy into them. The other nomads darted between the stalls, grabbing anything that came to hand and lobbing it at the Raiders. Bits of cheap jewellery and food flew through the air.

The Raider pushed the nomad boy into a stall. The boy raised his arms in time to block a punch. A spark of heat simmered in Isiah's chest.

It's not fair, he thought. *The nomads don't deserve this.*

The Raider slammed his fists into the nomad boy. One hit its mark and caught him across the ear. The merchant behind the stall yelled a string of curses and beat the pair with a stick.

Before Isiah could stop himself, his legs carried him toward the fight. The Raider grunted in pain and yanked the merchant's stick away. Isiah grabbed the downed nomad boy's arm and pulled him free.

"Thanks," the nomad said. He spat blood from a split lip. "Who are you?"

"I'm a nomad," Isiah lied. "I wanted to help you."

Before he could say anything else, the Raider recovered his senses and swung the stick at them. The nomad boy sidestepped and made a dive for a row of stalls. Isiah ducked instinctively and the stick passed inches above his head. The Raider gritted his teeth and advanced.

Isiah stumbled away. His earlier anger melted as his situation dawned on him. *What am I doing?* His heart flew into his throat as the Raider grabbed his collar and swung him through the air. He hit the hard stone and the wind exploded from his lungs.

The nomads scattered into the crowd, whooping and hurling insults at the Raiders as they went. Isiah groaned and pulled himself onto his elbows as the Raiders closed in. The one who'd grabbed him bore down on him, face red and chest heaving.

"We've got this one," a voice said. Isiah twisted around to see Lazaro.

"No you don't," the Raider said. Blood trickled down from a cut above his eye, and sweat glistened on his forehead. "This little rat is mine."

"I said we've got it," Lazaro replied. His voice took on a hard tone.

The Raider looked from Lazaro to Isiah, his chest heaving. After a moment he grunted and turned away. "Fine."

Isiah tried to scramble away, but a pair of Lazaro's friends grabbed his arms and yanked him to his feet.

Lazaro's friends dragged Isiah out of the crowd and away from the bazaar. Isiah fought against them, but his sides throbbed and each breath pained his chest. Lazaro took the lead and they slipped down a side road. Panic built in Isiah's insides.

"I say we throw him off the edge," one of the Raiders said. "Let's see if nomad boys can fly."

"Want to bet how many seconds it'll take before he hits the ground?" the other one—a woman—asked.

The noise of the bazaar faded behind them as they neared the edge of the city. Isiah kicked and tried to pull free, but the pair refused to budge.

"Don't even bother screaming," the woman said. "This is *our* city—and those nomad friends of yours are as loyal as dirt. They won't help you."

They reached the edge of the terrace, where a row of houses jutted over its side. The sight of the plain beyond sent a stab of fear through Isiah's chest.

Lazaro unlocked a door and disappeared inside one of the houses. The two Raiders shoved Isiah in after.

"Are you back from the bazaar so soon?" a voice asked. "You can't have bought everything we need."

"I found something better," Lazaro called back. The Raiders led Isiah into a cramped dining room. A table dominated the space, with chairs strewn haphazardly around it and a few bits of furniture against the walls. The female Raider yanked out a chair and shoved Isiah into it. They stood guard as Lazaro took a seat opposite.

Isiah scanned the room for an escape. The door stood behind him, and the only window looked out across the grassy plain. Lazaro cleared his throat.

"You have spirit," he said. "But I can't say the same about your intelligence."

63

The Raiders snickered. Isiah pulled his cloak tighter. His Mark itched, tugging at the edge of his attention. If the Raiders found it . . .

"It's hard to catch a nomad boy," Lazaro continued. He folded his arms on the table. "They're usually too fast and slippery."

"What do you want?" Isiah asked.

The female Raider clapped him across the back of the head. "Don't talk to Lazaro like that."

"Darla," Lazaro said, "a bit of spirit will help him here."

Isiah caught sight of the girl he'd seen earlier in the Badlands. She sat curled in the corner of the room, surveying him with a cold expression. "Why'd you bring him here?" she asked.

"I have a proposition for him," Lazaro replied. He turned his attention to Isiah. "We're looking to hire someone. Our last Scavenger met an untimely end a few months ago."

"Gorgons," the girl cut in. "Got her while we were inside a ruin."

Isiah remembered what Reuben had told him. *The Raiders look for treasure. Old crypts, burial sites, buried temples, the likes.*

"You're courageous, boy," Lazaro said.

"And reckless," Darla added.

Lazaro leaned forward. "We need people like you. We need someone to help us loot the ruins. What do you say you ditch the nomad life and become a Scavenger for us?"

"But—" Isiah started.

"Or," Lazaro said, cutting him off, "I could leave my friends here to bet on how far they can throw you off the mountain." His voice took on a hard edge. "Nobody insults the Raiders."

Isiah squirmed in his seat.

The girl stood up. "Wait—you want *him*?"

"Not now, Tess." Lazaro raised a hand. "I know what I'm doing." He turned to Isiah. "So what will it be?"

Isiah remembered his plan to find the oasis. "W—what do you want me to do?"

"Tess here will tell you everything you need to know," he replied. "We need someone to crawl into difficult spots, reach places we can't, and find safe passages."

"I don't have a choice, do I?" he asked.

"It depends," Lazaro replied. "Can you fly?"

Isiah gulped. "I'll do it."

Lazaro clapped his hands together. "A wise choice. Darla, show him to his room."

Darla pulled Isiah to his feet. She and the other Raider herded him from the room and up a narrow staircase. Lazaro and the girl disappeared from view.

"Get comfortable, boy," Darla said. "Because you're a Raider now."

Scavenger

TESSA WAITED UNTIL DARLA AND ANTONY had escorted the boy away, then stood and marched over to Lazaro. "What do you think you're doing?"

"We need a Scavenger," he replied. "And he's as good as any."

"He's a nomad," she spat. "Don't you recognize him? He was with those ones we crossed paths with in the Badlands."

"So he knows how to survive." Lazaro gestured to the street outside. "He'll be better than a merchant's offspring."

"Nomads are useless." Tessa crossed her arms. "He doesn't have what it takes. He can't possibly become a Raider."

"That doesn't mean you can't teach him," Lazaro replied. He pushed out his chair and ran a hand through his short-cropped hair.

Tessa frowned. "Me? Why do I have to teach him? I don't have time for babysitting."

"You're the same age, Tess," Lazaro replied. "You two will get along fine." He straightened up. "I'm not letting you risk your life as a Scavenger any longer."

"I know how to look after myself."

"It's my job to protect you," Lazaro said. "And not just because I'm in charge."

Tessa huffed. "Just because you're my brother doesn't mean you can boss me around."

"I'm trying to look out for you, Tess," he replied. "You know that. I won't have you putting yourself in harm's way—no matter how independent you think you are."

"You don't trust me to look after myself?"

"There's no point arguing." Lazaro's voice took on the tone it always did when he was giving orders. "You know as well as I do that the Badlands is an unforgiving place. I'd be a terrible brother if I let you put yourself on the front line. No." He paced about the room. "It's time we got a replacement Scavenger. The boy's perfect."

Tessa turned up her nose. "He'll be dead within a month."

Lazaro gave her a wry smile. "Then you'd better make sure he lasts longer than that. Train him up, show him the ropes, and he'll make a fine Scavenger."

"But—"

"I've made up my mind," Lazaro said, cutting her off. "And my word is final."

Tessa grunted. "Don't expect any miracles." She marched from the dining room.

"I'm not expecting miracles," Lazaro called after her. "I expect you to make a half-decent Scavenger out of him!"

'Just a Nomad'

ISIAH CLIMBED THE STAIRCASE TO THE SECOND level of the house. The wooden boards creaked beneath his feet. Thin shafts of sunlight illuminated the dust floating in the air. He reached the top and found a narrow hallway. Darla swung open a squat door.

"Make yourself at home," she said. "Because this is where you'll be living from now on."

She pushed Isiah and he stumbled inside. The door slammed shut behind him. Isiah found himself in a small room filled with crates and barrels. A bed took up half the space, which was no more than a bundle of blankets on a frame. He studied the single window. It overlooked the street beyond—too small to climb through.

Alright. Isiah racked his brain. *Think.* The Raiders hadn't found his Mark. They didn't know who he was. He tried to spy Reuben or one of the other Nomads on the street below, but he knew they'd still be at the tavern.

"I can make this work," he told himself. He paced back and forth, stepping over boxes and rolled-up rugs. The Raiders explored ruins, and Reuben said the oasis might be hidden in one. Maybe they were exactly who he was looking for.

I'll stay with them, he thought. *I'll find the oasis, and as soon as I do, I'll slip away.* He nodded, mentally cementing his plan.

His Mark itched. He'd gone without healing ointment for days. Isiah peeled back his layers of clothing and inspected it. The burns and scars stretched from his chest over his right shoulder, then across his upper back and shoulder blades. He probed the angry red blisters. Some had burst after being thrown by the Raider in the bazaar, leaving his skin raw and painful.

Footsteps sounded in the hall outside. Isiah hurriedly yanked on his cloak as the door swung open. He spun around to see the girl from before.

"Am I interrupting anything?" she asked. She ran her eyes over him with a scowl.

"No . . ." Isiah hesitated. "You're Tess, right?"

Her nose crinkled. "Tessa," she said. "Only Lazaro can call me that."

Isiah extended a hand and introduced himself. "Is he your father?"

"No." Tessa folded her arms. "He's my brother." She paused. "I don't want to talk about it."

An awkward silence descended. Isiah caught sight of straps and harnesses among the pile of crates—for their eagles.

Tessa sighed after a minute. "Lazaro wants me to teach you," she said. "So from now on, you take orders from me."

"Fine," he replied. He paused. "Lazaro mentioned something about ruins. What are they like?"

Tessa rolled her eyes. "They're buried structures," she said. "Sometimes they're even whole towns. Nobody knows how many there are, but they're buried beneath the Badlands. Rockslide and earthquakes expose new ones all the time."

"And then?" Isiah asked.

She snorted. "What do you think? We loot it. There are valuables in there. Gold artefacts, treasure, even magic."

A bubble of hope welled in Isiah's chest. "What kind of magic?"

Tessa shrugged. "All sorts. Magic runes, spellbooks, elixirs, the works. Whoever gets there first can carry away anything they find." She lowered her voice. "But you're just a nomad. You won't last five minutes in a ruin."

Isiah frowned. "Why's that?"

"You can't figure it out? You don't know the first thing about being a Raider. That's why Scavengers keep dying." Tessa plucked one of the harnesses up and turned it over. "Down there, the eagles can't help you. And there are *so* many ways to meet a grisly end." Her voice seemed to taunt him. "Packs of gorgons, sudden ravines, hidden traps, not to mention the danger of getting lost and slowly running out of torches and food . . ." She tilted her head. "Get the picture?"

Isiah puffed himself up. "You think I can't do it?"

"I *know* you can't," she replied. "Lazaro might as well have thrown you from the city and saved you the trouble, nomad boy." She nodded to the window. "But you could always run away. If you did, the city is *far* too big for us to ever find you again."

The thought of escape played on Isiah's mind. He could go back to Reuben and continue looking in the bazaar . . . He shoved it away. "No. I want to explore the ruins."

"Then good luck." Tessa swung the door shut. Her footsteps sounded as she departed.

Isiah clenched his jaw in determination. *She won't scare me off.* He adjusted his cloak to ease the itch under his skin, then went after her.

* * *

The next morning, Isiah found himself in the cramped dining room with Tessa and Lazaro. The girl had spoken little to him the previous day after their encounter, and he'd spent an uncomfortable night squashed into the bed the Raiders had given him.

He'd spotted the remaining two members of the household that morning—a young man they called Luca, alongside a tall and mean-looking woman named Helen.

Lazaro studied Isiah. "You can't be a Scavenger looking like that."

"What's wrong with how I look?" he asked.

"Your cloak is a mess, and you don't have any gear." He fished around in his pocket, then tossed a pouch of coins to Tessa. "Go into the bazaar with him and buy him some new things."

"We don't have money to waste," Tessa told him.

71

"We're not wasting it—not if we can pick his gear off his corpse when he's done with it." Lazaro flashed him a wry smile. "Then we'll use it to equip the next Scavenger."

Tessa folded her arms. "Suit yourself."

Isiah hurried after her as she left the dining room and exited the house. They stumbled into the city, and the hot Badlands air washed over him. Isiah blinked, trying to make his eyes adjust. Tessa melted into the crowd.

"Wait up!" he called. He jostled past people to keep up with her. She moved effortlessly, weaving in and out of groups of merchants and ducking through side streets. Isiah strained to keep her in his sight.

"You're going to need a new cloak," Tessa called over her shoulder. "Eagles don't like it when it flaps around. It spooks them."

Isiah found himself at the entrance to the bazaar. No sooner had he regained his senses than Tessa disappeared inside. He ducked past a pair of mules and redoubled his pace.

He found Tessa standing in front of a merchant's stall. Robes, dyed a deep yellow and orange, hung over the merchant's head. The woman haggled with Tessa over the price. Isiah fished around in his boot for his pouch of coins.

"I could pay for that," he offered. He tipped a few coins on the counter. Tessa narrowed her eyes at them.

"Paradon coins?" she said. "Where'd you get those from?"

"At the border," Isiah lied. "I traded for them."

Tessa stuck her nose up at them, but the merchant scooped them into her own pouch and passed them the cloak. Isiah exchanged it for his ripped and battered one. Tessa then bought him a harness to pin his cloak closer to his body and keep it from flapping around.

"We need more rope," Tessa said. "Lazaro was supposed to buy some before he found you."

"Why can't you just use the eagles?" Isiah asked.

"We need it for *inside* the ruins, stupid."

Tessa led him deeper into the bazaar, where another merchant sold coils of cordage and rope. Others crafted eagle harnesses and sewed leather into saddles. Isiah stuck close to Tessa as they navigated past a group of Raiders. He hoped none would notice him from the previous day's fight.

"Here." Tessa dumped a coil of rope into Isiah's arms. He awkwardly shrugged it onto his shoulder.

"Follow me." She took off again. Isiah went after her. She led him out of the bazaar and further into the city. Ahead, hammer strikes rang out alongside the grind of sharpening wheels. Coils of smoke curled into the air from forges. The houses grew closer together, forming three-story high towers with walkways and arches in between.

"You'll need a way to defend yourself," Tessa said. "Unless you can shoot a bow, that is?" She raised an eyebrow at him.

"I never learned," Isiah replied.

"Thought as much." Tessa kept walking. "And that measly knife of yours won't do anything against a gorgon. It's useless."

Isiah's hand fell to his knife, which was still tucked into his waistband.

"You think I didn't notice it?" Tessa asked. "If you don't notice things out here, you die. You can't rely on anyone other than yourself."

She reached a storefront. Curved sabres sat on a rack behind the merchant's head. Tessa ran her eyes over them, then pointed to one.

"Got any more of those coins?" she asked. "Sabres aren't cheap."

Isiah handed her the last of his money. The merchant took it and passed Isiah the sabre.

"Don't lose it," Tessa ordered.

The sabre had a wooden scabbard, painted with colourful patterns and sporting brass clasps that let it fit to a belt. The sabre's wooden hilt formed a curve, with a smooth pommel and a metal guard. Isiah pulled the blade free. Its sheen reflected the sunlight.

"It's worth nothing if you don't know how to use it," Tessa said. She backed away and grabbed the hilt of her sabre. "Or did you never learn that either?"

The crowds moved aside. Merchants leaned over their stalls to watch. Tessa stood on the rim of a sandstone ring, and Isiah found himself on the opposite side.

"What's the matter, nomad boy?" she said. "Are you scared?"

Isiah tucked the scabbard into his belt. "Did Lazaro say we should do this?"

Tessa drew her sabre and took a fighting stance. "Lazaro won't want to waste money on you if you're going to die inside the first ruin we find."

"Get in there, boy," someone in the crowd called. "Show her what nomads are worth."

Isiah tried to mirror Tessa's stance. He adjusted his grip on the sword. It felt weird and unwieldy in his untrained hand. The bottom-third of the blade was blunt, while the top-third fanned out to form a double edge.

"They're sharp!" Isiah said. "What if I cut you?"

Tessa scoffed. "Do you think I'll let you do that?" She darted forward and aimed a cut at him.

Isiah raised the sword instinctively. Tessa's blade struck it.

"Angle it," she said. "Make my sabre slide off."

She swung at him again. Isiah staggered away and blocked. The ringing of steel made his heart leap. He tilted the sabre to redirect her blade.

Tessa circled him. Isiah's palm grew sweaty, making it hard for him to grip the sabre.

Tessa darted forward. Isiah pulled away. She laughed. "You're too jumpy."

Isiah regained himself and launched a half-hearted cut at her. She parried it and brought her sabre around. Isiah barely blocked it in time. He felt her edge bite into his.

"Block with the dull part, closer to the hilt," she said. "Didn't those nomads teach you *anything*?"

Isiah blocked another flurry of attacks. The crowd parted as he stumbled out of the ring. People steadied him and pushed him back toward her.

Isiah batted away another one of her attacks. The impact sent a shock up his arm. "You're gonna hit me!"

"Then defend yourself," Tessa replied. She flicked her wrist and brought her sabre arcing toward his head.

Isiah sidestepped and blocked it. A surge of adrenaline overtook him and he countered with a strike of his own. Tessa parried and their sabres clashed together.

Isiah's arm lurched as she stepped toward him and drove their blades upwards. Her hand clasped around his wrist and she locked his arm against her body. His sword now hung uselessly behind her. Isiah went cross-eyed as the tip of her sabre came level with his nose.

"And now you're dead," Tessa said. She released him and stepped away. A sly smile crossed her face. "Ready to give up yet?"

Isiah rubbed his arm. His legs quivered. He took a deep breath and waited for his pulse to return to normal. Tessa sheathed her sabre. "I'll take that as a yes."

The crowd lost interest and drifted away. As it parted, a figure wandered into the sandstone ring.

"You put on quite the show," he said. A beard hugged his chin, with gold rings tied into it. The sun had left his bald head with a deep tan, and his hands were tough and leathery. Patches of armour hung over his thighs and shoulders like fish scales. "It's a shame you're not as good at being a Raider."

Tessa scowled. "What do you want, Enrik?"

Enrik raised his hands. "I couldn't help but notice you as I was passing, is all." The corner of his mouth upturned. "Lazaro taught you well."

"Don't talk to me about Lazaro," Tessa replied.

"If only he was as good at raiding as he is with teaching the sabre," he said, ignoring her. "Then maybe you wouldn't need to be training *another* Scavenger." His eyes darted to Isiah. "How many has it been now? Four? Five?"

"Three," Tessa snapped. "And you know that."

Enrik grinned. "I guess I'd better be on my way before you challenge *me* to a duel. But of course, you know the rules." Enrik raised his hand. Isiah gasped as his fingers melted into sand. "Magic is allowed."

"Don't show off your party trick again," Tessa said.

Enrik's smile dropped. "Suit yourself." His body dissolved into a spinning vortex of sand and dust. The crowd parted as he flew past and re-formed. As he marched away, Isiah ran to Tessa's side.

"Who was that?" he asked.

"Enrik," Tessa replied. "And he's not good news."

"What did he want?"

"He and Lazaro are rivals," she explained. "They got into a fight over some ruins a while back. Enrik never forgot."

Isiah watched where Enrik had disappeared. "And that sand thing?"

"Remember when I told you that you could find magic in the ruins?" Tessa asked.

Isiah nodded.

"Enrik did. His entire group can do that."

"What about you?" Isiah asked. "Do you have any magic?"

Tessa scowled. "We don't need magic." She took his hand. "Now come on. Forget about Enrik. I'm not done with you yet."

Vyrro

A LONG SERIES OF STAIRCASES LED TO THE higher levels of the city. As they climbed, the wind rushed through the streets and whipped Tessa's hair. The bustling crowds faded behind them as they neared the mountain's summit.

Isiah's lungs strained at the thinning air. Ahead, wide awnings stretched over storehouses and open plazas. Wooden platforms jutted from the mountainside, forming landing pads for eagles.

"Where are we going?" Isiah asked between panting breaths.

"The eagle roosts," Tessa called. She reached the top of the staircase and marched into the highest parts of the city. "I come here all the time."

The top of the mountain loomed several hundred feet above them, its blocky sides sheer and unscalable. Isiah paused to catch his breath, then turned to survey the way they had come. The city, with its tight-packed streets and labyrinth of houses, covered the mountainside. Beyond, an ocean of grass and maize swayed gently on the plain.

"I hope you're not afraid of heights," Tessa said, making him jump.

Isiah followed her into the eagle roosts. The storehouses and landing pads gave way to rows of tall, curved wooden pillars, like the ribcage of a giant dragon. Awnings were strung between them, offering protection from the wind and the sun.

"We keep the eagles here," Tessa said. "Handlers look after them while we're away."

Isiah saw that the pillars formed makeshift pens, with walls behind and gates in front. Eagles sat atop perches, surveying him as he passed. Some wore masks that covered their eyes, while others were chained to their perches.

Groups of Raiders stood around talking and laughing, while others fitted their eagles with harnesses in preparation for flight. Handlers scurried past, pushing wheelbarrows laden with meat for feeding.

"Where's your eagle?" Isiah asked.

"Here." Tessa pointed ahead. They stopped in front of one of the pens. Isiah's breath caught in his throat as he gazed at the same eagle he'd seen Tessa flying on over the Badlands.

"Does it have a name?"

Her nose crinkled. "Of course." She swung open the gate and approached the perch. Her eagle tilted its head as she approached, surveying her with beady black eyes. "His name is Vyrro." She stroked his foot. Each toe was as thick as her arm, armed with hooked talons. Isiah hung back.

"They're dangerous," she said. She leaned in. "They can see their prey from miles away, and their claws can rip open a man in a single kick." A cruel smile crossed her lips as she spoke. "The wild ones have even been seen feasting on the bodies of dead nomads."

Isiah swallowed. Vyrro ruffled his feathers and adjusted his grip on the perch. His black, beady eyes studied Isiah with an unrelenting intensity.

"And *we're* going to go flying," Tessa said.

Isiah choked. "What?"

"You heard me," she replied. "Every Raider can fly. You can't be scared of them. Unless, of course," she added, "you've decided you don't want to be a Raider after all."

"No," Isiah said quickly.

Tessa's smile dropped. "Then come on. He's already harnessed."

Isiah tentatively gripped the gate. He avoided Vyrro's piercing gaze.

"He won't bite," Tessa said. "Not unless I *want* him to." She clicked her fingers and coaxed the bird from his perch. Vyrro thudded to the ground. Tessa clambered onto his back and took a seat in the harness. "What's the matter," she called. She giggled. "Are you scared?"

Isiah puffed himself up, but inside he wanted to cower. Vyrro dwarfed him, standing like a soldier on guard. His hooked beak glistened, razor-sharp.

"I'm not scared," he forced himself to say.

"Then stop being such a coward," Tessa replied.

Isiah approached Vyrro. He passed behind the bird and grabbed the harness, then awkwardly clambered up behind Tessa.

"You won't win any awards for gracefulness," she said.

Isiah shifted his weight until he was firmly seated in the harness. "Are there any straps?"

Tessa scoffed. "Raiders don't fall off. Only *nomads* do."

She spurred Vyrro forward. Handlers scurried aside as the bird exited his pen and bounded down the street. Isiah locked his arms around Tessa's middle as Vyrro picked up speed. The eagle reached the landing pad and his wings unfurled.

They soared into the sky, leaving the mountain behind them. Isiah's heart leapt into his throat as a feeling of weightlessness seized him. Vyrro sailed over the open air for a moment, before beating his wings and carrying them away from the city.

Tessa pumped her fist and let out a whoop. Vyrro mirrored her cry with a screech that sent a stab of pain through Isiah's head. He didn't dare cover his ears in case he slipped and fell. The wind roared around him, tugging at his clothes and chilling his face.

The city grew smaller. Tessa pulled on Vyrro's reins and he dropped, sailing toward the plain far below. Isiah closed his eyes, trying to quell the nausea roiling in his gut.

"Ease up," Tessa grunted. Isiah realized he was gripping her with white knuckles. He peeled his hands away and steadied his breathing.

"I bet you've never seen the Badlands like this before, huh?" she said.

"No," Isiah managed to say. Even in his homeland, Ward had never taken him flying. *Not until your Ceremony*, he'd said.

Vyrro settled into a steady flight, his mighty wings carrying him on the air currents. His head darted about as he scoured the plain for any sign of movement.

"Watch this." Tessa tugged on his reins again and the bird went into a dive.

Vyrro dropped like an arrow, wings pulled close and tail feathers outstretched. Isiah clung to Tessa as the force threatened to lift him from Vyrro's back.

They shot toward the plain. At the last minute, Vyrro pulled up. Isiah's insides jolted as Vyrro blasted over the Badlands, stirring the grass with the force of his wingbeats.

"What are you doing?" he exclaimed.

Tessa ignored him. She dug her heels into Vyrro's side and the bird responded by climbing rapidly. Isiah gripped Vyrro's harness with his legs and braced himself against the eagle's back. He didn't dare look behind at the ground as it grew further and further away.

With a flick of the reins, Tessa made Vyrro spin. He swept his wings and twirled in mid-air.

"They have to be agile," she said. Isiah barely heard her over the whistle of wind. "Fighting dragons is dangerous. They're faster and stronger than us, so we have to outmanoeuvre them."

Vyrro levelled out. Isiah twisted around to study the city. Its packed streets and elevators looked tiny from so far away.

"Hold on," Tessa said.

Isiah stifled a cry as Vyrro did a barrel roll. He felt his legs begin to slip out of the harness. He hung weightless in the air for a split second—but as soon as it had begun, it was over.

Isiah panted. "Why—why did you do that?"

"Because," Tessa replied. "It's fun." She gave him a wry smile. "You did well, nomad boy. I expected you to fall off at least once."

Tessa directed Vyrro to fly over the hills. The grassy plain changed to arid rock and spiky trees. The shape of Alcabaza faded into the distance. Isiah swivelled around to look at the plain behind them. A few silhouettes of eagles flew towards them—gaining fast.

"What are they doing?" he asked.

Tessa frowned. "I don't know."

The eagles drew closer until the Raiders atop them materialized. Vyrro lurched aside as the birds erupted past.

"Hey!" Tessa yelled. "What do you think you're playing at?"

The Raiders hollered and spurred their eagles, circling around Vyrro. Isiah flinched as they darted close and then broke away.

"It's just a bit of harmless fun," a voice called. Isiah spotted Enrik flying among them. His eagle was larger than the others, its plumage a golden-brown. "My boys thought they'd give you and your new Scavenger a fright."

"Remember the Oath," Tessa spat. "If your birds attack us . . ."

"Accidents happen all the time in the Badlands," Enrik replied. "People lose control." He winked at her. "Come on, boys. Let's get out of here."

The Raiders spurred their eagles and the group pulled away. Tessa glared at them as they went.

"What was that?" Isiah asked, steadying his breathing.

"Enrik thinks he runs the place," Tessa replied. "His Raiders are a bunch of thugs."

Isiah watched the silhouettes of Enrik's gang fade into the Badlands. "Where do you think they're going?"

"Beats me," Tessa replied. "To look for ruins to loot, I guess. Hopefully the Royal Guards finally get him."

Vyrro stretched out his wings and glided toward one of the mesas. When they drew close, he stretched out his legs and landed.

Isiah slipped from the eagle's back. He hit the ground and took a few shaky steps, trying to regain his balance. Vyrro ruffled his feathers and watched Isiah with a knowing gaze.

"Impressive," Tessa said. She hopped from the harness and sauntered over. "Maybe I'll make a Scavenger out of you yet."

Isiah regained his composure. "Do you always use eagles to get around?"

"Of course," she replied. "There's no better way. We can go anywhere we like—and we get to ruins before anybody else."

They wandered to the edge of the mesa, where the ground dropped away with crumbling layers of rock. Behind them, a heap of cracked boulders climbed into the sky, as if placed there by a giant. Tessa put her hands on her hips and surveyed the Badlands.

"It's beautiful, isn't it?" she said.

Isiah held a hand to his forehead. The Badlands stretched out before him, a mass of orange and yellow. Flat plateaus and tall, lopsided buttes loomed over gorges and ravines. Bushes and trees grew around babbling streams and waterholes. Far above, the twin suns looked down on them like a pair of eyes.

"People say there are two suns because of the dragons and eagles," Tessa said. "One for the dragons, and one for our eagles." She paused. "If you want to believe the stories, that is."

Isiah squinted at them. The blue-white sun cut through the clouds and basked the Badlands in heat. Its cousin roamed across the sky on a separate orbit, rising and falling whenever it pleased.

"Sometimes the dark sun is out with the moon," Tessa said. She sighed. "The Badlands look incredible then."

"Do the Royal Guards believe the same thing about the suns too?" Isiah asked. He never recalled Ward saying anything about it.

Tessa kicked the rock beneath her. "No. Paradon and their Royal Guards don't appreciate what we have here. They think they can fly in here and terrorize us—that just because we don't submit to their rule, they can kill our eagles and burn our cities." She turned to him. "You've seen that, haven't you?"

Isiah shifted his weight. "I—" He swallowed. "Of course. They fly over the border. I had to run away from a dragon once."

"We all have," she replied. She started to say something else, then paused. "What's that?"

Isiah raised a hand to his forehead. A flash of movement caught his eye, further in the Badlands. "It looks like more eagles." He shrugged. "Maybe they found a ruin."

"There are no new ruins so close to Alcabaza," she replied. "They've all been looted." She jumped onto one of the boulders. "I'm going to get a better look."

"Why don't we fly?" Isiah asked.

"Because I don't want them to spot us, stupid."

Tessa clambered onto the pile of broken boulders. Isiah went after her, grabbing half-dead plants and slipping his hands into cracks for purchase. He hoped no snakes or scorpions were hiding inside. Rocks shifted under his feet, threatening to come loose.

He neared the top of the spire and balanced on a narrow ledge, pressing himself against the rock for balance. Tessa leaned out, her head darting about like one of the eagles.

Isiah mimicked her. "Do you see anything?"

Tessa didn't reply. Isiah caught a glimpse of one of the eagles— one with golden-brown plumage.

"Enrik," he said.

"Why did he land?" Tessa asked. "He can't have found a ruin so close to the city."

"Maybe it was one of those earthquakes," Isiah suggested.

Figures, no more than dark dots obscured against the backdrop of the rocky terrain, moved about. Isiah readjusted his footing on the ledge.

Tessa hopped from her perch. "Whatever. I'm going back now."

Isiah started after her, but a loud bang made him freeze. It crackled across the heavens. The ground beneath him began to tremble.

"Earthquake," Tessa called. She scurried off the boulders as loose stones rained around them.

Isiah stumbled, struggling to keep his balance. Dust fell from the spire, settling in his hair and making his eyes water. Boulders shifted and rocks clattered to the ground. Vyrro squawked in alarm.

"Get down from there," Tessa said.

Isiah tried to obey, but the trembling rocks made it impossible to keep his footing. A stone the size of his head struck a boulder next to him and shattered. The trembling stopped, but the damage was already done.

Tessa grabbed Vyrro and pulled him out of the way as the heap of boulders collapsed. Isiah scrambled away as the sound of grinding stone split the air. Large rocks tumbled around him, dislodging more and more as they went.

Isiah jumped as the boulder beneath him tumbled. Panic flared in his chest as the ground seemed to rush to greet him. His feet connected with the hard rock and a burst of pain ricocheted through his knees. Tessa grabbed his arm and dragged him away as the boulders landed with a crash.

A plume of dust billowed into the air. Vyrro screeched in panic and flapped his wings. Isiah found himself lying on the ground among a pile of loose pebbles and shattered rock. Tessa sat up, coughing.

"Are you alright?" Isiah asked. He winced at the pain in his knees as he stood.

Tessa ignored his question. "That was too close to be miners," she said.

Isiah looked in the direction of Enrik and his eagles. The Raiders scurried about, calming their birds.

"Maybe they found a door," Tessa said. She dusted herself off. "Ruins weren't built to be easy to break into."

Isiah took a moment to collect himself. The boulders were strewn across the surface of the mesa. A few rocks clattered down its sheer side. Tessa calmed Vyrro, then climbed atop his shoulders. "I'm going back now."

Vyrro unfurled his wings and kicked off, taking to the air. Isiah ran after them.

"Hold up!" he called. He swore. He should have known she'd try to get rid of him. She was only waiting for a chance—

Tessa laughed and Vyrro swung around. "Did you think I was going to leave you behind?" she said.

Isiah folded his arms. "Yes!" He felt his cheeks begin to burn.

Vyrro landed and Tessa beckoned him. "If I was going to abandon you somewhere, I would have flown further away."

Isiah climbed onto Vyrro before she could change her mind. He steadied himself in the harness. "Don't do that again."

Tessa giggled. "Like I said, you're too jumpy."

Vyrro took to the skies. With a flick of the reins, Tessa directed him toward Alcabaza.

Archive

MONTHS PRIOR . . .

Isiah hunched over the table. He squinted in the darkness, scanning the dusty old pages. A lingering pain rippled across his skin. He gritted his teeth against it.

The shadows of the palace archives hung thick around him, obscuring ancient bookshelves and piles of crates. Isiah had visited the archives with Ward when learning about dragons—now, he needed them for a different reason.

There has to be something. Isiah turned the page faster. If the healers discovered him out of bed, they'd drag him back to the medical ward. His freshly grafted skin itched like a thousand ants. He still felt a simmering heat deep inside his flesh.

Marks were uncurable. Everybody knew that. Isiah raised his candle, tracing faded sentences and diagrams with his finger. With every second that passed, he inched closer to the day he'd have to leave. The Royal Guard's dragons were already getting twitchy. Ward wouldn't be able to control them for much longer.

I knew I wasn't ready. The voice in his head told him. *Ward was wrong.*

Isiah knew what happened to people who were Marked. He'd be cursed to wander the wild, hunted by dragons until they finally caught up to him . . . or he died from something else.

Isiah's hands flew across the pages. He fought the urge to scratch his Mark. It would only tear the skin and infect it.

A page ripped and Isiah swore. He carefully smoothed it out, then paused. Something caught his eye, the text so faded it was nearly illegible.

Unusual ailments and their treatments. The heading jumped out at him. Clutching his candle tighter, he scanned the page.

The sound of creaking hinges echoed across the space.

"Isiah?" a voice asked. Isiah recognized it as the archive-keeper. "The healers told me not to let you down here."

"Just a moment," Isiah called back.

"I'm locking up for the night. Don't make me fetch Ward."

Isiah turned the pages faster. The book listed off rare diseases and poisons, before he stumbled upon a section about dragons.

Isiah's hands began to shake as he turned the pages. He forced himself to breathe slower. Footsteps sounded on the archive stairs.

"I said I'm locking up," the voice called.

Isiah ignored him. His eyes flitted across the page. A diagram of a dragon's cursed blackish fire marked the page, alongside handwritten notes. Isiah's eyes widened.

"Isiah." The archive-keeper stopped beside him. "What are you doing down here?"

"Alcabaza," Isiah stammered. "That's what it says."

"What are you talking about?" In the shadows, Isiah saw the man's brow furrow. "Isn't that some Badlands city?"

"It says there's a healing spring," Isiah said. He squinted at the page. "Like an oasis. It's supposed to be able to cure anything."

The archive-keeper exhaled. "I know you're worried," he said. "You need to rest. Your skin still hasn't healed, and this is no place for a patient like you."

Isiah hardly heard the man. A faded sketch of a map stared at him from the page, burning itself into his mind. The single word *Oasis* echoed in his mind.

The archive-keeper took his arm and flipped the book shut. His voice took on a sterner tone. "You have to go. You can talk to Ward about it later."

Isiah reluctantly broke away from the table. The archive-keeper herded him toward the stairs.

"I'm going to be banished," Isaiah said. "They can't let me stay here."

"I'm sure your father and the nobles will figure something out," the archive-keeper replied.

"No," Isiah insisted. "The dragons will hunt me. I need to see if that book is telling the truth."

"The Badlands is a terrible place," the archive-keeper said. "They hate us—they'd kill you the second they see your Mark."

They reached the stairs and the archive-keeper shut the door behind them, locking it. "Back to the medical ward you go, boy," he said.

Isiah did as he was told. His mind buzzed with thoughts. Despite the fear gnawing at his gut, a spark of hope began to well inside him.

What if the oasis was real?

The Arena

ISIAH SPLASHED A HANDFUL OF WATER ON HIS FACE. The cramped washroom at the Raiders' house penned him in, with no more than a washbowl and a rusted handpump that drew from the groundwater beneath the plain.

Several days had passed since flying with Tessa. Since then, she'd continued to train him with the sabre. Isiah turned over his hand, inspecting the cut that now snaked across it. He'd been too slow to parry.

"Relax," she'd told him. "It isn't deep. Your hands and arms are the biggest targets. You have to protect them."

Checking to make sure the door was locked, Isiah peeled back his clothes and washed his Mark. The water sapped the heat from it, giving him a momentary relief.

As soon as I cure my Mark, I'm out of here, he vowed.

His mind drifted to Reuben and the nomads he'd travelled with. He hadn't seen the group since joining Lazaro. He'd meant to sneak away and talk to them, but someone was always watching him.

Isiah finished treating his Mark, then unlocked the door and left the room. The washroom was attached to the kitchen. Pots and pans hung from a rack over a grimy counter. He passed the dining room, where the Raiders Luca and Darla sat.

"I heard you're skittish around eagles," Luca said. He twisted a pipe in his mouth, peering up at Isiah through a mop of frizzy hair. "I wish I could have seen the look on your face when Tessa tricked you. I'd pay all the gold in the city to see that!"

Isiah ignored him. Darla sat opposite, tinkering with harnesses and sharpening their sabres. He slipped out of the house and lost himself in the street beyond. Lazaro and Tessa had gone out flying, giving him a brief window when nobody was around to keep an eye on him. He hastened down the street, studying the taverns and passing nomad groups. He owed it to Reuben to at least say goodbye.

Animals grunted and supplies rattled somewhere in the crowd ahead. The rumble of elevators met Isiah's ears. A fresh wave of merchants and travellers streamed into the city, driving their animals ahead of them and hauling goods to trade. Isiah ducked through the crowd until he reached the tavern Reuben had taken him to.

"Isiah!" a voice called. Isiah spotted Reuben and his group near the wooden platform that led down to the elevators. He hurried over. People jostled him back and forth. The familiar smell of animals made his nose crinkle.

"Good timing," Reuben said. "We were getting ready to set off today. I tried looking for you, but I couldn't find you anywhere." He leaned in and lowered his voice. "I assumed you were already at the bazaar."

Isaiah nodded. "I've found some possible leads." He decided not to mention the part about joining the Raiders.

"Good for you, lad," Reuben said. "Maybe we'll bump into each other on the trail sometime, ey?"

"Yeah," Isiah replied. He knew that once the nomads were gone, he would be stuck with the Raiders. "You know where I'll be."

Reuben extended a weathered hand. "Was good meeting you, kid." He dropped his voice. "Just don't let any dragons catch wind of you again."

Isiah shook the man's hand. "I won't."

He bid Reuben and the nomads farewell, before breaking away and heading back to Lazaro's house. As he approached, Tessa and Lazaro appeared.

Lazaro raised an eyebrow at him. "Where have you been?"

"I took a walk," Isiah said quickly. "I didn't think you'd be back so soon."

Before Lazaro could reply, Tessa stepped forward and grabbed Isiah's hand. "I want to show you something," she said.

Relieved at the opportunity to break away, Isiah let Tessa take him into the city.

"Did you find any ruins?" he asked. He tried not to sound impatient.

"We were exercising the eagles," Tessa replied. "You'll know when we find something. All the Raiders scramble to be the first to claim it."

Tessa led him to the second terrace, to the far side where the houses met the mountainside. Above, the third level led to the eagle roosts, but Tessa ignored the staircases.

"Where are we going?" Isiah asked.

"You'll see."

Ahead, a crack in the mountain beckoned them. It snaked up the rock, narrow at its tip but wide at the base. Merchant stalls and squat buildings spilled out from it.

"Labourers carved this place out decades ago," Tessa said. Her voice bounced off the walls. The rocky ground beneath them sloped downward, its cracks clogged with sand and dirt. Shafts of sunlight made it through the entrance to cast dappled light across the space.

They stopped as the passage fanned out to form a wide cavern. A stone ceiling spanned overhead, with a wide space beneath. Inside it, a half-circle of chairs surrounded a wrought-iron dome. A large gate, sealed shut, led into a circle of sand.

"It's an arena . . ." Isiah started. His mind flashed back to his Ceremony at the palace.

"It gets better." Tessa pulled him toward one side of the cavern. On the far side of the arena, metal bars blocked off a passageway. Isiah's pulse quickened as he realized what was inside.

"We captured it from the Badlands," Tessa said. "Lazaro and I went with a bunch of other Raiders."

Something moved behind the gate, and claws clicked against the stone. Isiah tried to pull away, but Tessa had an iron grip around his wrist. She seemed not to notice his apprehension.

"The last one died, so we had to find a new one," she said. "We feed prisoners and Royal Guards to it." She gave him a cruel smile. "Fitting, huh?"

Isiah gritted his teeth as his Mark began to burn. The pain crept across his skin, red-hot needles penetrating his flesh. A guttural hiss emanated from beyond the gate.

Isiah jumped as a dragon slammed into the metal. The bars shook and chains rattled. The beast's jaws parted to reveal strings of saliva and rows of razor teeth. Manacles were secured around the dragon's ankles, with thick rings chaining it to the wall.

Tessa raised an eyebrow at him. "What's wrong with you? Why are you so pale?"

Isiah tried to speak, but his throat felt sealed shut. The dragon cracked open its jaws and bellowed at him. He ducked, waiting for the stream of fire to arc overhead.

"We took care of it," Tessa said as if reading his mind. "Look."

Isiah opened his eyes a crack. At the base of the dragon's neck, a small metal valve protruded from a ring of red and inflamed flesh.

"It's blocking the fire tubes," Tessa explained. "The Raiders put it in. The dragon can't breathe fire as long as the valve is in there."

The dragon threw itself against the bars again. Its eyes bored into Isiah's soul.

Tessa frowned. "It really hates you."

Isiah's Mark throbbed, stinging him like thousands of ants. He staggered back, willing himself to tear his eyes away from the dragon. The pain made it hard to think straight. His mind flashed back to the arena in Paradon when the dragon rejected him and—

Tessa made a grab for his cloak. Isiah pulled away, but she caught the edge and the material slipped, exposing his shoulder. Tessa froze.

"You're from Paradon," she said slowly.

Isiah hurriedly covered his skin. "I know I'm Marked," he admitted. "I tried to hide it." He checked around to make sure nobody else had noticed. "I didn't want anyone to know." He winced, waiting for her reaction.

Tessa narrowed her eyes. Her voice took on a hard edge. "Lazaro will kill you if he finds out . . ."

"Please don't tell him," Isiah begged. "I'm not like the Royal Guards, honest. The dragons rejected me." He tried to read Tessa's expression, but her face gave away nothing.

Her dark eyes flitted over him. "I can't trust you."

"Then let me prove myself to you," he said quickly. "If you keep my secret, I'll show you that I can be a Raider."

Tessa shifted her footing. An eternity seemed to pass. Isiah tried not to let his unease show.

"Fine," Tessa said at last. "I won't tell anybody. But if you even *think* about betraying us to Paradon—"

"I won't," he replied.

Tessa pushed past him and headed for the exit. "You'd better get out of here before the dragon breaks out." She marched away. "I liked you better as a nomad."

Low Profile

YEARS EARLIER...

Tessa tightened her arms around her mother's middle as they soared over the Badlands. Below, ravines and gorges split the landscape. She looked into the distance, where the flat Tablelands marked the border.

Half a dozen eagles flew around her. Their wingbeats stirred the air and made Tessa's heart sing. She spied her father in the lead, twin sabres dangling from his belt.

"Do you think we're going to find treasure?" Tessa asked.

"You never know," her mother replied. "The other Raiders don't often fly this close to the border. Hopefully they'll have missed it."

Tessa wriggled in her seat. The excitement made her want to bounce up and down. It was supposed to be Lazaro's turn, but she'd convinced him to stay behind and let her explore this time.

They passed a wide gorge and flew over the flat, empty Tablelands. A few scraggly bushes whipped past far below. A herd of mountain goats scattered at the sight of the eagles.

"I can't wait to fly on my own," Tessa said.

"When you're older," her mother replied. "You can rear your own eagle chick and fly on him whenever you like."

Her father scoured the land below, searching for the tell-tale signs of the ruin entrance. Butterflies welled in Tessa's insides. This was the first time she was allowed to go looting.

One of the eagles let out a sharp cry. Her mother's head twisted around.

"What is it?" Tessa asked.

"Company," she replied, her voice even.

A trio of dark shapes materialized on the horizon—far too large to be eagles. Tessa's heartbeat quickened.

"Keep a low profile," her father called. "We're not on their land. We should be able to slip right by."

"Should we be worried?" Tessa asked. She watched the figures draw steadily closer.

"We'll be fine, Tess," her mother replied. Even as she said it, Tessa noticed her spur their eagle to fly faster.

The eagles dropped to a lower altitude and raced across the Tablelands. Tessa glanced over her shoulder. The figures were gaining. She made out their intense blue-purple scales and wide, leathery wings. She tightened her grip on her mother. "They're coming after us, aren't they?"

Her father swore. "We can't outrun them. We'll have to engage."

"Not with Tess here we don't," her mother snapped.

"I'll distract them. Once we start fighting, you scatter." He drew one of his sabres. "You can lose them deeper in the Badlands."

Tessa's heart thudded against her ribcage as her father's eagle spread out its wings and dropped away. The rest of the Raiders did the same. Her mother powered their eagle on, away from the group and toward a distant collection of spires.

"Will they be okay?" Tessa asked.

"They've dealt with dragons before," her mother said. "The Royal Guards are no match for them." Tessa caught the wobble in her voice.

She twisted around just in time to see the dragons bearing down on her father. They cracked open their jaws and an inferno scorched the Tablelands.

Tessa screamed. The eagles scattered as the dragons attacked, twisting away with a flurry of slashing talons. One shrieked as a dragon clamped its jaws around its wing. A Royal Guard ignored the eagles and spurred his dragon past the battle.

"It's coming for us!" Tessa cried.

Her mother urged their eagle on, but the dragon kept gaining. As her father and the Raiders wheeled through the sky, too far away to help, the Royal Guard and his dragon closed in on them.

"Hold on!" her mother yelled.

Tessa clung to her middle as their eagle flipped upside-down and the dragon blasted overhead. Their eagle clawed at the massive beast's underbelly. The dragon's hind legs flashed forward and a pained shriek split the air.

Tessa screamed again as their eagle went into a freefall. Blood sprayed from its underside where the dragon had struck it. It pivoted around and dropped toward the Badlands below.

Then it hit the ground.

Tessa's world spun. She flew free of the harness and was thrown across the flat earth. An explosion of pain went through her side as she hit the ground and rolled. Dust billowed into the air as the lifeless eagle skidded across the ground.

The dragon circled overhead. Tessa swallowed her pain and staggered to her feet. She ran to her mother's side.

"Hide!" her mother said. The eagle's body pinned her to the ground. Its entrails spilled out of the gaping wound in its underbelly. The bird's head was twisted at a weird angle, blood seeping from its open mouth.

Tessa looked around for somewhere to go. The Tablelands offered no protection. The dragon roared as it approached. Her mother shoved the eagle's body, trying to free herself, but it held fast.

"Use its body," she said. "It's the only way."

With tears pricking in her eyes, Tessa dropped to her knees and pried the eagle's ribcage apart. Warm blood seeped into her clothes and stained her skin as she forced her way inside the corpse. She stifled a gag. Hot air blasted her face, radiating from its freshly exposed organs. The stench invaded her nostrils, tightening her throat, suffocating her lungs...

The ground shook as the dragon landed. Tessa shrank away, curling herself into a ball. The eagle's slimy innards pressed against her. She fought the urge to vomit. Footsteps sounded as a Royal Guard approached.

"You're too close to our lands, Raider," a voice said. "We warned you once. Now you've forced our hand."

Tessa heard her mother spit on him. "I'm not afraid of you."

A sword unsheathed. "You should be."

A thud sounded. Tessa squeezed her eyes shut and tried not to sob. The Royal Guard's boots moved away. The dragon bellowed, then launched itself into the air. Its wingbeats grew fainter and fainter.

Tessa wrapped her blood-drenched arms around herself and wished he'd killed her too.

* * *

Tessa jolted awake. A cold sweat covered her forehead and made her nightclothes stick to her skin. She rolled out of bed and leaned against the open window, sucking in the night air.

The city lay still. The faint sound of Lazaro snoring reached her ears from the room opposite. Tessa wrapped her arms around herself and sank into the bed.

I'm too old to go running to Lazaro. She wiped her eyes. She calmed her breathing and buried the memories into the darkest recesses of her mind.

She knew that further down the hall, Isiah slept. Part of her urged her to grab a sabre and kill him. She wanted to split him open like his people had done to her family. A fire burned in her chest, hotter than anything a dragon could ever muster.

No. Tessa pushed it away. Isiah wasn't like them. He *couldn't* be. She turned away from the window and pulled the covers under her chin.

But if Isiah ever tried to betray them, she'd make sure she killed him before he got the chance.

Finders Keepers

ISIAH GROANED AND THREW OFF HIS COVERS. Voices yelled somewhere below him. Doors slammed and footsteps thudded back and forth.

Lazaro's voice wafted up. "Luca! Go and ready the eagles. I want them harnessed and prepared to fly once we join you."

Isiah hurriedly pulled himself out of bed. A bubble of excitement welled inside him. He threw on his cloak and, checking his Mark, ran downstairs.

He burst into the dining room, where the Raiders were readying their gear and slipping sabres onto their belts. Darla grabbed an armful of rope and tossed it to Antony. Tessa tied her hair back into a bun and adjusted her cloak.

"What's going on?" Isiah asked.

"Darla spotted a ruin while flying at dawn," Lazaro said. "And it's nearby, too. It must have been exposed by a recent earthquake. We want to get there before anybody else does."

"Get your stuff ready, Scavenger." Darla tossed him a bag. "Every minute counts."

Isiah fumbled and caught it. Slinging the bag onto his shoulder, he hurried back to his room. His sabre lay on one of the barrels. He grabbed it and slid it onto his belt. His knife sat on the bedside table. Isiah's hand hovered over it for a second, before he added it to his gear.

Better safe than sorry, he thought.

He rejoined the Raiders as they piled out the door. Lazaro beckoned them, ushering them out.

"Don't run," Antony warned. "The other Raiders will get suspicious."

"With a ruin so close, someone else is bound to have seen it," Lazaro replied. "I'm not losing out on another one."

Isiah was the last out the door. Lazaro locked it behind them and they hurried in the direction of the eagle roosts. Isiah got a chance to inspect the Raiders. Lazaro and Tessa took the lead, with Antony and Darla behind. The siblings sported matching cloaks and sabres, and Darla's hair whipped behind her as she ran.

Alongside her ran Helen. Isiah had seen little of the woman since arriving. She was a tall woman with long limbs. Scale armour, like Enrik's, covered parts of her body, and her weathered features made her look tougher than any nomad.

They reached the first of the staircases and sprinted up. The crowd dispersed as Lazaro and Tessa shoved their way through. Isiah willed his legs to move faster. He struggled to keep pace with the rest of the group.

"Wait up!" he said between panting breaths.

The Raiders ignored him. They reached the eagle roosts and slowed their pace. Lazaro walked briskly. His eyes darted about. From up ahead, Luca beckoned them.

Then a figure stepped out in front of him.

"Morning, Lazaro," Enrik said. "Nice day for flying, isn't it?"

Lazaro and Tessa stopped. Isiah caught up to them and paused to catch his breath. Several other men and women stepped out to block the way ahead.

Lazaro's expression darkened. "Mind your own business, Enrik."

"The Raiders *are* my business," Enrik replied. He looked to his group. "Especially when there are ruins involved."

A snicker went around Enrik's gang. Isiah's heart sank.

"Stay out of this," Lazaro snapped. "This one's ours."

"You know the rules," Enrik replied. "It's finders keepers."

"And Darla found it first," Tessa cut in.

Darla stuck her nose up at Enrik. "Damn right. We've already claimed the entrance."

Enrik cracked a smile, but his eyes stared right through them. "There's more than one way into a ruin. Let's just hope you don't stumble upon any trouble while you're in there." He glanced at Isiah. "I wouldn't want you to have to train *another* Scavenger."

"We won't," Lazaro said. "Not unless you're going to break the Raider's Oath." He clenched his fist. "And if it's another fight you're after, I'd be happy to oblige."

Enrik's hand went to his forehead. Isiah made out a lump on the man's skull. "I didn't think your nose could survive being broken again."

Lazaro tried to push past the man, but Enrik stepped to block him. "Your hot-headedness will be the ruin of you, Lazaro. I'm not here to break our Oath—but I won't need to if you run head-first into a gorgon's den."

"Look after your own gang," Lazaro spat. "I've got mine covered."

Enrik stepped aside and let them pass. Isiah hurried to keep up with the others. He followed Tessa to Vyrro's pen and climbed onto the eagle after her.

"They hate each other, don't they?" he asked.

"They go way back," Tessa said. "Arguing over ruins is nothing new."

"Is that why Enrik has his magic?" Isiah asked.

He felt Tessa stiffen. "We lost out that time," she said. "He got there first. But don't mention it to Lazaro. He doesn't like to talk about it."

Lazaro's eagle let out a shrill cry and took the lead. Vyrro fell into formation behind them. Isiah gripped Tessa's middle as the troop of birds picked up speed and then launched themselves from the landing pad.

The eagles took to the skies and fanned out, flying away from the city and across the plain. Isiah settled into the rise and fall of Vyrro's wingbeats.

"I bet you're thankful that I took you flying before, huh?" Tessa said. She'd spoken little to him since discovering he was Marked.

Lazaro cupped his hands around his mouth. "Lead the way, Darla!"

Darla pulled on her eagle's reins and the bird veered to the side. Vyrro and the others fell in behind them. Darla took them out of view of the city, past the plain and into the mesas that surrounded them. A river snaked through the landscape below, painting the Badlands with flashes of green foliage.

"This is a rocky place," Darla called. "I'm lucky I spotted it."

Buttes and cliffs hugged close together, broken by narrow passageways and deep ravines. Mesas towered above them, forming a jumble of ledges and multi-layered platforms. Darla's eagle tilted its wing and they glided toward a patch of freshly exposed rock.

Vyrro descended with them. As they went, Isiah made out the crumbled stones littering the bases of cliffs. They landed by a pile of loose boulders beneath the side of a mesa. Pale orange rock, not yet weathered by the elements, stood out against the landscape.

"This is it." Darla hopped off her eagle and put her hands on her hips.

"There's nothing here," Isiah said.

"Look closer," she replied. She pointed to the base of the mesa, where a rectangular cave stood.

No, Isiah thought. *Not a cave. A doorway.*

He and Tessa climbed from Vyrro's back. Luca and Helen used ropes to secure the birds to trees and nearby boulders.

"This will keep them from flying away while we're gone," Helen said.

Isiah joined the others as they crowded around the ruin entrance. Pillars, carved into the rock itself, formed an elaborate front, with murals exposed by the earthquake. Isiah ran his fingers over one. Dust rained from its bumpy surface.

"It looks like a tomb," Darla said. "See all the artwork?"

Lazaro rubbed his hands together. "Then there should be plenty of good loot inside." He checked the skies over his shoulder. "Let's get to it."

Antony cracked open a bag and produced several torches. They were stout sticks with thick, padded cloth heads. Helen lit them with a firestarter and passed them around. "These will burn for a half-hour or so."

Lazaro stepped aside. "Scavengers first."

"Wait," Isiah started.

"What do you think we brought you here for?" He gave Isiah a push. "You go first and check the way."

Isiah stumbled into the ruin entrance. He waved his torch ahead of him. It cast a flickering light across the interior of the passageway. Worn sandstone walls descended into darkness.

Swallowing his fear, Isiah started into the ruin. His footsteps bounced off the walls. The Raiders walked in single file behind him. He felt Lazaro's hot breath on the back of his neck. Tessa came next, then Darla and Luca. Helen and Antony brought up the rear.

"I'm surprised nobody found this place sooner," Antony said. "It's practically on our doorstep."

"The cliffs here are like a maze," Darla replied. "If not for that earthquake—"

Lazaro raised a finger to his lips. "Keep it down. We don't know if anyone else found it first."

"We would have seen their eagles," Darla said.

Lazaro tugged on his sabre, revealing a few inches of blade. "Not if they're nomads or merchants, we wouldn't."

Isiah gulped. He expected something to come flying from the darkness at any moment. As they descended further, he became aware of the weight of the rock pressing in on all sides. Blood rushed in his ears, the only sound above the steady crunch of their boots on the stone.

A doorway materialized ahead of them, made from thick stone. Isiah lowered his torch. "Dead end."

Lazaro shook his head. "The builders always left some way to get out once they'd filled it with treasure. They used to put the door on early to keep out looters." He cracked a smile. "Like us."

Antony passed Lazaro a metal rod. Lazaro pushed past Isiah and felt the edges of the door. He stopped at the top corner. "There."

Rock crumbled as Lazaro struck it with the pole. He chipped away, revealing a narrow gap barely big enough for someone to crawl through. He raised his torch and inspected the other side. "All clear," he said. "Scavenger, you're up."

Isiah eyed the tunnel. "What am I supposed to do?"

"Go through there and see if there's a way to open the door."

"But . . ." He tried to form the words. "What if I get stuck?"

"Then we'll push you." Lazaro crossed his arms. "Save the questions. We're wasting time."

"Tessa will fit too," Isiah said quickly. "What do you need me for?"

111

Tessa wrapped her arms around herself. "I hate going through tunnels."

"Look," Lazaro cut in, "you're a Scavenger. That's why you're here. Now go and do your job!"

Reluctantly, Isiah grabbed the sides of the gap and hoisted himself up. He threw his torch through to the other side, then wiggled through himself. Sharp rock pressed into his sides and snagged his clothes.

"Almost there," Lazaro said.

Isiah pulled his waist through, then fell to the floor. He threw out his arms to break his fall. A bolt of pain stabbed his wrists. He swore.

"Are you alright?" Tessa's voice wafted through the door.

Isiah rubbed his wrists. "Fine."

"Good," Lazaro said. "Now find a way to open the door."

Isiah scooped up his torch and inspected the door. The flat square of rock fit snug against the tunnel walls. He probed it for any weaknesses. In the far corner, there was a cavity. An idea popped into Isiah's head.

"Pass me your metal rod," he called.

Lazaro passed it through. Isiah took the rod and, wedging it in the cavity, pushed against it. Dust trickled from the gaps in the door, but it didn't budge.

Isiah tried harder. Stone scraped against stone. "Give it a push!" he called.

A force struck the other side of the door. Isiah redoubled his efforts, leaning into the rod and using all of his weight to lever the door open. The grinding of stone filled his ears. The door came free and swivelled to form a foot-wide gap.

Lazaro ducked through. "Great work, Scavenger." He raised his torch and surveyed the space beyond.

The door guarded a long hall, with sandstone pillars supporting the ceiling. A series of passageways branched off. Piles of bricks and other leftover building materials littered the space.

Darla kicked a pile of wooden beams. "I wonder how old these are."

"Unless it's made of gold, I don't care," Lazaro replied. He passed around empty sacks. "Fill them with whatever you can find. Coins, statues, artefacts, anything of value." He stretched out his arms and sucked in a breath. "There's magic down here, I can feel it."

Isiah shifted his weight. "What about me?"

"I would send you ahead to check the way, but we're pressed for time. We'll split up and inspect some of these tunnels first. The good stuff must be around here somewhere."

"And remember," Antony warned. "Don't go too far. Keep your wits about you. I don't need to tell you about the dangers of ruins."

Lazaro produced a bottle and some bandages. "Take this. If you fall down somewhere and get hurt, you could be in serious trouble." He passed the supplies to Tessa.

The Raiders branched off into groups. Antony and Darla took one passageway, while Lazaro went with Luca and Helen. Isiah found himself alone with Tessa.

"Remember who's in charge," Tessa said, not looking at him. She picked one of the passageways and started down it.

113

Isiah hurried after her, eager to not be left behind. They exited the main hall and navigated the new tunnel. Alcoves branched off, with low stone coffins and various trinkets resting on top. Some had dust-covered robes and blankets. Others had wooden bows, too old and dried out to be useful.

Tessa paused in front of one. A handful of gold coins were scattered across it. She added them to her bag. Isiah spied a handful of golden goblets and cups. He grabbed them and passed them to Tessa. Part of him felt bad for stealing from the tomb, but a more important thought drowned it out.

What if the oasis is down here?

Tessa kept going. "Try not to get lost."

Isiah hovered behind her. He hesitated. "I'm sorry I lied to you, you know," he said.

Tessa whirled on him. "You told me you were a nomad," she spat. "Nomads aren't Marked."

"I had to keep it a secret," he said. "Paradon banished me. I couldn't let you know."

"But you're one of them. If you're Marked, that means you were a noble." Tessa's eyes narrowed. "You knew the Royal Guards."

Isiah raised his hands. "They only protected us—"

"*Protected* you? How? By invading the Badlands and killing everyone they found? How is that supposed to protect you?"

"I didn't know they did that!" Isiah struggled for the words.

"Well, they do," Tessa said. "And you nobles sit back and watch it happen. If you weren't Marked, you wouldn't care about any of us.

You'd still be in that palace of yours." Her voice echoed, and then silence descended. Tessa turned away. "Just look for treasure."

Isiah did as he was told. *Find the oasis,* he told himself. *That's all that matters.*

They searched the tunnel, gathering anything of value they could find. A few dusty books, their pages crumbling and text illegible, sat on a shelf.

Tessa found more coins and goblets alongside ceremonial knives, their blades long rusted. Isiah added a few small statues to his bag.

"We should turn back," he said. "Antony told us not to go far."

Tessa grunted.

The passageway sloped down, intersecting a new tunnel. Isiah ran his hand over the rock. Deep cracks snaked across it. He furrowed his brow. "Why do you think it's so damaged?"

A rumble cut him off. The ground trembled beneath him. Tessa's eyes widened.

"Earthquake!" she cried.

Dust rained from the ceiling. Rocks split and stones clattered to the floor. Isiah steadied himself against a wall for balance. The shaking made his legs weak.

Cracks fractured the passageway until part of the ceiling collapsed. Isiah squeezed his eyes shut as a wave of dust ripped through the tunnel.

The shaking faded. Isiah coughed, covering his nose. He opened his eyes as the dust settled, exposing a pile of rock that blocked the way they had come.

With a sinking feeling, he realized they were trapped.

MORGAN LEE CLASPER

Another Way

ISIAH RAN TO THE BLOCKED TUNNEL EXIT AND pressed his hands against it. He shoved the rock with all of his strength. Nothing budged.

"What are we going to do?" he asked. Their torches illuminated a wall of crushed boulders, packed tightly against one another.

"There has to be a way," Tessa said. He caught the hint of panic in her voice. She clawed at the rocks. "Don't just stand there. Help me!"

Isiah obeyed. Loose stones clattered to the floor—but not enough to change anything. Huge slabs of rock blocked the way, far too big to hope to shift. Tessa's breathing bounced off the tunnel walls, faster than usual.

"Keep going," Tessa urged. She grabbed a boulder and tugged it. Nothing. She swore. "Help me with this."

"We can't move it," Isiah said. "It's too heavy."

She whirled on him. "Then what are we supposed to do?"

"We need to stay calm," Isiah said. He stepped away from the boulders and tried to clear his head. "There has to be another way out."

Tessa paced back and forth like a caged animal. "You don't know that," she replied. "We might be stuck down here. We could die and nobody would ever find us!"

"Enrik said there's more than one way into a ruin," Isiah said. "Maybe one of these other tunnels joins up to the main hall."

Tessa stopped pacing. "Yeah." She nodded as if trying to convince herself. She glanced at their torches. "We don't have much time." Flames curled around the torch heads, already half-burnt. "We were supposed to go back so Antony could give us more."

"What happens when the fire dies?" Isiah asked.

Tessa's voice dropped. "Then it's lights out."

Isiah shivered. Tessa took off at a jog and he hurried after her. Their torches cast flickering shadows across the narrow walls. They found an intersecting tunnel and followed it. Isiah strained his ears for the sound of Lazaro's voice or one of the other Raiders. Tessa slowed down and wrapped her arms around herself.

"Are you alright?" Isiah asked.

"I'm fine," she replied. She hesitated. "Is it getting harder to breathe in here?"

Isiah sucked in a mouthful of air. The dust irritated his throat. "I don't think so."

"Good." She sighed. "Sometimes you get bad air. People suffocate."

They continued along the tunnel for what felt like an age. Their footsteps echoed ahead of them. Isiah cupped his hands to his mouth and called out.

"Lazaro! Are you there?" His voice echoed, unanswered.

The tunnel opened into another hall, larger than the first. Shadows shrouded its corners. A few collapsed pillars lay like the broken bones of a giant skeleton, alongside more piles of old wood. Isiah swept his foot over the floor. Beneath the thick layer of dust and sand, worn tiles gleamed.

"Weird," Isiah said. "What do you think they used this place for?"

Tessa knelt and inspected it. "I don't know. It doesn't look like a tomb."

Isiah wandered further into the room. Several passageways branched off. Parts of the floor dropped to form large rectangular holes.

"It's like a bathhouse," Tessa said.

Isiah peered into the holes. "It dried up a long time ago."

He moved to the far wall. More murals, similar to the ones around the entrance to the ruin, were etched into the sandstone walls. He raised his torch and studied them.

"Come on," Tessa said. Her voice echoed through the hall. "We need to keep moving."

"Hang on a minute." Isiah ran his fingers over the mural, dislodging centuries of caked dust. Some depicted dancing figures, while others formed elaborate landscapes. A large scene of a bustling city street dominated half of the wall. Isiah furrowed his brow. His gaze came to rest on a large mural of a shining pool.

His breath caught in his throat. He studied the mural closer. Bent and decrepit figures lined one shore, while people frolicked and danced on the other. Words were etched beneath it, too faded to read.

Is it the oasis? Isiah thought. A twinge of excitement pulled at his heart.

He jumped as Tessa grabbed his arm. "What is it?" she asked.

"Uh—nothing," Isiah said quickly.

Tessa pulled him away from the mural. "Then let's go. I found something."

Isiah hurried after her. Part of him wanted to slip away from Tessa and search for the oasis himself, but he didn't dare in case he became lost in the pitch-black tunnels and ended up starving to death. At least with Tessa he'd have a better chance of getting out alive.

"Look." Tessa pointed to the far side of the ceiling. Shafts of light peered through, illuminating a thin strip of the floor.

They ran over. Isiah craned his neck. Through the crack, he spotted a patch of blue sky. Twin walls of rock, dozens of feet high, formed a fissure.

"The ground must have split," Tessa said. "Maybe during an earthquake."

"How are we going to get up there?" Isiah asked. He felt the wall nearest to the crack. Its murals offered him some handholds. He hoisted himself up, but the sandstone crumbled and he slipped to the ground.

"This means we're close to the surface," Tessa said.

Isiah started to speak, but a noise cut him off. Stones crunched in the darkness. He turned to the source of the noise.

"Lazaro?" he called.

A guttural growl replied to him.

Tessa swore.

"What is it?" Isiah asked.

"Draw your sabre." Her sword flashed into her hand.

Isiah fumbled with his belt. The growling grew louder. From the other tunnels, more voices joined it. With a sinking feeling, Isiah's mind flashed back to what Reuben had told him in the Badlands. *They like to hide in dark and cool places.*

"Gorgons," he stammered.

A creature stepped into a shaft of light. It rippled across the beast's muscular body. Short, barb-like fur covered thick limbs armed with curved claws. It stood taller than Isiah's chest, its wide shoulders giving way to narrow hips and a long tail. A huge set of jaws cracked open, revealing four tusk-like fangs.

"Stay close," Tessa warned. She pointed her sabre in the gorgon's direction. "They like to ambush."

The gorgon snapped a warning at her. Its long jaws clapped together, echoing across the hall. Other gorgons appeared in doorways. Tessa swung her torch at it, making it shrink away.

Isiah adjusted his grip on his sabre. His palm made the handle slick and sweaty. He locked eyes with the gorgon. Thick ridges protected its small eyes, while its ears were nothing more than holes in the sides of its head.

"This is a den," Tessa said. "They must have moved in when the fissure formed."

The gorgon snapped again, and spittle flew from its jaws. Isiah shrank away instinctively.

"Aim for their mouths," Tessa said. "They don't have many teeth. Avoid the fangs and hit their gums."

The gorgon lunged. Isiah stepped away and lashed out. His sabre caught the gorgon across the side of the face and left a long cut.

The beast seemed not to notice. It spun on him and Isiah stumbled away. Other gorgons erupted from the doorways and circled them, waiting for their chance to dart in and bite.

The lead gorgon advanced on Isiah. His mind grasped for his training, but everything Tessa had said deserted him. He waved the sabre in an attempt to keep the beast away.

"Back off!" he yelled. His voice came out more like a squeak.

The gorgon attacked. Isiah struck its shoulder and the blade glanced off. The beast kept coming.

Isiah backed away, swinging wildly. The gorgon reared on its hind legs and loomed over his head. Tessa yelled and lobbed a rock at it. The rock exploded into dust on its shoulder, but the gorgon paid it no attention.

Then Isiah tripped.

His foot caught one of the fallen pillars and he hit the ground. A jolt of pain went through his spine, making him drop his torch. The gorgon bore down on him, its massive jaws cracked open to deliver a killing blow . . .

Isiah yelled and thrust his sabre at the gorgon's underbelly. The tip pierced its tough hide and sank in.

The gorgon barked in pain and reeled away. The force nearly ripped Isiah's arm from its socket.

Tessa yelled and swung her sabre at the circling gorgons. They darted away from her blows. The gorgon Isiah had stabbed bounded away, blood seeping from its wound. Isiah scrambled to his feet in time for another gorgon to attack. This time he was prepared. He side-stepped and the gorgon flew past him.

Isiah's torch had fallen on a pile of old wood. He scooped it up. Coils of smoke appeared as the wood began to smoulder. A few small flames took hold.

"Good idea!" Tessa yelled. She torched a second pile, then produced the bottle Lazaro had given her and doused the wood with it.

The gorgons leapt away with cries of alarm as the bottle's contents took hold and flames ripped across the ancient material. Isiah joined Tessa as it formed a ring around them, leaping into the air to form a flickering wall.

Heat baked his face and made sweat drip into his eyes. His Mark itched, but he didn't dare scratch it. One of the gorgons tried to leap through the fire, but Tessa kept it at bay with her sabre.

The fire grew brighter, dispelling the shadows. Smoke pooled on the ceiling and escaped through the narrow crack. With a bark of panic, the gorgons abandoned their den and bolted down the tunnels. Several scaled the wall with their long claws and climbed out into the ravine.

Isiah and Tessa waited until the gorgons had left and the fire had grown weaker, before hopping out of the ring.

"What if they come back?" Isiah asked.

"They won't," Tessa replied. "They're just animals. The fire will have scared them away." She glanced down the tunnels. "There must be another path to the surface. Maybe the gorgons know a way out."

Isiah eyed his torch. The flames had died, leaving behind glowing embers that cast a weak light. "I hope you're right."

They picked the tunnel the other gorgons had disappeared down and followed it. Their torches illuminated only a few feet ahead of them. Isiah kept his sabre at the ready in case a gorgon flew from the darkness. None did, and the tunnel began to climb. A bubble of hope welled in his chest.

They followed the tunnel for a few hundred feet, before the ground turned to sand and the walls disappeared. Isiah held out his torch and strained his eyes.

"It looks like a cavern," Tessa said. Their torches revealed a low, rough-cut ceiling.

"Maybe someone was building another room," Isiah said.

Tessa pushed past him. "The gorgons must have gone somewhere. There *has* to be a way out." She marched deeper into the cavern until her light faded to a faint glow.

"Be careful," Isiah called out.

Tessa scowled. "You're telling *me* to be careful? I've fought gorgons before. I can handle myself."

Isiah began exploring the cavern, following the wall to keep from getting lost. As Tessa's light disappeared behind him, something caught his eye. A doorway beckoned him, cut into the rock. It blocked the way like the one at the entrance to the ruin—but instead of being smooth, dozens of lines and symbols were carved into its surface. Isiah opened his mouth to call Tessa, then paused.

In the centre of the door, a carving like the pool on the bathhouse wall stared back at him. Isiah raised his dying torch to get a better look and his heartbeat quickened. A strange object, shaped like a rough-cut crystal, sat on a pedestal next to the door. It glowed with a faint light, the same smouldering colour as one of their twin suns.

It's like some kind of artefact, he thought. He sheathed his sabre and turned the artefact over in his hand. It seemed to pulse, filling his arm with an odd sensation. His gaze drifted to a hole in the rock next to the door. Without thinking, he slotted the artefact inside. Nothing happened for a second, before something clunked and dust billowed from the cracks in the door.

Covering his mouth with his sleeve, Isiah gave the door a tentative push. It moved an inch. He glanced in the direction Tessa had disappeared. His torch barely cast enough light for him to see his own hands. If it fizzled out, he'd be lost in the darkness.

Swallowing his unease, Isiah braced himself against the door and pushed it until it formed a gap wide enough to slip through. The anticipation made him lightheaded. With every second, his breathing grew shallower until he thought he'd pass out. The image of the mural and the oasis was burned into his mind.

Isiah stumbled into the room beyond.

Beneath the faint glow of his torch, a shallow pool filled a small cave. Ripples danced across its vibrant blue surface, making it swirl as if alive. A slick layer of water coated the porous ceiling above.

Isiah sank to his knees. He jammed the torch into the ground beside him and, with his hands shaking, dipped them into the pool.

The water chilled his skin, shimmering with an ancient, mysterious power.

It can't be, he thought. He remembered the faded parchments in Paradon, the ones that had pointed him to Alcabaza.

Isiah carefully peeled away his clothes and splashed a handful of the water onto his Mark. He gasped as it sapped the heat from his flesh. Blisters lost their angry glow. The water seeped into his skin, driving out the itch and the pain.

Isiah sucked in a breath. His mind raced with a million thoughts. He grabbed another handful of the water and dumped it on his shoulders, then another. The water trickled between his fingers. He gasped as his blisters faded. He wanted to tear off his clothes and throw himself into the oasis.

"Isiah!" Tessa called.

Isiah froze. He strained his eyes in the near-darkness. A lump of charred wood fell from his torch. Only a few embers remained.

"Where are you?" she said. "I found something!"

With every fibre in his body, Isiah forced himself to stand. The oasis beckoned him, but the fear of getting lost in the darkness made his insides churn.

I'll come back, he thought. *I know where it is. I'll return with more light and I'll cure myself.*

He slipped out of the cave and collected the artefact. The door slid shut with the grinding of stone and locked into place. Isiah pocketed the artefact and stumbled through the darkness in the direction of Tessa's voice. A sliver of light illuminated her.

Isiah dropped his spent torch. "What is it?"

She peered up at the crack of light. "It's another fissure," she said. "Like the one in the bathhouse."

Isiah waited for his breathing to return to normal. He was thankful that the shadows concealed his expression. A series of boulders and rock ledges led up to the source of the light. "Do you think we can climb up?" he asked.

"It looks like it," Tessa replied. She threw away her burned-out torch. "It's our only shot."

Isiah scurried to the source of the light, squinting to make out handholds. The artefact pressed against his leg, reminding him of its presence with every movement. Below him, Tessa slipped and swore.

"I could help you," Isiah offered.

She waved him away. "I don't need your help."

Isiah shrugged. He fixed his eyes on the thin strip of daylight above and redoubled his efforts. Part of him urged him to return to the pool, but he pushed the thought away. *Soon.*

As soon as he had the chance, he'd sneak back to the oasis and cure his Mark forever.

Escape

TESSA DUG HER FINGERS INTO THE ROCKY HANDHOLDS. The walls pressed against her, restricting her movements and grating against her skin. Isiah climbed above her. His feet dislodged dust and pebbles, making them rain onto her head.

"Careful!" she said. She blinked the dust out of her eyes and kept climbing. Sharp rocks dug into her palms. It felt like the earth was pressing against her, squeezing her like a vice. When she tried to breathe, the fissure restricted her ribcage until she could barely suck in a breath.

Just keep climbing. She gritted her teeth and forced herself to climb. The rock seemed to encase her, locking her into a suffocating tomb. Panic welled in her insides. Her throat seized until it felt like she was gasping for air.

"I can't do this," she managed to say. The rock seemed to crush her, pressing in on every side.

"What are you talking about?" Isiah replied. "I thought you said there's no other way."

Dust and stones pelted her head and filled her nostrils. Tessa coughed. "I mean I can't climb up it. I'm going to suffocate!"

Her heart thudded against her chest until she was sure it would break free from her body. A familiar sinking dread filled her body and made her limbs turn into dead weights. The image of hiding inside the eagle's corpse played into her mind. She could almost smell the sickly stench of its blood . . .

"You'll be fine," Isiah said. "There's a ledge here. It gets wider."

Tessa fought for breath. Her head swam. The earth seemed to close up to swallow her . . .

Isiah's hand appeared. Tessa grabbed it and he pulled her free. She clawed her way to the ledge, coughing and spitting dust.

"Are you alright?" he asked. "It sounded like you were panicking."

Tessa wiped the dirt from her eyes. Dust caked her clothes and hair. She blinked, trying to clear the image of the eagle. "Isiah," she said.

"What?"

"Don't leave me down here, okay?"

He furrowed his brow. "Why would I do that?"

"Just don't."

They waited for a few minutes for her breathing to steady, then continued their climb. The fissure widened, as Isiah had said, forming ledges and bigger handholds. As they drew away from the darkness and its crushing rock walls, a breath of fresh air beckoned them from above. Tessa scrambled the last few feet to safety and hauled herself to the surface.

They dragged themselves to their feet and Tessa dusted herself off. "Made it."

"That wasn't so hard," Isiah said. He paused. "Where are we?"

Tessa surveyed her surroundings. They were in the centre of a wide bowl, with half-dead trees and bushes surrounding it.

"It's like a dried-up lakebed," she said. "I wonder what was here."

Around the lakebed, cliffs penned them in, with sandbanks leaning against them and overhangs sloping over to leave only a strip of light. The cliffs continued a few hundred feet, before growing narrower and twisting out of view.

Tessa craned her neck and spun in a circle. "This place is so well-hidden. It must be impossible to spot from the air." She studied the cliffs, searching for a way up. Narrow ledges formed a trail that curved out of sight. "We can go up that way," she said. "We can't be too far from the entrance. Lazaro must be worried sick about me."

A breath of wind stirred the loose sand in the lakebed. Trees and bushes waved. A flash of colour caught Tessa's eye, hidden beyond them. A plume of sand swirled in the air, heading towards them . . .

Isiah started to walk, but she grabbed his arm. "Wait—"

Swirling vortexes erupted from the foliage. Tessa's sabre flashed into her hand. The colour drained from Isiah's face as the sand materialized to form Raiders.

Enrik put his hands on his hips. "Look who decided to sneak into our camp," he said. "I thought Lazaro had already claimed the entrance."

131

Tessa searched for an escape, but Enrik's Raiders had them surrounded. One darted out a hand and grabbed her arm. She struggled against him, but he pried the blade from her grip. The other Raiders overpowered Isiah and confiscated his sabre.

"We can't have you meddling in our business, can we?" Enrik said.

"Leave us alone," Tessa spat.

Enrik laughed. Two of the Raiders grabbed her arms and pinned them behind her back. "You're not in a position to be telling us what to do." He turned and marched toward the flash of colour she'd seen earlier—*tents*, she realized.

"Bind them and bring them with us," Enrik ordered. "Lazaro and his ilk have been a thorn in my side for far too long."

No Choice

THE RAIDERS DRAGGED ISIAH AND TESSA INTO THE CAMP. Isiah struggled against his binds, but the ropes held fast. His captors dumped him next to Tessa against a boulder near the camp.

"Don't try to run," Enrik said. "You don't want to make this worse on yourselves than it already is."

The Raiders knelt and bound Isiah's ankles together. He shifted his weight, feeling the hard rock pressing into his back. Tessa flexed her binds.

"Lazaro will find us," she spat.

Enrik laughed. "This ravine is the most hidden place in the entire Badlands." He gestured to the overhangs. "It's invisible. We're the only people who know it exists." His voice dropped. "At least, we *were*."

He paced back and forth in front of them. "But Lazaro won't ever be able to find you. I've had my Raiders cause a rockslide. He's trapped. Nobody will ever find the ruin entrance."

Tessa stopped struggling. "You're breaking the Raider's Oath," she said slowly.

"I haven't killed anyone yet," Enrik replied. "Starvation will be their fate—if they don't suffocate first."

A snicker went around the Raider group.

"I'm keeping you two here until we have what we need. I can't have you causing any trouble." Enrik stopped in front of her. "Then I'll throw you into the ruin and you can join Lazaro's fate."

Tessa tugged at her binds. "You can't keep this a secret. Once the other Raiders know you've broken the Oath—"

"Please," Enrik said, cutting her off. "Do you think any of the other Raiders care about Lazaro? There isn't a group in the city he hasn't made enemies with. Why else are you stuck living in that hovel of yours on the lower levels?"

Enrik knelt in front of her. "But if you behave yourselves, maybe I'll let you live. I'm tempted to sell you to passing merchants." His hand darted out and grabbed Tessa's chin. "You could spend the rest of your days working in a salt mine in some far corner of the Badlands." Tessa tried to pull away, but his grip tightened. "Maybe it will do you good. You always were a spoiled brat."

Enrik released Tessa and stood. "Keep an eye on them," he ordered. "The rest of you can get back to work."

He turned and marched away. Tessa glared at him as he went. Isiah took a second to collect his thoughts while Tessa redoubled her efforts to break free. A couple of Raiders loitered nearby.

"Stop trying to escape," Isiah told her.

Tessa glared at him. "Why?"

Isiah lowered his voice. "They're still watching us. We have to wait until their guard is down."

He saw the gears spinning in Tessa's head. She sighed. "Fine. But we need to help Lazaro."

Isiah shifted his weight. He racked his brain for some kind of plan. Enrik had confiscated their sabres. Isiah shifted his position and his knife handle jabbed him in the side.

Of course! A spark of hope bubbled inside him. He studied their surroundings. A few Raiders sat next to a clump of bushes. Several trees obscured the Raider camp beyond.

"We'll wait until nightfall," he said.

"What? That will be hours yet!"

"It's our only hope," he replied. "Once the Raiders are asleep, we can escape under the cover of darkness."

"What about Lazaro?"

"We'll free him afterwards."

Tessa groaned and rested her head against the boulder. "We have no choice, do we?"

Isiah eyed the Raiders. One kept glancing over at them. "No, we don't."

* * *

The shadows lengthened as dusk fell upon the Badlands. The activity in the Raider camp grew quiet as they sat and talked around their campfires, then retired to their tents as darkness settled over the lakebed. Isiah waited, pretending to be asleep, listening for their chance.

A single Raider wandered by to check them periodically—but as the evening grew older, his checks became less frequent. The binds had begun to bite into Isiah's wrists, making them red and sore. Tessa sat slumped next to him, but he caught the flicker of her eyelids.

Once the light of the campfire grew dim, Isiah straightened up. Silence cloaked the lakebed, broken only by the soft chirp of insects in the trees nearby.

"Finally," Tessa whispered. "Now how are we supposed to get out, wise guy?"

Isiah twisted his body. "Do you see my knife?" He kept his voice low so as not to alert any Raiders who might still be awake.

Tessa squinted. "You brought it with you?"

"Pull it out."

Tessa obeyed. She awkwardly grabbed the hilt and drew the blade. "Now what?"

"Cut through my binds."

Tessa positioned the knife so that it lay over the ropes, then began sawing it back and forth. Isiah grimaced as its tip poked him. "Try not to stab me."

"This is harder than it looks, you know."

An eternity seemed to pass, before Isiah's binds slackened and he pulled his wrists free. He rubbed them, wincing as the blood returned.

"Now do mine," Tessa said.

Isiah took the knife from her and sliced through her binds. He then did the same to the ropes that bound their ankles. "Not so useless now, is it?" he asked.

Tessa scowled. "You can gloat later." She stood. "We need to get our sabres. Lazaro will kill me if I lose them."

Isiah sheathed his knife, then they crept forward. Through the bushes, the embers of a dying fire illuminated the camp. A haphazard collection of tents were clustered around the campfire. Further off, pickaxes and shovels lay next to piles of earth. A heap of crates, covered by a tarp, stood beside it. Isiah spotted the silhouettes of their eagles sleeping further off.

"They're excavating," Tessa said. "What do they think they're doing?"

Digging to the ruin, Isiah realized.

Something moved in the darkness. Tessa ducked and dragged Isiah after her. Isiah peered through the foliage as a Raider wandered through the camp. His sabre dangled at his side, and a whistle on a chain bobbed against his chest. He hummed a low tune as he went.

"He must be the watchman," Tessa said.

Isiah shifted his weight. "Maybe we should just go. What if they catch us again?"

"No," she hissed. "We need those sabres. They'll be inside Enrik's tent. He always takes the best stuff for himself."

Isiah studied the tents. The vibrant red and purple material rippled in a breath of wind. His gaze settled on the largest one. "That must be it."

Ducking low to the ground, they scurried through the camp, avoiding the ring of firelight. The Raider watchman strolled out of sight on the far side of camp. Isiah hoped he wasn't going to check on where they'd been bound.

They reached the tent and paused. Tessa held a finger to her lips, then parted the material. Faint snoring came from within. Eager not to push their luck, Isiah ducked inside.

Enrik snored, asleep on a low bed. His armour and sabre lay on a squat table beside him. A chest dominated most of the space, alongside various sacks of supplies.

Tessa grabbed the chest and eased it open. The squeal of hinges made Isiah wince. Their sabres lay inside. They both made a grab for them. Isiah bumped into Tessa and her grip on the chest slipped.

The lid fell with a bang. Isiah's blood froze. He tensed, waiting for Enrik to yell.

Nothing happened. Isiah breathed a sigh of relief. Tessa glared at him and he gave her an apologetic look. They secured the sabres to their belts, then exited the tent.

Right into the watchman.

The Raider's eyes widened when he saw the two of them. Tessa swore and threw herself at the man. She collided with him and he let out a grunt as they hit the ground.

Isiah spurred into action. He helped Tessa up and they sprinted away from the Raider. The man stumbled to his feet and raised the whistle to his mouth. Isiah winced as a shrill sound split the night's calm. The camp exploded into action.

Tessa grabbed Isiah's arm and drew her sabre. "Stay with me!"

Isiah fumbled for his sword. The shriek of the whistle cut through his head, painfully loud. Bleary-eyed men and women burst from their tents, half-dressed and clutching their weapons.

Enrik stumbled out of the tent behind him. When he saw them, his expression darkened. "Stop them!"

Tessa dragged Isiah away from the tents. The Raiders went after them. One transformed into a sand vortex and whipped past them, materializing to cut them off.

Tessa let go of his hand. "I hope you can fight," she said.

Isiah gulped. One of the Raiders charged at him. His sabre flashed through the air. Isiah parried the blow. The Raider aimed a thrust at Isiah's middle. Isiah sidestepped and lashed out instinctively. His blade sliced across the Raider's forearm.

The Raider spat a curse. With blood staining his sleeve, he swung again. A flare of panic seized Isiah's chest. He batted the man's sabre away seconds before it could bite into his flesh.

Tessa stood with her back to him. Raiders hung back, searching for an opening.

"Don't let them escape," Enrik ordered.

"What about the Oath?" one asked.

"Forget about the Oath."

The Raider from before launched another attack at Isiah's head. "You're dead, boy!"

Isiah raised his sabre and parried the blow. The Raider twisted his sword until its curved tip was hooked over Isiah's blade, hovering inches from his face.

Isiah pushed against it. The Raider's arm tensed as he tried to break Isiah's guard. The tip moved forward an inch, ready to sink into his eye socket . . .

Isiah yelled and twisted away. He pushed Tessa aside and the Raider's sabre stabbed the air where his face had been seconds earlier. The momentum made the Raider stumble. Isiah swung his sabre and left a long cut across the man's middle.

The Raiders closed in around them. Isiah backed away. A campfire burned behind him, cutting off his escape.

"I have an idea," he said. He grabbed a burning log from the campfire and hurled it into the dry, half-dead foliage surrounding them.

Enrik's eyes widened as he realized what was happening. "Protect the tents!" he yelled.

The bushes erupted into flames. One of the female Raiders transformed into a vortex and flew at Isiah, but he sidestepped before she could materialize.

The fire grew stronger. Raiders broke away to unpeg their tents and move them before they could catch alight. Tessa grabbed a second log and lobbed it into another patch of bushes. The Raiders' eagles shrieked cries of alarm and tugged at their ropes.

The Raider from before charged. Blood stuck to his clothes, and his eyes burned with hatred. "I'm not done with you, boy!"

Isiah took a step back. The man's sabre arced through the air. Sparks flew as their blades collided. The force sent a shockwave up Isiah's arm.

Tessa aimed a cut at the man. He diverted it and she struck again. A nearby tree went up in flames, baking the camp in heat and making their shadows look tall and disfigured.

Tessa forced the Raider away. His teeth clenched, and his chest heaved with exertion. He parried another of Tessa's blows, then whipped his sabre around. This time Tessa was too slow. His blade caught her across the forearm. She gasped in pain and cradled her arm.

Isiah clenched his fist. Before the Raider could strike her a second time, he darted in and jabbed his sabre at the Raider's chest.

The man jolted. His eyes widened. Isiah felt the sabre slip between his ribcage and bury itself into his flesh. The Raider looked down at the wound as if in shock.

Isiah yanked the blade free and the man stumbled away. Blood streamed down Isiah's sabre. He tore his eyes away from the dying Raider and grabbed Tessa.

"We need to go," he said.

Still clutching her wounded arm, Tessa went after him. They slipped out of the burning camp before the Raiders had a chance to regroup and come after them. Isiah fixed his eyes on the narrow trail snaking up the ravine wall. He knew that somewhere on the other side, Lazaro was still trapped.

He hoped they wouldn't be too late.

'Dead Meat'

Iᴀʜ sᴄʀᴀᴍʙʟᴇᴅ ᴜᴘ ᴛʜᴇ ʀᴏᴄᴋʏ ᴘᴀᴛʜ. Gravel shifted underfoot and stones came loose in his hands, but he didn't care. Far below, the fire began to die as it ran out of foliage to burn, illuminating the camp with flecks of smouldering light.

Isiah's lungs heaved. The feeling of his sabre sliding into the Raider's ribcage made his legs weak and his palms sweaty. He paused near the top of the ravine to help Tessa.

"Are you alright?" he asked.

She grimaced. "Just keep moving."

They climbed out of the ravine and he surveyed his surroundings. Beneath the moonlight, the flat top of a mesa stretched in both directions. Its exposed surface gave them little protection from the elements. A cold wind had picked up, chilling him and making his sweat-drenched clothes stick to his skin. Tessa ran after him, her arm held tight against her body.

"Let me see it," Isiah said.

Tessa shook her head, but after a second she relented. She sat on a low boulder and Isiah pried her arm away from her body. His pulse fluttered. The moonlight exposed the slick, dark blood staining her clothes.

"It's just a shallow cut," Tessa said. "I'll be fine."

"We should stop the bleeding," Isiah replied.

She tried to pull her arm away. "We're still too close. We have to keep moving."

"It'll only take a second," he insisted.

Tessa let her arm go slack. Isiah carefully peeled her sleeve away. Blood oozed from a long line running down the inside of her forearm. He fumbled with his belt, then pulled out his waterskin. He used the contents to wash away the excess blood.

"The bandages," he said. "Lazaro gave you some."

Tessa fished about in her pocket, then produced them. Isiah began winding them around her arm. He tried not to disturb the cut and make it bleed even more.

Tessa watched him work. "You're very good."

"I used to work on dragon hatchlings," he admitted. "Sometimes they got hurt and needed patching up."

He finished securing the bandages, then tied them tight. He released Tessa's arm and she inspected it.

"Good as new, huh?" Isiah said.

"I guess I'll live," Tessa replied. She paused. "Does being Marked hurt?"

Isiah touched his shoulder. His clothes brushed against his damaged skin, rough and scratchy. "Most of the time."

Tessa dropped her gaze. "I'm sorry for being so mean to you."

Isiah hesitated. He shifted his footing. "You didn't know."

Tessa turned her arm over. "Thanks for helping me."

"It was nothing," he said.

"No," she said. "In the ruin too."

He frowned. "What do you mean?"

She shook her head. "Never mind." She hopped off the boulder. "Come on. Lazaro will be waiting for us."

Isiah went after her. "How do you know which way to go?"

"Raiders have a good sense of direction."

They set off at a brisk walk, navigating the desolate surface of the mesa. Isiah squinted, studying the moonlit ground in case they stumbled into another fissure or cliff. Somewhere far off, the roar of a gorgon sounded.

They travelled for a few minutes. As the end of the mesa materialized, Tessa crouched. "Enrik's Raiders might still be around," she said.

Isiah dropped low to the ground. He inched his way to the crumbling edge and peered over. The mesa dropped away for several hundred feet. The moon illuminated the exposed rock from the landslide. A pile of boulders and earth was slumped against the bottom of the mesa—right where the ruin entrance had been.

Movement caught his attention. A pair of Raiders paced back and forth, their eagles perched nearby. Vyrro and their own eagles were further off, heads pulled tight against their shoulders as they slept.

"Guards," Tessa spat. Her nose crinkled in disgust. "They were probably going to collect our eagles and sell them."

"How do we get rid of them?" Isiah asked. The thought of another fight made his stomach turn in knots.

"We can use Vyrro," she replied. "We'll scare them away."

Tessa scurried to the edge and began lowering herself down the rock wall. "Keep your voice down," she instructed.

Isiah went after her. With his muscles still aching from the fight, he carefully began the descent. The bumpy rock provided dozens of handholds, and the rockfall had formed a long, sloping channel that carried them to the ground like a slide. As they neared the bottom, Isiah waited for one of the Raiders to spot him and let out a yell of alarm.

None came. Isiah's boots met solid earth and he crouched next to Tessa. Vyrro and the other eagles were still tied to the trees where Lazaro had left them.

Doubled over, Tessa skirted the landslide and the Raider guards. Isiah scurried after her. The tip of his sabre dragged against the earth. They reached Vyrro's side and the eagle chirped a welcome.

"Shh," Tessa whispered to the bird to calm him. Vyrro ruffled his feathers and tugged at the rope that secured him.

"Keep it down, you stupid birds!" one of the Raiders snapped. Isiah froze. Vyrro's body shielded them from view. "You're lucky if we don't sell you to the butchers at the bazaar."

Tessa scowled. She waited until the Raider had lost interest, before untying Vyrro and climbing onto his back. Isiah joined her, and she drew her sabre. She whispered something to Vyrro and aimed her sword at the men.

Vyrro's neck feathers stood on end. He puffed himself up and unfurled his wings. He let out a cry of warning.

"I told you to—" the Raider started to yell again, but the words died in his throat as Vyrro let out a shriek and launched himself at the men. Isiah clung to Tessa's middle as the eagle descended on the Raiders with a flurry of wingbeats and swirling dust. The men screamed and scrambled away to avoid his talons. They grabbed their own eagles and spurred them into motion.

"How did it get loose?" one of the Raiders yelled.

"Doesn't matter!" the other replied. "I'm not getting mauled. Leave it to calm down!"

The Raiders abandoned their posts and flew away. Vyrro watched them go, chest puffed up and wings outstretched.

Tessa laughed. "Good work!" She stroked Vyrro's outstretched nape. The eagle lowered his wings and returned to his totem pole-like stance.

"What if they alert Enrik?" Isiah asked.

"They didn't notice us," Tessa replied. "And we'll be long gone before anybody comes back." She leapt from Vyrro's shoulders and sprinted to the site of the landslide. She pressed her ear against the rock. Isiah mimicked her. Faint scratching came from the other side.

"Lazaro!" Tessa called.

"Tess? Is that you?" Lazaro's faint voice wafted through. "How did you get out?"

Tessa clawed at the landslide. Rocks and dust came loose, but not enough. "Enrik was trying to kill you!"

Lazaro swore. "We're almost out of torches. Help dig us out."

Tessa went to work. Isiah joined her, shifting large boulders and rolling them away. After a few minutes, they'd only made a small dent.

"We're not fast enough," Tessa said.

"What about the eagles?" Isiah asked. "Can't they help us?"

Tessa clicked her fingers. "The rope!" She broke away and ran to the other eagles. She returned a moment later with a coil of rope. "We had some spare. Vyrro can help us shift the boulders."

Isiah helped her tie the rope around a large boulder. She then brought Vyrro over and coaxed him into taking the other end in his talons. Tessa climbed onto his back and instructed him to fly.

Vyrro took to the air. After a second the rope went taut, then the boulder shifted. Loose stones rained as Vyrro pulled it free. Tessa let out a whoop.

They shifted several more boulders until a hole big enough to crawl through formed. Isiah helped drag Lazaro out. Antony and Darla came next, followed by Luca and Helen.

Lazaro dusted himself off. "Good thinking, you two." He paused. "How did you get out? We searched for you in the ruin."

Tessa told him about the tunnel collapse, then their fight with the gorgons and capture by Enrik. Lazaro's face darkened.

"What does Enrik think he's doing?" he spat. He beckoned the others. "Get your eagles. It's time to remind him why we're not to be messed with."

"Wait," Tessa said. "We'll be outnumbered. Enrik has way more people than we do."

"It doesn't matter," Lazaro replied. "He's dead meat."

"Lazaro . . ." Antony warned.

Lazaro clenched his jaw. "Fine. We'll deal with him later. He won't get away with this." He turned to Darla and Antony. "Bring our bags through. We've got enough loot to survive a few months."

Lazaro pushed past Isiah and untied his eagle. "We'll return to Al-cabaza before Enrik can come after us."

Isiah joined Tessa and Vyrro. The eagles climbed into the heavens and they left the ruin behind. As they went, the memory of the oasis played on Isiah's mind. He patted his pocket, where the artefact pressed against his leg.

Soon he'd be cured.

Returns

THE MOON HAD CLIMBED HIGH ABOVE THE CITY by the time Isiah and the others had returned. They landed their eagles on the roosts and Luca led the birds away with a group of handlers. Isiah trudged down the staircases with the rest of the group, through the shadow-smothered streets in the direction of their house.

The darkness obscured Lazaro's features. The man marched in the lead, hand on his sabre's hilt. Aside from the rats in the alleys and the beggars sleeping against walls, nothing moved. Fatigue tugged at Isiah's eyelids. The adrenaline of the fight faded, leaving him ready to collapse in a heap on his bed.

They reached their house undisturbed and filed inside. Lazaro turned on an oil lantern, casting a warm, flickering shadow across the dining room.

"Enrik hasn't heard the end of this," Lazaro said. "If he thinks he can break the Raider's Oath and have us killed, he's got another thing coming."

"How can we prove it to the other Raiders?" Tessa replied. "Enrik hasn't killed anyone yet." She shifted her weight. "But we did."

Lazaro paused. The other Raiders stared at them.

"What did you do?" Lazaro asked slowly.

"It was Isiah," Tessa started. "We got into a fight trying to escape from Enrik. He stabbed one of them. I think—I think he died."

All heads turned to Isiah. He shifted uncomfortably.

"Well, that's just great, Scavenger," Darla said. "We let you join us and the first thing you do is break the Oath? The other Raiders will have our heads!"

"I didn't mean to." Isiah looked to Tessa for her help. "He was trying to kill me. Tessa set their camp on fire. I thought you didn't like Enrik!"

"We don't," Darla replied. "But there's a big difference between arguing over ruins and killing each other!"

Lazaro stepped between them. "It sounds to me like it was fair game," he said. "Enrik shouldn't have kidnapped them."

"But will the other Raiders believe us?" Antony said. "You know how popular Enrik is with them. What's stopping him from simply denying it?"

"This." Tessa stuck her arm out. "One of them cut me."

Lazaro's jaw clenched. "Who did it? Was it Enrik?"

"No," she said quickly. "It doesn't matter who it was."

"Tess…"

"It was just one of his Raiders, okay? It was self-defence."

"Even so," Antony said, "if Enrik tells the other Raiders about what happened, we could be executed, or driven out of the city. Maybe we should get out of town for a while."

Lazaro shook his head. "I'm not going anywhere. We can take anything Enrik throws at us." He looked around the group. "Isn't that so?"

"Damn right," Helen said. Darla gave them a salute.

"Then it's settled," Lazaro replied. "We should sort through this before any thief catches wind that we've been busy."

He dumped their bags of loot on the table. Gold glowed with a soft light. Various bits of antiques and artefacts were jumbled among it. They all crowded around to get a good look. Isiah found himself squished between Darla and Tessa. He became aware of the woman pressing against the artefact hidden in his pocket. She frowned.

"Hang on a minute." Darla grabbed Isiah's arm. "What's that in your pocket, boy?"

Isiah tried to pull away. "It's just my knife," he lied.

"It doesn't feel like a knife." Darla reached in and pulled out the artefact. Isiah's heart sank.

"Just a knife, ey?" She narrowed her eyes. "Thought you could pocket something for yourself while you were down there, did you? That's just like a filthy nomad."

"I—" He searched for the words.

Lazaro stood. "Scavengers don't get to keep secrets from us," he said. He plucked the artefact from Darla's hand and added it to the pile.

"I wasn't going to steal it," Isiah said.

"Lying only makes it worse," Lazaro snapped. "If you hadn't saved us, I'd be tempted to punish you for it." He gathered the artefact among an armful of gold and walked to the corner of the room.

"What are you going to do with it?" Isiah asked.

"I'm keeping it safe," he replied. He knelt and peeled back a corner of the rug. A trapdoor was embedded in the floor beneath. Lazaro lifted it to reveal a safe. He unlocked it with a large key and placed the gold inside. "There are some travelling merchants who swing by every so often," he said. "They'll be due in a week, by my reckoning. They always pay a good price for loot."

Isiah racked his brains for something to say. He couldn't tell Lazaro about the oasis. It would bring up too many questions—ones he couldn't answer. Lazaro shut the safe and returned the rug to its place. "Now go to bed, the lot of you. We'll figure out what to do about Enrik and the Oath in the morning."

The Raiders filed out of the room. Isiah hurried after Tessa, eager not to be left alone with Lazaro. His earlier excitement had deflated, leaving him with an empty pit in his stomach.

I need that artefact, he thought. If Lazaro sold it to the merchants, he might lose his chance at the oasis forever.

He just had to figure out a way to get it.

* * *

Isiah pushed open the door to his room and collapsed onto his bed. The last of his strength left his muscles, leaving his limbs nothing more than dead weights. His Mark throbbed, but he couldn't be bothered to tend to it again.

The artefact was his only hope. He cursed himself for not hiding it better. He racked his brains to form some kind of plan, but fatigue left his thoughts fuzzy and jumbled.

"Were you really going to keep that thing for yourself?" Tessa asked. Isiah twisted around to see her leaning against the doorway. She'd untied her bun, letting her hair fall around her shoulders.

"I forgot it was there," he said. He winced at how unconvincing he sounded. "I grabbed it before we found the fissure. It slipped my mind."

Tessa shrugged. "I guess that makes sense."

They stood in silence for a moment.

"Is your arm alright?" he asked.

"Darla said she'll look at it tomorrow."

Isiah unhooked his sabre and placed it on a nearby barrel. Dust coated his cloak and seemed to fill every crevice, but fatigue won over the urge to wash.

"Why didn't you want to tell Lazaro who cut you?" he asked.

"I didn't want to worry him," Tessa said. She left the doorway and wandered into the room. "He might do something rash. He looks out for me too much."

Isiah rubbed his Mark. "Maybe that's not such a bad thing, you know."

Tessa broke away. "You've got to look after yourself out here. Nobody else will protect you." She paused at the doorway. "You of all people should know that."

She disappeared down the hall, leaving Isiah alone with his thoughts.

153

Pickpocket

YEARS EARLIER . . .

Tessa clutched her bag to her chest. She put her head down and slipped through the crowd, hoping nobody would notice her. The vibrant colours and nauseating smells of the bazaar invaded her senses, making her brain foggy. She slipped past a yelling merchant and ducked into a side street.

She risked cracking her bag open to peer inside. Gold coins shone with a soft light, alongside the fruit and bread she could grab from the merchant stalls when nobody was looking.

Tessa navigated the cramped alleyways, studying the many faded and boarded-up doors. A beggar—no more than a bundle of rags—lay across the path ahead. She checked to make sure he was asleep, then hopped over him before he could grab her.

Ahead, a decrepit building stood. Boards were haphazardly nailed across its shutters, and its door leaned open on a single hinge. Tessa swung the bag over her shoulder, then scrambled up the windowsills of a neighbouring house to reach the balcony. The bustling of the city faded to the edge of her senses as she rolled onto the balcony and slipped into the building's second floor.

"Lazaro," she called. She studied the dimly lit interior. Parts of the ceiling had crumbled, exposing patches of the sky above and wooden beams. Broken furniture, long since looted by Scavengers and squatters, slumped against walls and were strewn across the floor.

Lazaro popped his head out from a hole in the floor. "I didn't think you'd be back so soon." He climbed through the hole. Dust stained his moth-eaten clothing, but bright eyes shone through his unwashed, boyish face.

Tessa dumped her bag on a three-legged table. "The merchants were distracted today."

Lazaro inspected the contents. He cracked a smile. "That's my sister!" He ruffled her hair. "It looks like we'll be eating tonight."

Tessa beamed. She always liked it when Lazaro was happy.

"I'm working on that Raider idea," Lazaro said. "I've found a couple of groups who might want to take us on as Scavengers."

Tessa grabbed an apple and plopped herself on the bundle of rags that formed their mattress. It was the only source of comfort in the dilapidated house. "You really think so?"

"If we can join the Raiders, we'll be out of here in no time," Lazaro said. "And they'll pay us a share of whatever loot we find."

Tessa smiled. "We could be like real Raiders—just like Mum and Dad." Her smile faltered.

"Hey." Lazaro sat next to her. "You're alive. That's all that matters to me. As long as we're here, we can make them proud."

Tessa sniffed. Losing their parents felt like a lifetime ago. Without Lazaro to protect her from squatters or rival thieves, she didn't know how she'd survive. "Do you think the Raiders will be able to protect us from dragons?"

"Forget the Raiders," Lazaro said. "*I'll* protect you from dragons. Once we're Scavengers, we'll make more money. Then I can find you an eagle chick." He pulled her close. "I know how much you always wanted one."

Tessa hugged him. "I'd like that." She pushed the memory of the Royal Guards back to the edges of her mind.

Lazaro pulled her tighter. "As long as I'm looking out for you, you'll never have to worry about dragons again."

Celebration

Bright sunlight illuminated his cramped bedroom when Isiah woke. The muffled voices and grumbling carts of the city wafted up from the street outside. Isiah stretched his aching limbs, then wiped the sleep from his eyes and stumbled into the hall.

Talking reached his ears from down below. He hurriedly treated his Mark and straightened out his cloak, before jogging into the dining room. Tessa and the other Raiders sat talking over bowls of greyish porridge.

He took a seat beside Tessa and she passed him a portion of his own. Despite the growling of his stomach, the events of the previous night left his insides in knots.

"If Enrik talks to the Raiders, we're in trouble," Antony said. "It's been years since anyone has broken the Oath."

"What if we give the Scavenger boy here to him as payment?" Luca piped up. "He's the one who did it. Let him be the scapegoat."

Tessa glared at him. "Raiders aren't supposed to desert their own."

"And he's not a Raider," Luca said. "*You* didn't even want to make him part of our gang."

Isiah shifted uncomfortably. The safe in the corner of the floor seemed to beckon him. He could almost feel the artefact calling out . . .

"We're not giving Enrik what he wants," Lazaro cut in. "He wouldn't be happy with it anyway." He balled his fist. "I won't let any of my Raiders be pushed around by the likes of him."

"So do we just wait and bide our time?" Darla asked.

"Enrik has a lot to answer for if he goes around spreading rumours," Tessa said. "He's not stupid. He knows what sort of chaos this could make."

Isiah remembered what Reuben had told him. *They'd be at war if they didn't have some kind of agreement among themselves.*

"What will happen to the city if they discover the Raider's Oath is broken?" he asked.

"Nothing good," Antony replied. "There are more than a few rivalries that have only fallen short of bloodshed because of the Oath."

"There's a celebration in the city," Darla interrupted. "I heard the Raiders talking about it when I visited our eagles this morning. Word is they've captured a couple of Royal Guards."

Isiah nearly choked on his porridge.

A sly grin appeared on Darla's face. "And we all know what happens to *them*."

"A spectacle, ey?" Luca said. "When does it start?"

"They'll be in the arena at midday," Darla replied. "When our dark sun is at its highest."

158

Lazaro clapped her on the shoulder. "What better way to take our minds off Enrik and celebrate our newest haul?"

Isiah gulped. "What are they gonna do?"

"You've never seen what happens to Royal Guards before?" Lazaro laughed. "Then you're in for a treat, Scavenger."

* * *

As the twin suns neared their highest point, Lazaro and Tessa filed out of the house. Isiah tagged along with them. The crowd swept them up in its fold, jostling him from side to side. Their excited chatter climbed to a chorus as they migrated in the direction of the arena.

Darla and Luca followed them, alongside Helen. Antony had stayed behind to watch over their treasure. As they went, Isiah quelled the unease in his gut. Part of his mind urged him to break away. With the house almost deserted, there was no better time to retrieve the artefact . . . but without stealing the key, he had no idea how to get in.

I'll find a way, he thought. *And before Lazaro sells it, too.* As soon as he had the artefact, he'd abandon the city and trek out to the ruin. Then he'd cure himself with the oasis and he could leave it all behind.

They climbed to the second terrace and navigated their way to the crevice in the mountainside. The crowds grew denser. People were fighting to secure seats in the cavern inside. As they drew near, Isiah's stomach did backflips. Cheering echoed from the direction of the arena.

"Come on!" Darla said. "We're gonna miss it!"

Isiah dreaded to think what *it* was—but deep down, he already knew.

Get the artefact, the voice told him. *Then you can run. Leave the Raiders before they figure out who you are.*

Isiah nodded to himself. He knew if Lazaro discovered his Mark, he'd join the fate of the Royal Guards.

Isiah bumped into a group of merchants and stumbled.

"Watch where you're going!" one snapped.

Tessa hurried back and took Isiah's arm. "Stick close," she said. He felt her warm breath against his ear. "It's easy to get separated."

Isiah found himself hurrying after her. The bandage he'd secured to her forearm was still there. He remembered the way she'd thanked him after their fight with Enrik. The voice in his head faltered.

They made it through the crowd and emerged in the cavern. Looking around, they found a handful of empty chairs on one wing of the arena. The rest of the seats were soon filled, and other people lined up against the far wall. Trumpets blared an announcement. The crowd's cheering invaded Isiah's head like insects burrowing into his eardrums. He fought the urge to scratch his Mark.

The crowd cheered as a gate on the far side of the arena opened and a handful of rag-clad people were thrown through. They turned and tried to run back to safety, but the gate slammed shut in front of them. The people pressed their backs against it, watching the far side with wide eyes.

"Prisoners," Tessa said. A cruel smile crossed her face. "They're just the warm-up. They save the Royal Guards for last."

Isiah squirmed in his seat as a gate creaked opened and a deep, guttural hissing sounded.

A serpentine head came into view like an eel slithering from its den. At the sight of it, his Mark began to burn.

No. Isiah tightened his cloak. It couldn't possibly notice him in such a giant crowd. The dragon lumbered into view and extended its wings with a throaty roar. Manacles hung around its ankles, and a gleam of metal shone from the valve lodged in its neck.

The prisoners screamed and ran. They skirted the edges of the arena, trying to get away from the beast. The crowd hollered and jeered at them from the other side. Isiah closed his eyes as the dragon whirled on one of the prisoners and a sickening crunch ran out.

The dragon finished with the prisoners, then scanned the crowd.

Tessa laughed. "You can look now."

Isiah cracked open one eye. Nothing remained of the prisoners except for a few body parts and stains of blood. The dragon's jaws salivated. He felt its eyes sweeping over the crowd.

Then they rested on him.

A new trumpet sounded, distracting it. A second batch of prisoners were thrown into the arena, this time with makeshift spears and daggers. The dragon made short work of them. With every kill, the crowd grew more frenzied. Isiah clamped his hands against his ears as their voices swirled around his head. His mind flashed back to the crowd for his Ceremony, when the dragon—

Tessa grabbed his arm. "The Royal Guards are here."

A voice told him not to look. All the same, he found his eyes glued to the gate. It creaked open and two Royal Guards, clad in their shining armour, entered the arena. The Raiders tossed them swords.

"We like a show," Darla explained. "The dragons bash them around a bit before killing them. It's more entertaining that way."

Isiah hardly heard her. He squinted at one of the Royal Guards. He could have sworn that despite the man's bloodied face and scuffed armour, he looked familiar. A sinking dread welled in the pit of his stomach.

"Ward," he whispered.

"What?" Tessa said.

Isiah checked to make sure none of the other Raiders were listening. "I know him."

The other Royal Guard swung his sword in the direction of the dragon, but Ward let his fall to the floor. The dragon bellowed at them, spittle and blood drenching the sand. It whirled on the first Royal Guard and attacked. The crowd cheered as the dragon catapulted him a dozen feet into the air. The man crumpled into a heap.

The dragon closed in. Lazaro pumped his fist into the air. Darla and Luca yelled. The injured Royal Guard dragged himself to his feet in time for the dragon to seize him in its jaws and shake him violently. Isiah shrank into his seat, unable to look away.

The dragon released the man and threw him into the bars. But before it could attack again, Ward ran between them. He raised his hands and yelled at the beast. Isiah's heart skipped a beat as the dragon skidded to a halt. Its serpentine head swayed back and forth, ready to strike.

Tessa frowned. "What does he think he's doing?"

Ward puffed out his chest. Even from a distance, Isiah made out the tremor in his legs, but the man pinned the dragon with his gaze. The dragon made a mock lunge at him, but he stood his ground.

Lazaro dropped his arm. "Hurry up and kill them!" he yelled.

People in the crowd jeered at Ward and threw things into the arena. Isiah's fingers dug into the edges of his chair. The dragon stood frozen, as if unsure what to make of Ward.

It took a step backwards. Ward's wounded companion dragged himself to his feet.

Chains rumbled as the gate lifted and a flood of Raiders spilled into the arena. Ward faltered. The dragon rose to its full height and snarled at them. The crowd booed as Raiders grabbed the two Royal Guards and dragged them away.

"What are they doing?" Isiah asked.

"The dragon won't bite," Tessa said. She glared at the men. "It doesn't want to kill them."

The dragon advanced on the Raiders, but several produced long sticks topped with swirling orange crystals. The dragon hissed and shied away. Waving the crystals, the Raiders forced it back into its prison.

"More magic," Tessa said, seeing Isiah's expression. "It's rare, too. We find them in the ruins sometimes." She watched as the Raiders sealed the dragon's gate. "It's the only thing the dragons fear."

"The stories say it has something to do with our suns," Darla added. "It repels them or something."

Isiah watched the Raiders carry Ward and his wounded companion out of the arena. "What are they going to do with them?"

"Execute them, probably," Lazaro said. He sneered. "Shame we couldn't watch."

"We might get lucky," Darla replied. "Executions take time to be scheduled."

The gate slammed shut and the arena fell still. The crowd began filing out, grumbling among themselves. Lazaro and the other Raiders joined them.

A figure stepped out in front of them. Isiah's blood ran cold as his eyes settled on Enrik's face.

"Nice day, Lazaro," Enrik said. "Celebrating your haul? I would as well. There must have been good riches in that tomb."

Isiah exchanged looks with Tessa. Her hand rested on the hilt of her sabre. Lazaro's eyes narrowed. "What do you want, Enrik?"

Enrik raised his hands in mock surrender. "Nothing at all. I just thought I'd tell your Scavenger here to be more careful. One of my men must have *fallen* on his sabre. Now I'm down a Raider."

Isiah spotted several other Raiders in the crowd—all part of Enrik's gang. The crowd around them didn't seem to notice what was going on. He tensed, waiting for a fight to break out.

"After you tried to bury us?" Lazaro snapped. "Do you think—"

Tessa grabbed Lazaro's arm. His fists unclenched. "We'll look the other way if you do, Enrik."

Enrik cracked a smile. Isiah caught the same cold, emotionless eyes behind it. "Now you're a man with a shred of sense, Lazaro. We'll call it *our little secret.* I can't imagine what would happen to Alcabaza if word got out about the Raider's Oath being broken."

Enrik's Raiders melted into the crowd. Isiah realized he hadn't been breathing. He sucked in a mouthful of air.

"One other thing," Enrik said. His eyes flitted between Isiah and Tessa. "Stay away from the ruin."

Enrik turned and disappeared into the crowd, leaving Lazaro and his friends to hasten out of the arena. Isiah hurried after them. He rubbed a hand across the back of his neck and breathed a sigh.

Lazaro scoffed. "Some truce. He'll sell us out the moment he gets the chance."

"Then we'd better watch our backs," Helen replied. "And keep a low profile until the heat dies down."

"We're not hiding from Enrik," Lazaro said. "What are we? Nomads? We don't scurry under rocks to hide."

Isiah let their conversation fade to the edges of his mind. Despite Enrik's warning and their standoff, one thing dominated his thoughts.

The Raiders had Ward.

Ward

"I THOUGHT YOU HATED PARADON!"

Isiah held a finger to his lips. He nervously glanced at the door. "I told you. I used to know him."

"They banished you," Tessa said. "Isn't that what your Mark is about? Why are you defending them?"

"They had to banish me," Isiah replied. "Ward isn't like them. He was my dragon-trainer."

Tessa's nose crinkled. "That's two reasons to hate him."

"He doesn't care about the Badlands," Isiah said. "He was probably just on some scouting mission or something."

"They're all evil," Tessa replied. "The second they cross the border, they're our enemies."

Isiah paced about his cramped room. "What about me, then?"

Tessa eyed him. "You're different. You're Marked."

"I need to help him," Isiah said. Since returning to the house, he couldn't get the image of Ward facing the dragon out of his head. *Maybe he was looking for me.*

"What do you want me to do?" Tessa asked.

"Show me the prisons. You know all the other Raiders, right?"

She tossed her hair. "What are you suggesting?"

"I mean you're friends with the guards?"

She hesitated. "I sometimes talk to the people who work there."

"Maybe you can distract them. If I get a key, I could free him—"

"No." Tessa jumped off the barrel she had been sitting on. "We'll both be fed to the dragon ourselves."

Isiah racked his brains. "Then at least let me talk to him. You don't need to see him yourself. He doesn't even need to know you exist."

Tessa shifted her footing. "If Lazaro finds out—"

"He won't," Isiah said quickly. "Nobody needs to know. All I want to do is talk to him."

Tessa sighed. "Fine—but you owe me." She gathered her things. "We'd better be fast in case the Raiders want to execute him today."

They slipped out of the house and into the streets. Butterflies welled in Isiah's insides.

"Why do you even need to talk?" Tessa asked. "You know what Royal Guards are like. They kicked you out. They hate you."

"No they don't," Isiah insisted. "It—it was for my own good."

Tessa snorted. "Yeah, right."

"The dragons will kill me on sight," Isiah said. "How could they let me stay? If I ever found a way to cure myself, they'd accept me with open arms." He willed himself to believe it.

"And how are you going to do that, wise guy?"

Isiah wrung his hands. "I'm working on it."

Tessa frowned. "Remember who you're with. We're Raiders here." She poked a finger into his chest. "Unless you want to skip town?"

"I won't." He raised his hands in surrender.

"Good." Tessa whirled around. "Because you know how we feel about your kind."

Tessa took the lead and they navigated the city in the direction of the arena. The excitement had died down since the celebration, leaving the streets quieter than usual.

"They keep the prisoners in the mountain nearby," Tessa explained. "To keep them from escaping."

"How many prisoners are there?" Isiah asked.

"Not many," she replied. "Only the people the Raiders can catch. Most of the time we're lawless around here."

They neared the arena. As they drew closer, Tessa took him aside to a jumble of squat buildings that hugged the mountainface. Bars covered the windows, and thick wooden doors sat on sturdy hinges.

Tessa took a deep breath. "Here goes nothing."

She knocked on the door. A face appeared at the window. "Hey, Tessa."

Tessa faltered.

"Surprised to see me, right?" the boy said. He looked about their age, with youthful features and bright eyes. "Enrik sent me here as punishment."

Isiah glanced around, half-expecting Enrik to be watching them. Tessa leaned into him. "He's a Scavenger," she said. "I used to know him before Lazaro made our gang. His name's Aron." She returned her attention to the boy. "What did you do this time?"

"It was only a few coins," Aron said. "I didn't take much."

"Once a pickpocket, always a pickpocket." Tessa laughed. "Think you could let us in?"

"Give me a minute." Aron's face disappeared, and moments later the door gave a clunk. "The Raiders said no visitors before the celebration, but they didn't say anything about *afterwards*."

Isiah and Tessa piled inside. Bars divided the room in half, with a locked gate leading to the prisons beyond. Isiah craned his neck to see down the dimly lit passageway.

"Why do the Raiders run this place?" he asked.

"We're the only ones with authority," Tessa replied. "Someone has to do it."

Aron coughed. "What can I do for you?"

"My Scavenger friend wanted to see a Royal Guard for himself." She cupped her hand to her mouth and lowered her voice to a whisper. "He's new. He used to be a nomad."

"Inexperienced, then," Aron said. "I guess you've never seen one up close before, have you?"

Isiah ignored the boy's mocking tone. Aron unlocked the door for Tessa. "Don't tell Enrik about this. If he sees us together, he'll throw me off the mountain."

Tessa thanked him, then ushered Isiah through.

"Be quick," she hissed. "And don't let the guards see you."

"Where's Ward being kept?" Isiah asked.

"In the furthest cell," Aron replied. "They shoved him in there after the dragon failed to kill him."

Isiah thanked him and hurried down the tunnel. It wrapped around the cavern that held the arena, crude-cut windows offering faint slivers of light. Shadows shrouded the cramped cells. Isiah's eyes watered at the musty smell hanging in the air.

A handful of other doorways branched off of the main tunnel, with passages heading deeper into the mountainside. Footsteps sounded. Isiah retreated into the shadows as a figure emerged from one. The woman's clothes identified her as a Raider. She paused, raising an oil lantern to check one of the cells, before continuing. Isiah breathed a sigh of relief.

He darted down the way the woman had come. The tunnel led deeper into the mountain, shadows growing thicker as he went. He squinted into the cells. Most stood empty—or at least, he didn't see anything in the darkness.

"Ward," he whispered.

A voice sounded somewhere ahead. Isiah hastened toward it. His gaze came to rest on a cell. This one was occupied.

"Isiah?" Ward asked. "Is that you?" The man leaned against the bars. One of his eyes was swollen shut, and blood crusted a split lip.

"I saw you in the arena," Isiah replied.

"You're the last person I expected to see here," Ward said. "How did you end up in this place?"

"I'm looking for a cure," Isiah whispered. He paused to make sure nobody was listening. "I found a group of Raiders."

Ward expression fell. "The damn Raiders brought us down. My dragon crashed in the Badlands. They said they were going to *teach me a lesson*." He chuckled. "But I guess I showed them."

A groan sounded from deeper in the cell.

"Is he going to be alright?" Isiah asked.

Ward lowered his voice. "He's dying. The dragon got him real good."

At the mention of the dragon, Isiah shivered. "One chased me. It tried to kill me because of my Mark."

Ward clenched his fist. "I knew the nobles shouldn't have pushed your Ceremony forward. Now look at you." He paused. "Still, you're not the one in a cell."

"Let me help you escape," Isiah said.

"No," Ward replied. "Don't put yourself in danger. I'll figure things out myself."

"They're going to execute you," he blurted out. "The dragon didn't want to kill you, so they're going to do it themselves."

"I figured that," Ward said. "Don't worry about me. I'll fight my way out of here unarmed if I have to." He gave Isiah a wink, but the man's confidence did nothing to soothe him.

"I'm sure I can break you out," Isiah said. "If I just found the key."

"And then what?" Ward asked. "Smuggle me out looking like this?" He gestured to his armour. "They'll recognize me from a mile away." He shook his head. "No. I've caused you enough trouble already."

"That's not true," Isiah insisted.

"I should have been there inside the arena during your Ceremony," Ward said. "The dragon wasn't supposed to attack you. If I was closer, I could have stopped it."

His words made Isiah's Mark sting.

"But I'm sure you'll set things right," Ward continued. He reached through the bars and patted Isiah's shoulder. "Good luck with your cure."

Part of Isiah wanted to protest, but he knew Ward was right. He slumped his shoulders, defeated.

"One last thing," Ward said. "That dragon in the arena—it isn't so bad."

At the mention of the dragon, Isiah's legs went weak. His Mark prickled with heat.

"It's not a killing machine," Ward continued. "You saw how it didn't attack me. They're smarter than eagles. They can sense what you're really like."

But I'm Marked, Isiah thought. "I don't want to see another dragon in my life."

"Don't give up on them," Ward said. "Promise me that."

Isiah tried to answer, but the words wouldn't come.

"Now get out of here before anyone finds you," Ward told him.

Isiah navigated the tunnels back to the safety of the entrance. As he went, his Mark tugged at his mind. He could almost feel it calling out his presence to the dragon locked inside its cage.

If the Raiders discovered him, he knew he'd join it.

Deserted

ISIAH PACED BACK AND FORTH OUTSIDE VYRRO'S PEN. He watched as Tessa ran a comb through the giant bird's feathers. Vyrro sat like a statue, but Isiah caught his eyes keenly watching the handlers as they passed.

Isiah had spied Lazaro's key after returning from seeing Ward. The man kept it in his pocket. But even the thought of sneaking in and trying to steal it made his palms sweaty.

I'm not a pickpocket. He dreaded to think about what would happen if Lazaro caught him in the act. His gaze drifted to Tessa. Maybe she could . . .

"Done." Tessa finished brushing Vyrro and hopped down. She dusted her hands together. "Do you want to fly with me?"

Isiah shrugged. "Why not?"

He and Tessa climbed atop Vyrro and the eagle bounded toward the landing pad. As they went, Isiah returned to the world inside his head.

I can't tell Tessa, he thought. She would have too many questions . . . and he'd have to tell her his plan.

Vyrro unfurled his wings and took to the skies, climbing with a flurry of wingbeats. A few shreds of cloud wafted overhead, swirling around the mountain and drifting hazily on the horizon.

Tessa sighed. "I'm glad to finally get out of the house. You don't realize how stuffy it is until you go flying again."

Isiah gripped Tessa's middle. The sight of the ground so far away still unnerved him, but he settled into Vyrro's rhythm.

"Lazaro is paranoid," Tessa said. "He says he's not worried about Enrik, but he's looking out for us all the same."

"If that's what you call it," Isiah replied.

"Just because he can be bad-tempered doesn't mean he doesn't care about us." She gave Vyrro's reins a flick. "He's always been there for me."

"I thought you said you can't rely on anyone but yourself?"

"You can't." Tessa gestured to the sky. "Do you see anyone here? Nobody would come to our rescue if we got into trouble. We could have died to the gorgons, or to Enrik. No one would have cared."

Isiah sensed something in her voice. He decided not to push the matter further.

"Do you want to go scouting for more ruins or something?" he asked, trying to change the conversation.

Tessa paused. "I suppose so. There was another earthquake last night."

Vyrro veered to one side and they flew away from the city. The Badlands rolled below them. Isiah caught a flash of colour as a group of merchants trekked in the direction of the city.

"You're better at flying, Scavenger," Tessa said. She nudged him. "How about we go for round two?"

Isiah barely had time to respond before she spurred Vyrro and he spun in mid-air. Isiah felt the weightlessness of his insides as Vyrro barrel-rolled.

"They do this to fight," Tessa said as they swung back around. "They lock talons or scratch at each other's bellies."

"I thought Raiders didn't fight?"

"We don't," Tessa replied. "But our eagles don't always like each other." She lowered her voice. "And it works on dragons sometimes, too."

A distant boom caught Isiah's attention. It rumbled like a crack of thunder in the distance. Below, rocks trembled and dust rained from cliffs.

"Miners," Tessa said. "They must have found a vein nearby."

"More explosives?" Isiah asked.

She nodded. "They just caused a little tremor, this time."

They kept flying. The land fell still and they continued for several minutes. The wind rushed in Isiah's eardrums, the only sound other than the steady beat of Vyrro's wings. Isiah shifted his weight.

"Tessa," he said.

"Yeah?"

"I want to swing by the ruin again."

He felt her tense. "Enrik will see us."

"Not if we're careful, right? You said the lakebed was invisible from the air."

"It is," she replied. "But Lazaro won't be happy if he finds out."

Isiah nudged her. "Hey, I thought Lazaro said we weren't going to be pushed around? What's Enrik doing that's so important he doesn't want us to know?"

The seconds ticked past. He could almost see the gears turning in her head. "He *did* sound pretty suspicious," she said after a moment. "Or maybe he's just angry that we burned his camp down."

"Well," Isiah said, "do you want to go find out?"

* * *

The site of the landslide materialized. Vyrro soared towards it, his wings outstretched as he rode the air currents. Isiah scanned for any sign of activity.

"It's deserted," Tessa said. "Nobody has been here."

The tunnel Isiah and Tessa had dug to free Lazaro remained unchanged. Tessa frowned. "Why don't they want to go through the front entrance?"

Isiah already knew the answer.

Vyrro flew over the landslide and glided across the flat mesa that he and Tessa had crossed. Narrow ravines and valleys snaked between them, forming a complex labyrinth of crevices.

"Few travellers visit here," Tessa said. "It's too dangerous. Gorgons love it."

Isiah studied the ravines as they passed, trying to catch a glimpse of the beasts. Vyrro veered to the left as Tessa guided him toward the lakebed. Isiah fixed his eyes on a narrow crack that seemed to split a mesa in two.

"You were right when you said the lakebed was well-hidden," he said. "We could have flown right over it and not seen anything."

"I wonder how many Raiders have done exactly that," Tessa replied.

She pressed her legs into Vyrro's flanks and the giant eagle descended. He fell in line with the ravine and flew low over it. Isiah leaned over, craning his neck to glimpse the ground below.

"I don't see anything," he said. "Are you sure this is the right one?"

"Are you doubting my sense of direction?"

Before Isiah could reply, another boom sounded—much closer. He clamped his hands over his ears as the sound crackled across the heavens. Rocks dropped from cliff faces and shattered in clouds of dust.

Vyrro let out a panicked cry and lurched away. Isiah grabbed his harness to keep from falling off. Tessa fought to control him.

"Calm down," she said. "The miners can't hurt you."

Vyrro regained his composure and drifted back over the ravine. Isiah caught a flash of the lakebed below.

"I don't think those are miners . . ." he started.

Enrik's camp came into view. Burned foliage surrounded it, the earth stained black from the previous fire. Raiders scurried back and forth, carrying pickaxes and barrels. One rolled a long fuse across the ground.

Tessa swore. "You're right."

Vyrro tilted his wings, giving them a better look. Isiah prayed none of the Raiders would look up and notice them. Enrik stood in the middle of the camp, waving his arms and giving out orders. Their faint voices carried on the air.

"What are they doing?" Tessa asked.

Isiah caught a glimpse of the strange boxes he'd seen when they escaped from his camp. The sheets that had covered them lay strewn on the ground. Raiders dragged the boxes toward the excavation site.

"They're excavating," he replied. "They must be trying to reach the ruin."

"But why?" Tessa said. "Why not just go through the front door? Enrik wouldn't stay away just because we claimed it. Why go to so much effort?"

The oasis. Isiah swallowed. "He must be looking for something in particular."

Tessa nudged Vyrro and he glided away from the camp before any of the Raiders could spot them. "It's so weird. What are they after?"

Isiah hesitated. "I don't know."

Vyrro turned in the direction of Alcabaza. When the lakebed and the mesa had faded into the distance, Isiah let his shoulders drop.

Enrik won't reach it, he thought. *Not without the artefact.*

But as long as it was inside Lazaro's safe, he couldn't reach it either.

Breach

"Fire in the hole!"

Enrik covered his ears as a blast ripped through the camp. A plume of dust exploded upwards from the excavation site. Tremors rippled underfoot. One of the Raiders steadied himself against a burnt tree trunk as pebbles rained from the overhang above.

The rumbling died. Raiders scurried in to inspect the damage.

"Have we breached it?" Enrik asked.

A Raider coughed and covered her arm with her sleeve. She peered into the hole with her one good eye. "If not, we're close."

Enrik marched over. Pickaxes and shovels lay against piles of earth and rock. Their eagles stood further off, alongside their camp. Enrik reached her side and studied the hole.

A deep pit led into the earth, its edges rough-cut by pickaxes and explosives. Ledges of hard rock protruded from the soft earth, growing more jumbled the further down they went. Darkness obscured the bottom.

"There's only one way to find out," Enrik said. He summoned forth his magic.

A familiar tingling sensation seized his body as his power took hold. Enrik concentrated on a ledge at the bottom of the pit, then threw himself toward it.

His body dissolved. His senses ceased. He re-formed inside the pit and the entire world came flooding back. He regained his composure as the other Raiders materialized beside him.

The ground shifted underfoot, loose and smothered with sediment. Enrik knelt and swept the pebbles away. Cracks crisscrossed the rock.

A smile crept across his face. "We're close," he said. "Bring me a pickaxe."

One of the Raiders teleported away, returning a moment later with a curved metal pickaxe. Enrik took it from him and raised it into the air.

He brought it down with all of his strength. A shockwave reverberated up his arms. Shards of rock pelted the sides of the hole. The other Raiders backed away as he raised the pickaxe and struck it again.

Earth shifted and stone crumbled. The floor gave way and collapsed into a cavern. Enrik wiped a hand across his forehead. "Easy."

He dropped into the cavern. An eerie silence cloaked the space. A handful of other Raiders joined him. Enrik took a torch from one and studied the interior.

"Where's Aron when you need him?" the female Raider asked. She glanced down one of the tunnels. An eyepatch covered one of her eyes—lost to a duel. "We could have used him to check if we were jumping into a gorgon den."

"It's better if he doesn't know, Iris," he replied. "He'd end up spilling our secret to every Scavenger in the city."

Enrik wandered into the cavern. His torch cast dancing shadows across the walls, illuminating the many hidden alcoves and ledges.

"Where are you?" he whispered. "You have to be here somewhere." The lakebed didn't lie.

A door materialized from the darkness. Enrik's smile widened. He called over his shoulder, "Get over here, boys!"

The Raiders hurried over.

"Do you think this is the one?" Iris asked.

Enrik placed his hand on the door. He sensed the magic coursing behind it. "I can feel it."

The other Raiders stepped aside as Enrik raised his pickaxe and brought it down on the door. The sound rang out, bouncing off the walls. Enrik struck it again. His pickaxe slid off and the door remained unmarked.

Enrik frowned. He swung at the rock next to it. The force reverberated through his hands. He swore and shook them to ease the pain.

"Something wrong?" Iris asked.

"Bring the explosives," Enrik ordered.

The Raiders broke away. They appeared a few minutes later with a crate. They placed it by the door, then laid a long fuse. They all sheltered inside one of the passageways as a Raider lit the end.

Sparks flew. The fuse hissed, burning its way into the cavern. Enrik braced himself as an explosion tore through the confined space.

Dust billowed into the passageway. The earth shook and stones rained. Enrik waited until the dust had settled, then inspected the door.

It stood unscathed.

"What if it's magic?" Iris suggested. "It makes sense, doesn't it? Some kind of protection spell?"

A hole in the rock caught Enrik's attention. Its smooth edges betrayed it, too perfect to be natural. "So it needs a key, does it?"

"Hey, Enrik." Iris pointed to an empty pedestal next to the door.

Enrik narrowed his eyes. "A key that's missing."

"But who could have taken it?" she asked. "We buried Lazaro with explosives. He couldn't possibly have found this place."

"No," Enrik replied. He dropped his voice. "But Tessa and that Scavenger of hers could have."

"Do you think they know what it does?"

"It doesn't matter." Enrik marched away. "Get the eagles ready. I think we'd best pay those two a visit."

Like Them

Isiah sat on his bed, watching the dust suspended in the air. After flying with Tessa, they'd returned to the house. The thought of Enrik and his excavation tugged at Isiah's mind, but he pushed it away. *Enrik can't do anything without the artefact.*

Isiah glanced out the window, where the sun hung over the mountaintop. He knew what room Lazaro slept in. When night fell, he could sneak in and take the key.

And then what? a voice in his head asked.

He'd run. Isiah nodded to himself as he thought it over. He'd cure himself just like he set out to do. Then he'd free Ward and they'd escape back to Paradon together.

His heart sank as the size of the task dawned on him. Even if he escaped the city, he still had to slip past Enrik. He slumped onto his bed with a sigh.

Footsteps sounded in the hall outside. The door swung open and Tessa piled in. She saw him and laughed.

"You're in a good mood," Isiah said.

Tessa walked past him to the window. "Lazaro says the merchants are going to arrive early. They'll be here tomorrow and we can sell all our loot."

Isiah's stomach dropped. He tried not to show his expression.

"Lazaro says we can find a better place to live," Tessa continued. "We might even make enough to move to the higher terraces."

Isiah forced a smile. "Sounds good to me."

Tessa pulled away from the windowsill. "You did well out there," she said. "Flying, I mean."

"I learned from a great teacher, I guess."

Tessa giggled. "I'm not *that* good."

"You didn't even want to teach me at first," Isiah said. His gaze dropped to her bandaged arm. "How are you doing?"

Tessa turned her arm over. "Darla said it will heal quickly." She paused. "What about you?"

Isiah furrowed his brow.

"Your Mark, I mean," she said.

Isiah glanced at the door. He adjusted his cloak to reveal the burns. The sunlight cast shadows over his warped, wax-like skin.

Tessa put her hand on her chin. "I could have sworn it looked worse when I first saw it."

Isiah still felt the chill of the oasis. "You might be right."

"I think I have something for it," she said. "Darla used it on my arm."

Tessa disappeared from the room. A moment later she returned with a vial of ointment. "Didn't anyone in Paradon give you anything?" she asked.

185

"I got robbed," Isiah admitted. "My guides. I shouldn't have trusted them."

Tessa popped the top off the vial and poured some onto his shoulder. "It's supposed to make things heal faster."

The ointment soothed the heat beneath his skin. Isiah rubbed it in. "It can't sweat," he said. "The burns went deep."

But soon I'll be healed. Once he grabbed Lazaro's keys . . .

"Let me help," Tessa said. Before he could stop her, she put her hands on his back, where the Mark extended out of his own reach. "I hope this isn't weird or anything, right?"

Isiah glanced to the door. "As long as nobody sees us."

"Sometimes in the summers we get sunburned," Tessa said. "You can't always reach the bits that get burned yourself."

The stairs creaked. Tessa paused. Isiah hurriedly pulled on his cloak—but not fast enough.

Lazaro's head appeared. "Scavenger—" he started to say, then stopped. "What were you doing?"

"Nothing," Isiah said quickly. He hurriedly readjusted his cloak as he tried to quell the alarm bells going off in his head.

"He got sunburned," Tessa added. "I was helping, is all."

"No." Lazaro stepped into the room. "Let me see."

Isiah took a step back. "It's nothing."

Lazaro caught his arm. "Sunburns don't make your skin melt off, boy."

Isiah tried to pull away, but Lazaro's hand darted out and grabbed his cloak. "You're *Marked*."

"I'm not," Isiah protested. He fought to stop the panic rising inside him.

"Don't lie to me," Lazaro snapped. "I know what being Marked looks like." He whirled on Tessa. "And you knew?"

"He said he's not like them."

"Of course he is!" Lazaro's expression darkened. "How long have you been keeping this a secret? Since the ruin? Sooner?"

Tessa avoided his gaze. Lazaro tightened his grip on Isiah's arm. "I should have thrown you off the city, Scavenger."

"He saved you!" Tessa exclaimed. "He saved me, too."

"He's a liar." Lazaro shoved Isiah towards the door. "A liar and a thief."

Tessa grabbed Lazaro's cloak, but she failed to slow him. "What are you going to do with him?"

"What I should have done when he tried to keep that artefact for himself."

Isiah tried to twist away, but the man had a grip of steel. He shoved Isiah down the stairs. Isiah caught sight of the open window looking out across the plain.

Tessa ran down the stairs after him. "Let him go."

"Don't try to stop me, Tess," Lazaro said. "You know what his kind are like!"

He dragged Isiah to the front door. Isiah dug his heels into the ground. Lazaro unlocked it and threw it open.

"I should kill you, boy," he spat. "You betrayed my trust, you lied about who you are, and you tried to steal loot for yourself. I should have disbanded you then, but I gave you a roof to sleep under."

Lazaro threw Isiah onto the street. The crowd parted as Isiah stumbled and collapsed on the hard stone. A bolt of pain stabbed his knees.

"I would throw you off the mountain if you hadn't taken out one of Enrik's ilk," Lazaro said.

Tessa started to protest, but he pushed her back into the house. "Keep away from my sister," he ordered. "If you set foot near my house again, I won't be so forgiving."

The door slammed shut. Isiah scrambled to his feet. He felt people's eyes burning into him. He limped away from the house, aiming for an alley he could lose himself in.

Isiah reached the alley and ran into its cool shadows. The crowd closed up behind him, stealing the house from view. The hatred in Lazaro's eyes was burned into his mind.

"Isiah!" Tessa's voice rang out. Isiah twisted around to see her sprinting down the alley behind him. The turmoil in his gut grew stronger.

She skidded to a halt. "Where are you going?"

"What happened to Lazaro?" Isiah asked.

"I jumped out a window," she replied. "What are you going to do?"

"I'm going away," he said.

"What? Where will you stay?" Tessa asked. "You don't know anyone here."

"I'll find something," Isiah replied. *I can't let her know.* He willed himself to speak. "I don't need a Raider's help."

Tessa's expression dropped. "What do you mean?"

"I said I don't need you," Isiah replied. He winced at the pain in Tessa's eyes. "You were right. I'm from Paradon. I lied to you."

"Isiah . . ." Tessa started.

"I can't be friends with people who hate Ward." Isiah willed himself to spit out the words. He turned and hobbled away.

"Fine," Tessa called out after him. "For a minute you'd almost convinced me that you were different."

Isiah rounded a corner and left Tessa behind. He bowed his head.

I have to do it. She'd only get in my way. I'll find Ward, then we'll leave. He'll know what to do.

The noise of the crowd faded as Isiah slipped into a cramped alleyway between stacked houses. Tall buildings and weather-beaten awnings blocked the sky from view, and a beggar lay slumped against a rusted water pump.

Movement sounded in a doorway. Isiah turned, but it was too late.

A bag slipped over his head. His hands flew up to his face, but something caught his arms and tackled him to the ground. Isiah cried out as a fresh bolt of pain stabbed his side.

"Good timing, boy," Enrik's voice growled. His hot breath blasted in Isiah's ear. "You're making my job too easy." Enrik dragged Isiah to his feet. "Now get moving. We've got some talking to do."

No Good

TESSA CLIMBED THE STAIRCASE TO THE SECOND FLOOR. She passed the cramped storeroom Isiah had slept in and kept walking. A second set of narrow, creaky steps led to a doorway. She opened it and sunlight flooded through.

Cold mountain air washed over her. Tessa stepped onto the flat, walled roof of the house. Lazaro sat on the low wall, looking out over the plain.

"Are you alright?" she asked.

Lazaro shrugged. "I came up here to think."

Tessa walked to his side. In front of her, beyond the low sandstone wall, empty air fell to the feet of the mountain far below.

Tessa took a seat next to Lazaro. She dangled her legs over the edge. Without Vyrro, the sight made her giddy. "What were you thinking about?"

Lazaro scratched his short-cropped hair. The fire in his eyes had faded, leaving him deflated. "I can't believe he duped us. I should have been more cautious. I should have seen it."

"He's too young to be Marked," Tessa replied. "I didn't think he was from Paradon either."

Lazaro turned to her. "How long did you know about him?"

Tessa hesitated. She shifted her weight, then told Lazaro about the incident at the arena. "The dragon tried to attack him. That's when he told me."

Lazaro shook his head. "He's one of our enemies, Tess. How could you have stayed silent after that?"

"He told me he was different," she replied.

"You know that's a damn lie."

No, a voice in her head told her. She knew Isiah didn't mean those things he said to her. "It didn't feel like a lie."

"You can't take chances," Lazaro said. "The second your back is turned, that's when they strike. We can't trust anyone. Merchants, nomads, other Raiders, they'll all dance on our graves." He put a hand on her shoulder. "We have to look out for each other."

Silence descended. The wind whistled past them, ruffling the clothes on washing lines. A few eagles soared far above, approaching the roosts to land.

"Tess?" Lazaro said.

"Yeah?"

"Do you remember when our parents died?"

A familiar creeping dread welled inside her. She shoved it away. "I've never stopped remembering it."

"You weren't supposed to be there, you know. You weren't supposed to see them die. It was *my* turn to fly that day." His words hung in the air for a moment. "I shouldn't be alive."

191

Tessa sniffed. "That's not true."

"It's my job to look after you," Lazaro said. "After we lost our home, the Raiders didn't help us. I did whatever I needed to so I could keep you safe." He clenched his jaw. "And I'm not having the likes of *him* ruin it for us."

Tessa wrapped her arms around her older brother. "But we've got a home now. We're safe."

"Not if Enrik tells everyone what happened," Lazaro said. "Antony's right. If you'd told me who Isiah was sooner—"

"Then he wouldn't have saved us," she replied. "We'd still be buried inside the ruin."

"We would have found a way out. No good has come of him, Tess. I won't let you put yourself at risk any longer."

Tessa pulled away from him. "I can look after myself."

"You'll thank me," Lazaro said. "I should have listened to you when we first met him."

Hideout

ENRIK SHOVED A FIST INTO ISIAH'S BACK. "Keep moving, boy."

Isiah stumbled, fighting to regain his balance. He strained to see through the bag over his head. The grumble of machinery echoed around him.

Wooden boards creaked underfoot. Isiah flexed his wrists. They were bound tightly behind him, cutting off the blood flow and making his fingers numb. Enrik's hand on his shoulder guided him through the underbelly of the city.

"We're almost there," Enrik said. "Then we have some chatting to do."

Panic flared in Isiah's insides. His Mark itched beneath Enrik's palm. He prayed the man hadn't overheard Lazaro's rage.

They came to a stop and Enrik ripped the bag from Isiah's head. Isiah blinked, trying to adjust his eyes. Uneven platforms and walls covered the floor, spanning the thick wooden supports that supported the elevators. Pulleys squealed somewhere in the shadows. Further away, thin cracks of light peeked through from the outside.

"Where am I?" Isiah asked.

"Isn't it obvious?" Enrik said. He stood with a group of other Raiders. A few low tables and chests were scattered around a makeshift room. "You can call it our *hideout*."

Isiah scanned for an escape. He calmed his shaky breaths. If he reached the light, maybe there was an elevator he could jump on . . .

"Nobody knows we're here," Enrik said. "Not even the pulley-boys who operate the elevators. And thanks to your *argument*, Tessa won't even bother coming to look for you." He leaned in. "Tell me, what *were* you arguing about?"

Isiah held his tongue. Enrik straightened up. "It doesn't matter. What matters is Lazaro won't have the faintest idea you're here."

A snicker went around the other Raiders. The creak and groan of machinery muffled their voices.

Isiah forced himself to stand tall. "What do you want?" His voice came out more like a squeak.

"You have something I'm searching for," Enrik said. "Something very valuable. You got away from us when I captured you the first time, but I'm not the kind of man to make the same mistake twice."

Enrik paced in front of him. "We breached the ruin," he said. "And don't think I didn't see your eagle spying on us. I figured you were nothing more than a thorn in my side—until I realized you might have stolen something very important while meddling in the ruin." The man stopped in front of him. "An artefact."

Isiah tried to mask his expression.

"You know what I'm talking about," Enrik said. "I can see it in your face. Still, I'm not unreasonable. I'm a Raider, not a monster . . . but after you killed one of my friends, I figured the time for negotiations was over."

"We want to know where you hid it," the female Raider said.

Isiah swallowed. "I—I don't have it."

Enrik scowled. "Don't lie to me, boy."

"It's true," he insisted. "I saw the artefact on a mural—but when I found the door, it was missing. I don't know where it could have gone!"

"Artefacts like that don't just *go missing*," Enrik replied. "I was prepared to release you if you told us what we wanted to know, but you're testing my patience."

Enrik motioned to the Raiders. A knife appeared in the woman's hand. Isiah winced as she sliced through his binds. Two of the other Raiders grabbed his arms and led him further into the hideout.

"I heard what Lazaro said." Enrik walked in front of them, arms behind his back. "I have eyes all over the city. Even after I learned who you really are, I was prepared to look the other way."

Isiah's pulse quickened. The Raiders led him toward a pair of supports. Chains were embedded in the wood. He struggled against his captors. "What are you doing?"

"If you won't tell me what I want to know, then you need some encouragement," Enrik replied.

The Raiders dragged Isiah between the two supports and secured the chains around his wrists. Enrik's hand curled around the hilt of his sabre.

"I know you're Marked," he said. "That would be a death sentence at the hands of most Raiders." A cruel smile crept across his face. "I wonder how you fooled Lazaro for so long."

Enrik drew his sabre. Isiah yanked at the chains, but they held fast. With a flick of his wrist, Enrik sliced through the material covering Isiah's chest. Isiah gasped in pain as the tip left a long line across his skin.

"That should be nothing compared to what you've been through," Enrik said. He grabbed the loose material and exposed Isiah's Mark.

"I've dealt with Marked people before," Enrik said. "I noticed how little they like the sun. It seems to cause them a lot of distress. Something about the skin being so damaged, I presume."

The female Raider pulled on a rope. Pulleys squealed and wood creaked in protest. A sliver of light appeared next to Isiah. His heart leapt into his throat.

"And so I designed something to make people like you *talk*," Enrik continued. "The perfect interrogation device."

The sliver of light grew wider. Isiah looked up to see a trapdoor sliding open.

"The sun will be reaching its midpoint soon," Enrik remarked. "The midday sun is harsh, even for Raiders."

The gap of light grew wider. It washed over Isiah's bare skin. He squinted at the brightness. A wide glass circle sat above him, like Reuben's spyglass.

"The hatch is open," the female Raider said.

Enrik marched up to Isiah and stared him in the face. "Where is the artefact?"

Isiah squirmed under the sun's heat. His Mark began to burn, like ants crawling over his skin. "I don't know," he stammered.

Enrik's nostrils flared. He raised his hand. Footsteps sounded on the platform above their heads. A second magnifying glass rolled into position, concentrating the light on Isiah's Mark.

"I won't take denial for an answer," Enrik said.

Isiah's skin grew hotter, stabbing at him with needles. He bit his tongue to keep from crying out. A voice told him to give in, but he refused to betray Tessa.

"Higher," Enrik said.

A third magnifying glass slid into position. Isiah gritted his teeth. The cut from Enrik's sabre oozed lines of blood down his chest.

"Lazaro took it!" The words burst from Isiah's mouth. "He accused me of stealing it for myself and took it away."

"Now we're getting somewhere," Enrik replied. "Where did he put it?"

"I don't know!" Isiah lied. "He was going to sell it to merchants. He doesn't know what it does."

"That's not good enough, boy." Enrik put his hands on his hips. "I asked you where he put it."

"Take it from the merchants," Isiah pleaded. The intensity of the sun made his skin feel like it was boiling. Sweat made his hair stick to his forehead, but his burned skin remained dry.

"It looks like I'll have to try again later." Enrik turned and marched away. The Raiders filed after him.

"Wait!" Isiah cried.

Enrik kept walking. The door to the makeshift room slammed, leaving him alone.

* * *

Isiah grunted in pain. He twisted his body, trying to pull the chains free. Every second passing felt like an eternity.

The sun reached midday, glaring through the magnifying glasses with a searing intensity. Isiah's skin crawled, waves of pain rippling across his Mark. He blinked away tears and refocused his attention on trying to break free.

The chains bit into his skin, warm under the sunlight. Isiah blinked the sweat from his eyes. It rolled off his neck onto his shoulders, the salt making his burns agonizing.

A door creaked open. Isiah waited for Enrik to march through. A head appeared—one Isiah recognized.

"You're that Scavenger," Aron said. He scurried over. "You're with Tessa, aren't you?"

Isiah managed a nod. He didn't open his mouth because of the pain.

Aron wrung his hands. "Enrik shouldn't be doing this. He's breaking the Raider's Oath." Aron gulped. "The other Raiders will kill us."

Aron scampered over to one of the tables. He pulled open a drawer. "I saw where he kept the keys."

The seconds ticked past, painfully slow. Aron rifled through the draws. He came up with a small key. He hurried to Isiah's side and unlocked the chains.

Isiah collapsed to his knees and crawled out of the light. He gasped and wiped the sweat from his eyes.

"Thank you," he managed to say.

Aron glanced at the door. "You should get out of here," he said. "Enrik can't know I helped you."

Isiah dragged himself to his feet. His skin shone an angry red. He searched for some water to douse himself with.

"They'll be back soon," Aron said. "I heard them."

Isiah pulled on his damaged cloak. The material made his Mark sting. He hissed in pain and let it drop.

"I have to go." Aron slipped out of the door. "If I were you, I'd run."

Isiah staggered toward the door. He leaned against it and peered outside. Aron had disappeared into the shadows. Further away, machinery grumbled as elevators were lifted to the city. Isiah left the room and hastened toward the sound.

Shafts of sunlight peeked through the patchwork of wooden platforms above his head. Wood creaked as he hobbled over loose boards, careful to avoid the precarious gaps and holes that riddled the rickety structure. A breath of fresh air beckoned him from somewhere ahead.

Footsteps sounded. Isiah leapt behind a makeshift wooden wall. A narrow crack snaked up the board, letting him peer through.

Enrik marched toward him, alongside several Raiders. Isiah shied away as the man passed. The floor beneath him wobbled.

"Do you think he knows where the artefact is?" one of the Raiders asked.

"He has to," Enrik replied. "He and Tessa are the only ones who could have found it."

"What if he doesn't tell us?"

Enrik paused. "He will."

199

Isiah crept away from the wall. His heart pounded, distracting him from his searing burns.

His foot connected with a loose board.

The ground beneath him dropped. Isiah waved his arms and grabbed a nearby beam for balance. The far end of the board lurched upward, teetering like a see-saw, before Isiah regained himself and it slammed down. He winced as the sound echoed through the space.

"What was that?" one of the Raiders asked.

Isiah froze, caught like a wild animal. A Raider rounded the corner. Isiah prayed the shadows were thick enough to conceal him. His stomach dropped when the Raider's eyes widened.

"He got out!"

Isiah turned and ran. He heard Enrik swear. Moments later the sound of pounding boots accompanied it. Isiah willed his fatigued muscles to move. The shaky platforms bounced beneath him, creaking in protest.

Isiah scanned for a way out. A series of ladders and wooden staircases climbed to different levels. He ran toward one and climbed as quickly as his aching arms allowed. Each movement made his burned skin feel like it was on fire, but he bit back the pain.

"Get back here!" Enrik yelled. "You're only making this harder on yourself, boy!"

Isiah clambered to the top of the ladder and kept running. Out the corner of his eye, he saw Enrik's Raiders climbing to his level.

He lowered his head and sprinted in the direction of the light he'd seen earlier. Through the spiderweb of supports, he caught flashes of the plain far below. Ropes whipped past him as they pulled unseen elevators and cranes.

The city came into view as Isiah came to the edge of a cliff. He skidded to a halt to avoid falling off. Far below, elevators collected travellers and merchants. He searched for one he could jump onto.

Footsteps sounded behind him. Isiah twisted around to see Enrik reach the top of the ladder, clenching his sabre between his teeth as he climbed.

Isiah followed the edge of the platforms, keeping the empty drop to his right. He willed himself to run faster. A few loose boards jutted over the edge. He knew if he stepped on one that it would give way and he'd fall to his death.

A flash of colour in the sky caught his attention. A handful of eagles soared over the plain. A bubble of hope welled in his chest. If Tessa was there . . .

One of the eagles veered toward him. Isiah made out the Raider on its back. His heart sank when he recognized one of Enrik's men. Enrik emerged in the light behind him. When he saw the eagles, he thrust a finger at Isiah. "He's Marked!"

The hope died in Isiah's chest as the eagles closed in.

Isiah ducked as an eagle swooped overhead. It landed among the supports, gripping them with its talons and beating its wings for balance. A new surge of adrenaline flooded his veins as more eagles landed ahead of him, cutting him off.

"You've got nowhere to run!" Enrik called.

A wooden beam caught Isiah's attention. It made up part of the crisscrossing lattice that hugged the mountainside. Swallowing his fear, he jumped onto it.

The beam was wide enough for him to run on. It angled sharply downward, connecting with several others to support the mass of platforms and elevators.

Isiah ran along the beam. The wind raced through the supports, tugging at his sliced-up clothes. He waved his arms, fighting for balance. Just a few inches to his right was an empty drop.

A second eagle blasted overhead. Isiah covered his head instinctively. The giant bird tried to land on one of the supports ahead. Isiah made a sharp turn left and ran across the rickety platforms. The Raiders' boots pounded on the floor above him as they sprinted to find a ladder down.

A few workers yelled at him as he passed. Raiders tried to force their eagles to give chase, but the birds tugged at their reins and refused to fly into the structure. Isiah had lost track of Enrik. He expected the man to step out in front of him at any moment.

Ahead, the platforms met the mountainside. A sheer wall of stone blocked his path. Isiah's gaze fell upon a trapdoor, cut into the rock. As footsteps rang out somewhere behind him, he hastened toward it.

Isiah reached the trapdoor and yanked on the handle. Hinges squealed in protest.

"Get back here!" a Raider yelled.

A surge of adrenaline powered Isiah on. The trapdoor groaned as it swung open and he crawled inside a tunnel.

The trapdoor slammed shut behind him. The Raider swore.

"You can't go far, boy!" he jeered.

Isiah ignored the man and crawled as fast as his aching muscles allowed. His breath swirled in his eardrums. The tunnel was barely big enough for him to fit in. Its rough sides scraped his already sore skin. The Raider yanked open the trapdoor and reached for him, but it was too small for him to give chase.

Feeling his way ahead, Isiah crawled deeper into the tunnel. As he went, the sounds of the Raiders grew quieter, then stopped. Minutes ticked past. The faint rush of water reached his ears. A handful of pipes, their sides smooth and metallic, were embedded into the tunnel walls.

It's like some kind of maintenance shaft, he thought.

The tunnel climbed upward, toward the city itself. A few other tunnels branched off, each with its own collection of pipes.

The minutes ticked past. Isiah crawled until his knees ached and his palms were bloodied. After what felt like forever, a light appeared ahead. He prayed for a storm drain to crawl out of.

Something soft met his hands, covering the tunnel floor in a thin layer. Isiah scooped up a handful and let it pour out.

Sand. He frowned. He scurried forward, to where a metal grate let a sliver of light into the tunnel. He pressed his face against it and peered out.

A wrought-iron wall greeted him, with rows of seats beyond. Isiah's blood ran cold as it dawned on him where he was.

He was underneath the arena.

Too Late

Isiah shoved the grate with his shoulder, trying to dislodge it. The impact sent a stab of pain across his burned skin. The grate didn't budge.

Calm down. He forced himself to slow his breathing. He pressed his face against the grate again, trying to get his bearings. He was beneath the centre of the arena. Ahead of him, the tunnel led under the dragon's cage. Thin slivers of light illuminated patches of the tunnel from other grates.

Maybe one of them is loose, he thought. Swallowing his fear, he crawled further along. A deathly silence hung over the arena. Isiah shuffled across the sand-covered floor, bracing himself as it carried him closer and closer to the dragon's cage.

He reached another grate. He shoved this one, with the same result. Long bolts fastened it to the rock. A voice told him to call out for help—but he knew if someone saw his Mark, he'd never get out alive.

Isiah kept crawling. A cold sweat broke out on his forehead. His skin crawled as his Mark began to itch. He braced himself.

The dragon snarled as it noticed him. A metallic boom echoed across the arena, followed by an ear-splitting roar that made him slam his hands against his ears. Metal scraped and groaned as the dragon snapped at the bars.

Isiah tried a third grate. Nothing. A lump formed in his throat.

I can't turn back. The Raiders might still be waiting. Isiah forced himself to move. The ground trembled as the dragon thundered overhead. He gritted his teeth as his Mark burned, stinging like a nest of wasps. It called out his presence, stirring the dragon into a frenzy . . .

A force slammed above his head. Isiah pressed himself against the floor as another grate shook. Hot breath flooded the tunnel. The dragon clawed at the metal, hissing and snarling at him. Spittle showered his exposed back and shoulders. Ahead, the tunnel stopped at a dead end.

The dragon's claws wrapped around the grate, talons gleaming with a cruel light. It cracked open its jaws to expose its cavernous throat. The metal squealed in protest, bars bending and bolts popping free.

Isiah's hand flew to the knife in his waistband. He let out a gurgled battle cry and lashed out. It found a gap in the dragon's scales and sank into its flesh.

The dragon screeched and wheeled away. Dark blood dripped down the blade. With his heart pounding against his ribcage, Isiah pulled his knees to his chest and kicked the grate.

The damaged bolts gave way and it popped free. Isiah carefully crawled into the dragon's cage.

What are you doing? a voice in his head screamed. The dragon stood curled in the far corner, neck poised to strike and its eyes fixed on him. It dominated the dark, cramped space. A few bones lay strewn on the floor from feeding.

Isiah clutched the knife to his chest and backed away from the beast. He scanned for an escape route. A tall, sturdy gate separated the cage from the rest of the arena. A lever jutted from the wall nearby. With trembling hands, he reached for it. The pain under his skin brought tears to his eyes. He knew the dragon could attack at any moment.

"Enrik said the tunnel leads here," a voice said. Isiah tore his eyes away from the dragon. A group of Raiders marched into the cavern.

"There are plenty of places the tunnel can come out. Why is this one so special?"

"You heard the man. We've got to cover every exit."

The dragon lowered its head and snarled. Isiah thrust his knife in the dragon's direction. It hissed and shied away. The faint light from outside reflected off his knife's amber-coloured hilt. Isiah's eyes widened. He remembered the crystals the Raiders had used to drive the dragon back into its cage.

"You're afraid . . ." he stammered.

The dragon puffed out its chest. Twin plumes of hot breath erupted from its nostrils. It kept its eyes trained on the knife hilt.

"The tunnel cuts underneath the arena," one of the Raiders said. They passed the rows of seating and entered the arena itself through a small door. "He might still be in there."

"We could smoke him out," one suggested.

"Or wait here and stab him when he shows his face."

Isiah racked his brains. He knew the Raiders would find him. The shadows wouldn't hide him for long. He cast another wary look at the dragon. Ward's advice echoed in his head.

"D—don't kill me, okay?" Isiah said. "Stay right there."

Taking a deep breath, he gripped the lever with both hands and pulled it with the last of his strength.

The gate creaked open. The Raiders froze. Isiah threw himself aside as the dragon bellowed and exploded past him into the arena.

The Raiders screamed. Isiah staggered out of the dragon's cage and made a beeline for the exit. The dragon's wingbeats thundered in his ears. Sand whipped into his eyes as the beast descended on the Raiders.

Isiah reached the door the Raiders had entered through and threw it open. Their panicked cries rang out behind him. Someone blew a horn to raise the alarm. Isiah ducked behind a row of seats as Raiders from the prison sprinted into the arena. One of Enrik's men screamed as the dragon flung him through the air.

Keeping to the cover of the seating, Isiah made his way to the tunnel that led out of the cavern. He pulled his clothes over his burned shoulders as best he could, then sprinted out into open air.

Someone collided with him.

Isiah hit the ground. Panic flared inside him. He pulled out his knife, waiting for a Raider to grab him.

"Isiah!" Tessa said. She stood over him.

Isiah blinked, adjusting his eyes to the daylight. "What are you–" Isiah started.

Tessa helped him to his feet. "I heard the commotion," she replied. She saw the state of his clothes and covered her mouth. "What happened to you?"

Isiah glanced in the direction of the arena. The dragon roared as the Raiders tried to get it under control. "We need to get out of here."

Tessa grabbed his hand. "I know a place you can hide." She frowned at him. "And don't tell me you don't need my help again."

* * *

Isiah's lungs heaved as he climbed to the eagle roosts. Tessa ran ahead, taking him up a narrow stone staircase cut into the mountainside.

"The handlers don't know about this place," she said. "It's an old part of the city."

Isiah gripped his cloak, holding it together. Blood soaked his clothes from cuts and scratches he'd received in the tunnel. Sand rubbed against his burned skin, making each move agony. He reached the final step and made it to the roosts.

"In here," Tessa said. A squat, sandstone building hugged the mountainside, below the shadow of the landing pads. Isiah kept a wary eye out for eagles.

"It's an old storehouse," she explained. She produced a key and unlocked it.

"We're too close to Enrik," Isiah said.

"He won't find you," she replied. "Nobody ever comes here—and it's the only place I know to hide you."

They piled inside. A hammock hung diagonally across the room. Various boxes and barrels filled the space. The smell of mouldy grain hung thick in the air.

Tessa unlocked a pair of wooden shutters and let a small square of light into the space. "It's not much, but you'll be safe here."

Isiah carefully lowered himself into the hammock, wincing at the pain of his burned skin. The ropes creaked, but it held. He let out a sigh as the adrenaline from his escape wore off. "Thank you for helping me."

Tessa wiped her hand over a crate. Her fingers came away thick with dust. "Maybe you do need me, after all."

Isiah swallowed. "I'm sorry I said that stuff."

Outside, the distant roars of the dragon fell silent. Wingbeats sounded as small birds made nests on the storehouse roof above. The sunlight made Tessa's hair shine and reflected off the hilt of her sabre. Isiah looked at his feet. "I guess I lost my sword, too."

"What happened back there?" Tessa asked. "You look half-dead."

"Enrik," Isiah replied. He told her what had happened after he was kidnapped. He peeled away his torn clothes. "He was trying to burn me alive."

Tessa clenched her fists. "And he warned *us* about breaking the Raider's Oath?" She swore. "When the other Raiders hear about this–"

"You can't tell anyone," Isiah said. "I'm Marked, remember?"

Tessa's shoulders dropped. "You're right."

"But I didn't tell him what he wanted," he replied. "He's looking for the artefact, but I didn't say where it is."

Tessa kicked the ground. "The artefact? Why does he care so much about a stupid rock? Something is going on here. He's up to no good."

"He wants the oasis," Isiah blurted out.

Tessa frowned. "That old story? Lazaro always told me it was just a myth."

"I saw it on the bathhouse wall, before the gorgons attacked us," he explained. "I think he needs the artefact to reach it." He watched Tessa mull it over.

"But why does he want to find the oasis so badly?" she asked.

"I don't know," he admitted. "He didn't tell me."

Tessa's expression softened. She gestured to his chest. "How bad is it?"

Isiah stood and she studied his burns. The skin shone an angry red, and dried blood streaked his chest from where Enrik had cut him.

Tessa tentatively placed her palm on his shoulder. "Does it hurt?"

Isiah grimaced.

She withdrew her hand. "I have more of that ointment," she said. "And I can get you new clothes, too."

"What should I do?" Isiah asked.

"Stay here," she replied. She started toward the door. "Don't let anybody see you. I'll be back soon. I promise."

She slipped out of the door and disappeared into the city beyond. Isiah slumped into the hammock. The rough material made his skin itch, but he didn't care. Despite the sunlight streaming through the window and the ache in his body, fatigue finally caught up to him and he remembered no more.

Enrik

ENRIK MARCHED INTO THE EAGLE ROOSTS. A group of his Raiders walked alongside him. Handlers scurried out of their way as they passed. One of the Raiders clutched a bandaged torso that was stained dark with blood. Enrik's gaze swept over Lazaro's eagle and he narrowed his eyes.

"That dragon should have killed the boy," Iris said. "He's Marked. Why didn't it attack him?"

"I don't know," Enrik replied, "but perhaps it has done us a favour."

"Alcabaza is huge. There are so many holes for him to crawl into. How will we ever hope to find him now?"

"Trust me," Enrik said. "I have a plan." He cursed himself for leaving the boy alone. His Raiders had seen Isiah fleeing the arena with Tessa—but where they had gone, he had no idea.

"How did he manage to escape?" Iris asked.

"Maybe he snagged a key or something," he replied. "Or the chains weren't tight enough. Either way, it's of no use to us now."

A handful of other Raiders groups stood talking while handlers harnessed their eagles. They paused as Enrik approached. A couple of them gave him nods of recognition.

"It's a fine day for flying, boys," Enrik said. "Off to find more ruins?"

"You know it, Enrik," one of them replied. "Or to capture more Royal Guards. The last pair was such a let-down."

"Indeed," Enrik said. "It's a shame some of my men won't have the luxury of flying anymore—or doing anything else, for that matter."

"The dragon got them, didn't it?" a Raider asked.

"And not by accident, neither," Enrik replied.

The Raider groups stopped talking. They all turned to him. One frowned. "What do you mean?"

"I mean," Enrik said, lowering his voice, "it was done on purpose."

"So a nomad let it out? Or a merchant? Why would they do that?"

Enrik remained silent. Muttering went around the group as the truth dawned on them.

"A Raider?" one asked. "That's impossible. It would mean breaking the Oath."

Enrik gave him a solemn nod. "And it's not the first time."

The Raiders burst into discussion. Some of the eagles ruffled their feathers, sensing the unease in the air. Handlers rushed to calm them. A flicker of a smile crossed Enrik's lips.

"Who did it?" one asked. "An Oath-breaker can't be allowed to walk among us."

"I warned him," Enrik said. The other Raiders fell silent as he spoke. "I thought that perhaps it was an honest mistake when he fought my men over a ruin. His Scavenger was inexperienced. Perhaps he killed one of my friends in the scuffle by accident."

Enrik paced in front of the gangs. More Raiders, attracted by the commotion, crowded around.

"But then he freed the dragon," Enrik continued, "and left two more of my people dead. These Raiders are Oath-breakers, through and through. I wanted to keep it quiet. After all, you know what would happen if word got out."

A murmur of agreement went around the Raiders. A few cast suspicious looks at one another.

"It's none of you here," Enrik said. "You're all far too proud and upstanding to resort to Oath-breaking. No, the Raider I'm talking about is one you've all had a scuffle with at one time or another." Enrik stopped. "I'm talking about Lazaro."

Enrik smiled as the crowd went into an uproar. He raised his hands to quiet them. "He was so sick of losing out on ruins that he must have decided to take drastic measures," Enrik said. "He's killing my gang, one Raider at a time."

"Why would he do that?" one of the Raiders asked. "He knows what happens to Oath-breakers."

"The same reason he's living with the dregs down in the city while we're up here," Enrik replied. "He can't control himself. He's always been a wild card." Enrik paused, his gaze flitting over the men and women in front of him. "And for his latest Scavenger, he found someone who was Marked."

Iris rubbed her hands together as the crowd whipped itself into a frenzy.

"That's right," Enrik continued. "Lazaro managed to let someone from Paradon slip into our ranks and infiltrate our city. Before you know it, we'll have Royal Guards banging on our door!"

The yelling intensified. A few Raiders grabbed their sabres. Enrik waited until the fury had died down.

"But we must be smart about this," he said. "If they catch wind, that Scavenger of theirs could flee back to Paradon and spill our secrets. If we want Lazaro to face justice, we can't act hastily."

"We need to stop him before he strikes again!" a Raider called.

"And we will," Enrik said. "Wait for my call, my friends. When I'm through with them, Lazaro and his Scavenger will never spill another drop of Raider blood again."

The Roosts

Isiah jolted awake. Shadows cloaked the storehouse. He paused, listening in the darkness for what had awoken him.

Knocking.

Isiah swung one leg out of the hammock, then peeled himself away from the material. He winced as the movement disturbed his burns. He staggered to the front door and fumbled for the handle.

The door swung open and Tessa greeted him. She carried a bag slung over her shoulder. Beyond her, moonlight cloaked the Badlands.

"Did I wake you?" she asked.

Isiah shook his head, clearing the grogginess. "What time is it?"

"Late." Tessa pushed past him and dumped the bag on a nearby crate. "I bought you some food," she said.

Isiah frowned. "You don't have to do this."

"Don't give me that again," she said. "Raiders are *supposed* to look out for one another." She paused. "Lazaro doesn't believe you're different, but I do."

Isiah avoided her gaze. Tessa pulled out a bundle of clothes, alongside some of the healing ointment he'd seen in the house.

"Darla won't notice it missing," she said.

Isiah inspected the cloak. Its silky material was too light to snag on his Mark and make it itch.

"Meet me outside," Tessa said. "I've got something to show you."

Isiah hurriedly changed into the new clothes. He bundled up his torn, bloodied old ones and hid them at the back of the storehouse. He used the ointment to take the worst of the pain away, before slipping out of the door and finding Tessa.

"This way," she said. She led him away from the storehouse, up a winding staircase to the roosts.

"Are you sure we won't be spotted," Isiah asked.

"It's deserted," she replied. "I already checked."

They reached the roosts. A few handlers slept beneath the awnings, their soft snoring the only sound aside from the occasional rustle of feathers and the chirp of insects. Tessa walked to one of the curved, ribcage-like beams that supported the eagle pens and began to climb.

Isiah went after her. The moonlight cast a strong, silvery light across the mountainside, letting him easily see where he was going. He gripped the beam and shimmied his way up. He reached Tessa's side and carefully perched on the edge. Below them, one of the giant eagles slept like a statue.

"Look at the sky," she said.

Isiah craned his neck. To one side, the full moon sat among a mass of papery clouds. Overhead, the smouldering sun crowned the heavens alone.

"Sometimes the dark sun crosses the sky on its own," Tessa said. "The Raiders think it means good luck."

Isiah watched the glowing orb. It shone with the same muted light as the artefact. "Good luck for who?"

Tessa shrugged. "It's just something Lazaro used to say."

Isiah shifted his weight at the mention of the man. "Does he know you're here?"

"He doesn't need to," she replied.

Silence descended. Somewhere further in the roosts, an eagle let out a quiet call. Pinprick lights shone in the city through its many windows.

Isiah hesitated. "Thanks for helping me again. You don't need to keep putting yourself in danger."

"I can handle myself," Tessa said. "Besides," she added, quieter, "I guess we're even now, after you helped me escape the ruin."

Isiah furrowed his brow. "You would have done the same for me."

Tessa shuddered. "No." She wrapped her arms around herself. "I don't think I could have."

Part of Isiah urged himself to question her, but he let the matter drop.

"You know," Tessa said after a moment, "that fight in Enrik's camp—I've never seen anything like that before."

Isiah shrugged. "The Raider's Oath, right? You're not allowed to."

"I mean, I've never seen anyone die like that." She paused. "I've never killed anyone, either."

Isiah wrung his hands. The sensation of driving his sabre through the Raider's ribcage made his stomach tie knots.

Tessa dangled her feet off the edge. "And I'm worried what will happen if I have to."

Isiah faltered. For a moment, Tessa's hard expression seemed to slip.

"I was thinking about the oasis," she said. "But I can't think of any reason Enrik wants it so badly. It's supposed to be able to heal people, isn't it?" She paused. Isiah watched as she pieced things together. "That's why you tried to take the artefact."

"That was my plan," Isiah said sheepishly.

Tessa nodded to herself. "I know where Lazaro keeps his key," she said. "If you had the artefact, you could get inside the oasis. That'll heal your Mark, won't it?"

"It's the only thing that can."

Tessa let out a low whistle. "Why didn't you tell me this sooner?"

Isiah shifted his weight. *If I tell her I want to go back to Paradon, she'll hate me. There's no way she'll want to help me.* "I didn't want Lazaro to find out," he lied. "It would make him too suspicious."

"We'll get to the oasis before Enrik does," Tessa said. "I can steal the artefact from Lazaro's safe. It'll be easy."

Guilt tugged at Isiah's insides. After everything Tessa had done for him, how could he desert her? But there was no place for him with the Raiders.

"You'd really do that?" he asked.

Tessa climbed down to the ground. "Wait in the storehouse," she said. "I'll come back for you. We can use Vyrro to fly there."

His nausea increased. "You don't need to. I could find a way myself . . ."

She waved him away. "Don't worry. I've got this, trust me."

Before Isiah could argue, she turned and raced away, hair flying behind her as she went. Isiah cursed himself for not telling her sooner. How could he keep lying to her like this?

Focus, the voice in his head told him. *First the oasis, then Ward. After that, it's only a few days' walk to the border. Then you can leave it all behind.*

Isiah wrung his hands. Could he really abandon Tessa without saying goodbye?

She's still a Raider, the voice said. *She won't understand.*

Part of him wanted to tell Tessa about Paradon, to urge her to come with him. He pushed it away. *She'd never leave Lazaro behind.*

Isiah bowed his head. As soon as he was cured, he'd have no choice but to give Tessa the slip.

'Better Plan'

TESSA SLIPPED A KEY INTO THE LOCK AND snuck into the house. She paused in the dark entryway, listening for any sounds of life. The dining room to her right lay dark and still. Lazaro and the others had already gone to bed.

Tessa darted to the stairs, watching for the loose, creaky boards. The faint sound of snoring wafted down from somewhere above. Taking a deep breath, she climbed the stairs and made her way down the hall to Lazaro's room. She paused at his closed door.

Why are you doing this? she asked herself. She'd never stolen anything from Lazaro before.

Tessa cleared her head, then pressed her ear against the door. Lazaro's familiar snoring greeted her. She nodded to herself, then slipped inside.

She squinted in the shadows. Lazaro slept on a low bed beneath a closed window, overlooking the plain beyond the city. The shutters were closed, letting only a few slivers of moonlight peek through the cracks in the old wood. Next to it, Lazaro's cloak hung from a hook on the wall.

Tessa tiptoed over and felt about in its pockets. A pang of guilt ate at her insides, but she quelled it. *Lazaro's wrong this time. Isiah needs my help.*

She searched the pockets and came up empty. She cursed under her breath. *He must be extra cautious right now.*

Lazaro shifted in his sleep. Remembering her years spent pick-pocketing, Tessa crept to his side and searched for his belt. She nimbly felt Lazaro's waist for the keys. After a moment her hands met something cold and metallic.

A ring of keys was hooked around his belt, half-squished under Lazaro's sleeping body. Tessa carefully tried to work one free. She slipped the key to the safe off the ring and pocketed it.

Tessa turned to leave. She ignored the nagging guilt. *I'm sorry, Lazaro.*

She took a few steps, then her foot caught on his sabre.

She made a grab for it, but the sword hit the ground with a metallic crash. Tessa froze. Lazaro's snoring fell silent.

"Tess?"

Tessa swallowed. "Hey, Lazaro."

Lazaro sat up. "What are you doing here so late?" he asked groggily.

"Uh—" Tessa's eyes darted to the exit. "Another nightmare, that's all it was. I'm okay now." It pained her to lie to him.

Lazaro wiped the sleep from his eyes. "Are you sure you're alright?"

"I'm fine," she replied quickly. "I'm too old for this."

Lazaro reached out and touched her arm. "You're never too old for my help." He squeezed her hand.

Tessa forced herself to smile. "You're right. I'm just sorry for waking you."

Lazaro's hand went to his belt. "I was bound to wake up anyway. Sleeping on these keys is like being stabbed all night." He frowned.

Tessa tried to smooth out her expression. "What's wrong?"

Lazaro felt the keys. "I swear there's one missing." He counted them. "Check the windows. There might be a thief afoot." After a second, he paused. Tessa's heart dropped as he slowly looked at her. "Have you been outside?"

"I was sleeping," Tessa replied.

"Then why are you dressed like that? You're still wearing your sabre." Lazaro stood. "Show me your pockets."

Tessa started to protest, but he caught her arm. "You snuck out, didn't you?" Tessa squirmed beneath his grip as Lazaro found the key in her pocket. "You stole the key to the safe. Why would you do that?"

Tessa tried to pull away, but his fingers were locked around her wrist.

"Isiah . . ." Lazaro said slowly. "He tried to steal that artefact." His eyes narrowed. "You know where he is."

"I haven't seen him," Tessa replied. She winced at how unconvincing she sounded.

"You're still talking to him," Lazaro insisted. "How can you do that after everything we've been through?"

Movement sounded in other parts of the house. Darla's voice called out, "Is everything alright?"

"Why are you stealing for him, Tess?" Lazaro said. "That loot is *ours*. We need it for a better life."

"It was only one little thing," Tessa replied. "We didn't think you'd notice it missing."

"You're conspiring against me as well?" Lazaro shook his head. "What have I ever done to make you go behind my back like this? You're putting an enemy over your own flesh and blood."

Tessa blinked back tears. "That's not true."

The smouldering sun high above cast a reddish light into the room, making shadows flicker across Lazaro's face. The sound of the other Raiders grew louder. It seemed to be coming from outside.

Lazaro's expression faltered. "Wait—"

Tessa realized too late where the sounds were coming from. Her heart leapt as something smashed the shutters on the floor below. A chorus of yelling erupted from the street.

"Arrest the Oath-breakers!" Enrik's voice called.

Lazaro swore. He pushed past her and grabbed his sabre.

"What's going on?" Tessa asked. Deep down she already knew.

Footsteps thundered on the stairs as Darla and the other Raiders grabbed their gear. Tessa stumbled into the hallway as a sand vortex spilled into the hallway. It materialized into one of Enrik's Raiders.

"Get to the roof!" Lazaro ordered.

The Raider blocked their way. Lazaro darted forward and lashed out with his sabre. The sound of clashing metal rang out. Boots pounded below as more Raiders flooded into the dining room.

Lazaro aimed a thrust at the Raider in their path. The man parried it and tried to attack, but the walls restricted his movement. Lazaro seized his chance and threw himself at the man. They collided and hit the ground.

"Go!" he yelled.

Tessa obeyed. She leaped over the two struggling men and bolted for the narrow staircase that led to the roof. Wood splintered as more shutters broke. Enrik's Raiders poured into the rooms like swirling tornadoes. Tessa clambered to the roof and burst into the open air.

Torches illuminated the street. A crowd of Raiders surrounded the house, blocking their escape. They pushed and shoved their way through the broken front door, spitting curses and brandishing their sabres.

Tessa ducked before anyone could see her. She ran to the far side of the roof and leaned over. Empty air greeted her. She searched for some way to climb down and escape before any of the others noticed her.

A rush of air sounded behind her. Tessa whirled around and drew her sabre. Enrik materialized on the roof. A cruel smile crossed his lips. "Evening, Tessa. Your brother has some explaining to do."

Tessa thrust her sword in the man's direction. She forced herself to stand tall, but the tip of her sabre wobbled. "You broke the Raider's Oath," she spat.

Enrik grinned. "But they don't know that, do they?" He gestured to the crowd. "Who are they going to believe? My word, or Lazaro's?"

Tessa lashed out at him. Enrik sidestepped and parried the blow. "Don't make this hard on yourself. Isiah saw what happens when you don't *cooperate*."

Tessa glared at him. "You'll never find him. Isiah is long gone."

"He'd never escape Alcabaza without one of my people spotting him," Enrik replied. "No, he's still here."

The shouting below grew louder. Raiders cheered as a bloodied Antony and Darla were shoved out of the house.

"What are you going to do to them?" Tessa asked.

"They broke the Oath," Enrik replied. "You know what happens." He darted forward, forcing her into a corner of the roof. "But I have a better plan for *you*."

Tessa swung her sabre at him. Enrik blocked and the edges bit together. Enrik drove her sword up and caught her arm with his free hand. Tessa cried out as he twisted her arm and pried the sabre from her grip.

"Isiah might have got away from me," he said. His hot breath swirled in Tessa's ear. She struggled against him, but he forced her arms behind her back. "But I don't need to find him, provided I can make him come to *us*."

Several other Raiders appeared on the roof. A woman handed Enrik a coil of rope. "The eagles are waiting."

Enrik gave her a nod. He bound Tessa's wrists behind her back. She gritted her teeth and pulled against him, but she was no match for the large man. "Good. We fly out to the lakebed tonight."

"And Lazaro?"

"Leave his fate to the others," he replied. "This is far more important than his miserable life will ever be."

Oath-Breaker

She should be back by now. He glanced out the window. The sun peered above the horizon, painting the sky a soft pink. After Tessa had run off, he'd made his way back to the storehouse to wait for her to return. Hours later, she was still gone.

Isiah wrung his hands for the millionth time. *She's coming*, he told himself. *She has to be.*

Outside, the muffled sounds of the city wafted through the walls. Raiders departed on their eagles, launching from the landing pads and soaring over the plain. Voices reached his ears from a bazaar on the terrace below. Isiah unlocked the front door.

Pulling his cloak tight around him, he exited the storehouse and followed the staircase to the city. He kept his head down in case any of Enrik's Raiders were around. He reached the safety of the street and melted into the crowd.

Isiah retraced his steps, past the crevice in the mountainside that led to the arena and toward the lowest level of the city. With the rim of his hood obscuring his face, he weaved through the crush of bodies and animals and made a beeline for Lazaro's house.

Maybe she's just distracted, Isiah told himself. *She might not have had a chance to slip away.*

He rounded the corner and his eyes came to rest on their house. His stomach dropped.

The door to Lazaro's house was kicked open, hanging from a single hinge. Shattered wood littered the street from broken shutters. Before he knew it, Isiah found himself running.

He reached the door and stumbled into the hall. Furniture lay smashed and broken. Chairs were strewn about in the dining room. A few patches of blood stained the floor, making his heart pound faster. He ran to the stairs and sprinted to the second floor as fast as his legs allowed.

Isiah checked Tessa's room, then Lazaro's. The house stood deserted. With his head spinning, he ran back to the dining room and checked the safe. He peeled back the carpet and breathed a sigh of relief to find the safe in-tact. Nobody had found it. Straightening up, he forced himself to calm down.

A piece of paper caught his attention. It rested on the table, pinned beneath a sabre—the same one Enrik had taken from him. With trembling hands, Isiah picked it up.

"Hello, Isiah," the note read. "Thought you could slip away from me? I know you're still slinking around. I want that artefact. Bring it to the lakebed and Tessa lives."

Isiah let the note flutter to the floor. He racked his brains for some kind of plan. Sickening dread gnawed at his insides.

229

I need to find Lazaro, he thought. *He'll want to save Tessa too.*

Isiah grabbed his sabre and bolted from the house in the direction of the eagle roosts. Someone there would have to know what had happened.

He was out of breath by the time he reached the roosts. He fell in with a group of handlers and followed them. Lazaro's eagle stood in its pen, alongside Darla and Antony's. All hope that they had escaped evaporated. Isiah found one of the handlers on her own.

"Who looks after these eagles?" he asked her.

"Luca," she replied. "That one's Lazaro's. He's really picky about caring for them."

"Do you know him?" he asked.

She shrugged. "We talk sometimes. Why?"

Isiah glanced around. He half-expected to see one of Enrik's Raiders. "Last night—something happened to them."

The handler nodded. "I overheard the Raiders talking. Enrik said Lazaro broke the Oath."

Isiah fought the welling hopelessness inside him. "Where are they now?"

"Probably due for execution," she replied. "That's what happens to Oath-breakers."

Isiah thanked the girl, then jogged out of the roosts before any Raiders noticed him. His mind flashed back to when Tessa had taken him to the prisons to see Ward. *That must be where they're keeping them.*

He arrived at the prisons and knocked on the door. Aron's head appeared at the window. When he saw Isiah, he swore and ducked.

"I need your help," Isiah said.

"Why are you still here?" Aron hissed. "Enrik went mad after you escaped."

"He arrested Lazaro."

"I know," Aron replied. "They're in the cells here. They're going to be fed to the dragon."

Isiah gulped. "We need to break them out."

"If Enrik sees us together, I'm dead," Aron said. "You need to go."

"Just let me in," Isiah replied. "I have to break them out."

"And how are you going to do that?"

"I don't know," he admitted. "But I have to do something."

Nothing happened for a moment, before the door gave a click and swung open.

"I'm only doing this because you're friends with Tessa," Aron said. "The Raiders are setting up an execution for that Royal Guard today. Lazaro and the others will be next."

Isiah swore under his breath. "Where are the keys?"

Aron gestured to the wall behind him. "They're keeping Lazaro on the third row. Most of the guards are distracted with the execution." He pushed past Isiah and exited the room.

"Where are you going?" Isiah asked.

"I've got to meet with Enrik's Raiders. If there's a prison break while I'm on duty, *I'm* the one they'll feed to the dragon." Aron paused at the door. "Don't come after Enrik. If I were you, I'd get your friends and run."

Before Isiah could tell Aron about Tessa, the boy was gone. Isiah collected himself and grabbed the keys for row three. He hurried along the carved tunnel, pausing every few steps to listen for guards. He passed one of the narrow windows and a flash of colour caught his attention.

A few Raiders stood inside a ring in the arena, banners fluttering around them. One held a two-handed axe. Isiah swallowed. *The execution.*

He kept going. *I'll save them all,* he thought. He couldn't let Ward die, not even for Tessa.

Boots crunched ahead. Isiah froze. He searched for somewhere to hide. Spotting an open cell door, he hurried toward it and slipped inside right as a Raider rounded the corner.

Isiah crouched in the shadows. The boots drew steadily closer. Isiah held his breath as the Raider walked into view. He felt the man's gaze sweep over the cells.

The Raider paused for a moment to look out the window into the arena, then kept going. Isiah waited a minute to make sure he had passed, then exited the cell and hastened toward the third row. He reached the line of cells and began inspecting them.

"Lazaro," he whispered.

Movement sounded up ahead. Lazaro pressed himself against a cell door. A purple bruise covered his left eye, and dried blood stained his arms from scratches. When he saw Isiah, he narrowed his eyes.

"I've come to break you out," Isiah said.

"You'd better," Lazaro hissed. "This is your fault. If you hadn't broken the Oath—"

Helen coughed and glared at Lazaro. She turned to Isiah. "Get us out of here, boy."

More footsteps sounded in the hall. Isiah fumbled with the key, then slipped it into the lock. Hinges squealed as Lazaro and Antony piled out. Lazaro snatched the key from Isiah and freed Darla, Helen, and Luca. Isiah winced at the noise.

The footsteps grew louder. "Who's there?" a voice called. "I told you, we're supposed to execute the Royal Guard first."

Lazaro swore. "Give me your sabre."

Isiah drew it and handed it to him. Lazaro shoved past Isiah and darted to the tunnel entrance. He paused, crouching in the shadows. The Raider guard appeared around the corner. His eyes flashed open in shock, before Lazaro drove the sabre into him. The man collapsed with a gurgled cry.

Lazaro yanked the blade free and handed it back. Isiah suppressed a gag. Lazaro drew the fallen Raider's sword, then beckoned them. "Move."

The others burst into motion. Isiah scrambled to keep up with them. They sprinted down the tunnel and piled into the entrance of the building. The pounding of their boots echoed, painfully loud.

"Hey!" a voice yelled. Isiah spun around to see a pair of Raiders running after them. They drew their sabres. "You're dead, Oath-breakers!"

Lazaro swore. He turned to Isiah. "Where are our sabres?"

"I don't know," Isiah said quickly. "I didn't see any."

"Then find them."

Lazaro turned to block the tunnel. The approaching Raiders slowed, sabres at the ready. Isiah ran to the entrance and began rifling through the chests and desks. Darla and Antony did the same. The clash of steel rang out further down the tunnel. Isiah's hands shook as he fumbled with the latch of a chest.

"You'd better hurry up," Helen called.

One of the Raiders aimed a thrust at Lazaro. He batted it aside, backing out of the tunnel.

"Give it up, Lazaro," one of them said. "We promise to give you a quick execution."

Isiah undid a latch and threw open a chest. His eyes came to rest on their sabres. "I found them!"

Darla and the others grabbed their blades and whirled on the two Raider guards. The Raiders' eyes widened. They backed away.

"Let's go," Darla said, "before anyone else notices us."

"You won't make it out of the city," one of them spat. "Enrik has eyes everywhere."

Lazaro grabbed the metal door and slammed it, sealing the tunnel. "Then good luck raising the alarm."

"Hey!" One of the Raiders grabbed the bars, but Lazaro kicked the door to the prison open and they piled into the street beyond. The enraged yells of the guards echoed after them. A few people in the crowd nearby lifted their heads. Lazaro sprinted into an alleyway in the direction of their house. Isiah raced after them.

"Where are we going?" Darla asked.

"Tessa is still out here," Lazaro replied. He vaulted over a sleeping beggar and ducked through an archway. "She might have returned to the house."

"Wait—" Isiah said between panting breaths.

Lazaro slowed. "Why are you still here? We don't need your help anymore."

"I know where Tessa is," Isiah replied.

Lazaro's nose crinkled. "I warned you about seeing her."

"Enrik captured her," he said. He quickly told the Raiders about his kidnapping and Enrik's interest in the artefact.

"He kidnapped my sister over a stupid rock?" Lazaro spat. He took off in the direction of the house. When they reached it, Lazaro marched into the ransacked dining room and knelt by a loose board.

"What are you doing?" Isiah asked.

Lazaro pried the board free and produced a key. "I always keep spares." He unlocked the safe and pulled out the artefact. "How many other secrets are you keeping from us, boy?"

"What are you going to do with it?" Isiah asked.

"Tessa's life is more important than this," Lazaro replied. "He can have it for all I care."

"I thought you hated Enrik!" Isiah exclaimed. "Look at what he's done!"

Lazaro whirled on him. "*You* broke the Oath, Scavenger. This is *your* fault. Once I have Tessa, we're getting out of here and I'm taking her as far away from you as possible." He glanced at Luca. "Get the eagles harnessed."

Luca saluted and ran off.

"I'm the one Enrik wants." Isiah's voice climbed higher. "You don't know where the lakebed is. You'll never find it."

Lazaro scowled. "So you're insulting me now, are you?"

"Enrik won't let Tessa go." Isiah grasped at the words. "He was going to kill us at the ruin—that's why he buried you. We have to fight him."

Lazaro grabbed his collar. "*We* won't be doing anything." His spittle made Isiah wince. "And I don't need the help of your kind." He dropped Isiah and marched away. "I'm taking the artefact to get Tessa back. Enrik can have the ruin."

Isiah looked to the other Raiders for help, but they filed out after their leader. He ran out of the house after them, but they were already sprinting toward the roosts. Without the eagles, Isiah knew he'd never reach the ruin in time. His gaze drifted to the crevice snaking up the mountainside. Ward was still stuck in the prison. He needed Isiah's help—and the more Isiah thought about it, the more he realized he needed Ward's help too.

A cold dread built inside him. The only way to help Tessa was to face the dragon.

Dragon

ISIAH SHOVED THROUGH THE CROWD, SPRINTING IN the direction of the arena. The mass of people and animals seemed to form a wall, holding him back. He caught a flash of colour out the corner of his eye.

"Hey!" a Raider yelled. Isiah twisted around. The man broke into a run toward him.

A new surge of adrenaline powered Isiah on. He rushed in the direction of the arena. With every step, his heart pounded harder. Behind him, the Raider shoved his way through the crowd. Merchants and nomads spat curses as the man threw them to the ground.

Isiah made it to the second terrace. Despite the labyrinthian crush of houses and bazaars, he navigated his way to the crevice in the mountainside that led to the arena. A quick glance over his shoulder revealed the Raider still giving chase. Isiah ran into the shadow of the mountain. He prayed he wasn't too late.

He stumbled into the main cavern. The rows of seats were deserted. A ring of Raiders stood below, inside the arena itself. Ward was among them, his wrists bound in front of him.

Isiah vaulted over a row of chairs and made a beeline for the arena door. He reached it and flung it open.

"Ward!" he yelled.

The Raiders paused. Behind him, the Raider who had been chasing him exploded into the arena. He spotted Isiah and thrust a finger in his direction. "Stop him! He's with Lazaro!"

Isiah stumbled back as the Raiders in the arena grabbed their weapons and advanced on him. His hand flew to his sabre.

What are you doing? a voice in his head screamed. Half a dozen Raiders closed in.

"Drop the sabre," one of the Raiders growled.

Isiah made eye contact with Ward. A single Raider stood guard beside him. With a sudden burst of movement, Ward wrenched the guard's sabre free with both hands and whipped it through the air. The Raider collapsed, clutching his neck.

"Free the dragon!" Ward cried. He gripped the sabre's hilt between his knees and used the blade to slice his binds. The other Raiders spun on him. "I'll hold them off."

On the far side of the arena, a roar sounded. A familiar searing pain crept across Isiah's skin. His stomach turned in knots. "I—I can't do it!"

"Trust yourself," Ward replied. One of the Raiders darted forward, but a mock thrust from Ward kept him at bay. "Remember what I taught you."

Isiah forced his legs to move. He tore his eyes away from Ward and the Raiders and ran toward the dragon's cage. The beast snapped at the bars. Metal groaned beneath its weight. Isiah sheathed his sabre and fumbled with his knife.

A soft amber light illuminated the interior of the cage. The dragon saw the knife and shrank away with a hiss of warning. After its countless assaults, several bars were bent and leaning—wide enough for Isiah to slip through.

"Stop him!" a Raider cried. "He'll free it again!"

A couple of the Raiders burst into motion.

Isiah took a deep breath. The Raiders faded into the edge of his awareness. Holding the knife out in front of him, he stepped into the cage.

The dragon snapped at him. Its mouth dropped open to reveal four rows of jagged teeth. Isiah met its gaze and forced himself to stand tall.

The Raiders slammed against the gate behind him. One shoved his arm through, but Isiah stood out of reach. He swore. "Someone fetch a bow!"

Isiah's mind flashed back to the Ceremony, when a dragon had Marked him. He ran his eyes over the beast in front of him. Its ribs protruded from its skin, and its scales were dull and muted. It pressed itself against the far wall, head poised to strike.

I have to do this, he thought. *Tessa needs me.*

Isiah's hand shook. He forced himself to drop the knife. The dragon's eyes followed it as Isiah kicked it away. He swallowed.

"There," he said. His voice trembled. Every muscle in his body screamed at him to run, but he stood firm.

"You don't need to be afraid anymore."

The dragon shifted its weight. Bones crunched beneath its talons. Isiah risked a step forward. He fixed his eyes on the valve embedded in the dragon's neck.

"You know I'm Marked," Isiah said. Being so close to the dragon made his skin ripple with heat. "But we can help each other."

Isiah inched his way forward. The dragon lowered its head to meet him. A blast of hot air hit his face, but Isiah refused to run. His heart thundered against his ribcage so hard he thought it would burst out of his chest.

His fingers met the dragon's neck. The valve the Raiders had embedded protruded from its scales, the skin still red and inflamed. Isiah placed his hand around its cap. He probed it, trying to work it free. The dragon hissed as it budged an inch.

"Th—this might hurt," he said. He gritted his teeth and pulled the valve free.

The dragon jerked away. Isiah stumbled back as a light welled in its chest. He covered his eyes and braced himself for the agony of being burned alive.

The dragon spewed a fireball at the bars. Heat blasted past Isiah's face, then it faded. He lowered his arm. The hole the valve had left was sealed shut, the edges singed and black. Isiah pulled himself to his feet.

"You . . . cauterized it," he stammered.

A new light bubbled inside the dragon's chest. It shifted from orange to a deep red, then softened to pale yellow. Isiah held his breath as the light grew brighter until it was a blinding white-blue.

Fire spilled from the dragon's jaws. Isiah squeezed his eyes shut, waiting for the pain to start. None came. The flames swirled around him—but this time it was ice-cold. Isiah remembered what Ward had told him in Paradon, what felt like a lifetime ago. *The fire they use to bond won't harm you.* As the fire evaporated, Isiah opened his eyes.

The dragon stood in front of him, head raised high. Isiah could have sworn some of the sheen had returned to its muted scales. Despite himself, he laughed. The adrenaline deserted him in a rush. He took a deep breath to keep from passing out.

A clash of steel distracted him. Several of the Raiders had cornered Ward against the arena wall. Isiah leapt into action. He unclasped the dragon's manacles, then yanked on the lever to open the cage.

The dragon let Isiah climb up its wing and onto the hump between its shoulders. A familiar thrill filled his body, just like when he used to see Royal Guards soaring over the palace.

Isiah braced himself as the dragon erupted from its cage and burst into the arena. It opened its jaws and let out an ear-splitting bellow. When the Raiders caught sight of it, they bolted. Ward lowered his sabre. Through the bruises and scratches covering his face, he grinned.

"I knew you could do it!" Ward said. He nodded at the dragon. "She's a strong one. We should fly her back to Paradon."

Isiah hesitated. "I can't. I still have to heal myself." He peeled away his cloak to reveal his warped, melted skin. "I'm still Marked. Paradon will never accept me." He paused. "And I have to help someone."

Ward frowned. "Help someone?"

"A friend," Isiah said.

242

"The Raiders aren't our friends," he warned. "Remember that."

Isiah shifted his weight. "I know, but I have to do this."

Ward put a hand on the dragon's flank. "Then I'm coming with you."

The dragon turned to the arena gate. A wooden wheel sat next to it. Ward ran to it and began slowly cranking the gate open—but not fast enough. Isiah stifled a cry as the dragon lumbered toward the widening gap.

Ward pulled the wheel as fast as he could. The gap widened as the gate swung open, first one foot, then two. Isiah threw his arms around the dragon's neck as it hit the gate and slammed its weight against the doors.

Ward grabbed its flank and scrambled onto its back as the desperate beast forced its way through. It clambered over the rows of seats, toward the crack of blue sky beyond. It escaped the crevice and spilled into the street with thundering wingbeats.

The crowd screamed and scattered. Merchant stalls fell over and clothing flew from washing lines. The dragon jumped onto the roof of a low building and launched itself off the mountainside. Sunlight hit its scales and reflected in a dazzling display, forcing Isiah to squint. The dragon threw back its head and let out a cry of victory.

"We did it," Isiah managed to say. He clung to the dragon for dear life.

"Which way do we go?" Ward asked.

Isiah fixed his eyes on a group of eagles on the horizon. "There."

The dragon shifted its course as if reading his mind.

"How am I flying it?" he asked.

"Do you remember what I told you?" Ward said. "Before your Ceremony? All you have to do is think. They do the rest." He put a hand to his forehead. "What do we do once we reach them?"

"Leave it to me," Isiah replied. "I—I have a plan."

The mountain and its city grew further away. The dragon wobbled on the air currents, its weakened wings readjusting to the feel of flight. Isiah carefully sank into the rise and fall of its wingbeats, all too aware of the empty drop on either side of him. He turned his gaze in the direction of the ruin.

Tessa still needed his help—and if Lazaro gave Enrik the artefact, he'd lose his chance at a cure forever.

Lakebed

THE DRAGON ROARED AS IT POWERED ITSELF toward the eagles in the distance. As they drew closer, Isiah made out the form of Lazaro and his Raiders hunched on their backs. He tensed as the man glanced over his shoulder and spotted them. A light welled in the dragon's chest.

"No," Isiah said quickly. He stroked the dragon's neck. "Don't do that." He hoped it could understand him.

The dragon hesitated, then the fire died. Isiah cupped his hands to his mouth as they grew closer. The dragon dwarfed the eagles, looming over them.

"Lazaro!" he yelled.

The Raiders fell into formation. Darla and Antony drew their sabres.

"I don't want to hurt you," Isiah called.

"Get out of here!" Lazaro replied. "Keep that dragon away from us!"

"I need the artefact!"

"Never," Lazaro snapped. He clutched the artefact to his chest. "I won't let you ruin this for us."

Isiah tightened his grip on the dragon as it picked up speed. One of the eagles let out a cry of alarm. The Raiders broke formation and fell away. The dragon went after them.

Towering spires and buttes pitted the terrain. The eagles weaved through them, tilting their wings as they soared inches from the rock. The dragon locked its eyes on them and gave chase. Isiah's insides flew into his throat as they dropped like an arrow. The ground whipped past. A group of merchants and their mules scattered as they blasted overhead.

"I won't let it hurt you!" Isiah cried. Darla's eagle appeared on his left, snapping at the dragon's wing. The dragon snarled and spat a fireball at the bird. Isiah tried to calm it. "You have to stop attacking us!"

"You're with Paradon," Lazaro said. "I should have killed you when I had the chance!"

The eagles climbed in altitude. Isiah's dragon powered after them. Helen and Luca closed in, sabres drawn. Ward drew his own blade to keep them at bay. Isiah ducked as an eagle whipped overhead with a piercing shriek. Its talons missed his head by inches.

Lazaro flew ahead of them. He clutched the artefact in his hand, gripping the reins to keep his eagle stable.

The memory of flying with Tessa flashed through Isiah's mind. An idea popped into his head. He tightened his legs around the dragon and braced himself.

"Hold on," he cried.

The dragon powered through the air with a burst of wingbeats. It closed the distance between them and spun into a barrel roll. Time seemed to slow. Lazaro's eyes widened as the dragon's shadow passed over him. As they swept overhead, Isiah reached out and snatched the artefact from Lazaro's grip.

The dragon righted itself and Ward let out a cry of victory. Lazaro's eagle shrieked in panic and lurched away. The man fought to control it. With his heart still pounding, Isiah urged the dragon to keep flying. The artefact pulsed in his hand seemingly with a mind of its own.

"Isiah!" Lazaro yelled. "Get back here!"

The Raiders gave chase. The dragon broke away from them, each powerful wingbeat furthering the distance. Isiah stuffed the artefact into his pocket, then guided the dragon in the direction of the ruin. Lazaro's yelling faded behind them.

Tessa, here I come.

* * *

The ruin materialized in front of them. The dragon flew over it, heading towards the crack in the mesa that obscured the lakebed.

"That was good flying," Ward said. He let out a low whistle. "You'll make a Royal Guard in no time."

"Only if I can cure my Mark," he replied.

"What's the plan?"

"We'll use the dragon," Isiah told him. "The Raiders have a camp. We'll fly in and destroy it, then we can help my friend while they're fleeing."

"You make it sound so easy," Ward said.

Isiah swallowed. "It's our best shot."

They neared the site of the lakebed. A flash of colour below betrayed the Raider camp. Isiah puffed up his chest, unsheathed his sabre, and directed the dragon to dive.

The mighty creature folded its wings and dropped like a stone. The ground rushed to meet them. The twin overhangs flashed past and the dragon threw out its wings. Sand billowed into the air as it flew through the ravine, soaring over the dried-up lakebed and then wheeling around with a deafening roar.

Raiders screamed and scattered. Isiah let out a battle cry as the dragon hit the ground in a shower of dust. Tents collapsed and eagles pulled at their reins in panic. Isiah scanned the camp for Tessa.

The Raiders regrouped. A few arrows landed around the dragon. It bellowed a warning and launched a fireball in their direction. The flames hit a tent and enveloped it. Enrik's Raiders transformed into sand vortexes and weaved through the camp, trying to surround the dragon.

Enrik marched into view. When he spotted Isiah, a cruel smile crossed his lips. He produced a long stick topped with an amber-coloured crystal and thrust it into the air. Ward swore.

The dragon's fire died in its throat. Isiah's blood ran cold as it hissed and backed away.

"No—" he started.

A force slammed into him. A Raider materialized and threw him from the dragon's back. Isiah hit the ground and the air escaped his lungs. The Raider tore his sabre free and threw it aside.

"Not so tough now, are you?" he spat. His hot breath blasted Isiah's face.

The other Raiders closed in on Ward. The dragon spun away from the crystal, throwing Ward from its back. He scrambled to his feet, sabre outstretched, but the Raiders closed in.

Isiah's captor dragged him to his feet. He strained against the man, but the Raider pinned his arms behind his back. Ward lashed out at the nearest Raider. Several more circled around behind.

"Watch out!" Isiah yelled.

A Raider darted forward and landed a cut on the back of Ward's knee. The man gasped in pain and collapsed onto it. The Raiders hovered around him like a pack of vultures. Isiah tried again to free himself.

"Hold still," his captor spat. "Or you'll join him."

Enrik marched over. "Drive the dragon into a corner," he said. "And make sure it stays there."

One of the Raiders landed a cut on Ward's arm. He tried to stagger to his feet, but his injured leg made him hiss in pain.

"Let's not drag things out," Enrik said to Ward. "You should know not to venture into our lands, Royal Guard."

One of the Raiders caught Ward's sword arm and wrenched the sabre from his grip.

"Leave him alone," Isiah yelled. He fought the panic in his voice.

"You're outmatched," Enrik said. "And deep in our territory, now. There's no way out."

Ward's face remained stony. "At least let me die on my feet."

Enrik nodded to the Raiders. They grabbed his arms and helped him stand.

"What do you have to say for yourself?" Enrik asked.

Ward spat on the dirt at his feet. "I'm not afraid of you."

Enrik wrapped his hand around his sabre. "You should be."

Isiah squeezed his eyes shut as Enrik's sabre flashed through the air. A spurt of dark blood stained the earth. Moments later Ward's body dropped with a thud.

"Ward!" Isiah yelled. He strained against the Raider holding him. The man grunted as he tried to keep Isiah under control.

Enrik calmly sheathed his sabre and wandered over to Isiah. "Isiah, I'm glad you could join us. With the Royal Guard out of the way, now we can get down to business."

Isiah ripped his arm free from the Raider's grip and swung at Enrik. His fist fell short. He felt like yelling curses, but his throat tightened until he could hardly breathe. Enrik scowled.

"Dispose of the body," he ordered. A couple of Raiders dragged Ward away. "Loot his valuables and toss him into a gorgon den." He turned to Isiah. "Where were we?"

Isiah blinked back tears. "What have you done with Tessa?" he spat.

"You'll see her soon enough," Enrik replied. "Breaking out the dragon, that was a daring move." He leaned in. "I'm surprised it didn't rip you apart."

Isiah's captor snickered. "They're harmless once you know their weakness."

Enrik turned the crystal over in his hand. "They're expensive, these crystals." He passed it to a female Raider, who joined the gang driving the dragon away. "Still, I wasn't about to take chances with people from Paradon running around."

The Raiders backed the dragon into the corner of the ravine. Enrik chuckled. "It's just as scared as you are, boy. What was your plan? To kill us all? That Royal Guard of yours couldn't even save himself."

Isiah held his tongue. He felt numb.

"Revenge for what we did to you?" Enrik asked. "Or maybe to play the hero? I don't think Lazaro will ever let you get near Tessa again. That is," he added, "if you all survive this."

"I freed Lazaro," Isiah said. "He's on his way now. I told him where the lakebed was."

Enrik shook his head. "You're a bad liar. Even if he does find us, he's outnumbered."

Isiah's captor shoved him. Enrik turned and strolled toward the excavation site. "You should know by now that it's foolish not to cooperate with us. Have you brought the artefact? Or do I have to start cutting off Tessa's fingers until you tell me where it is?"

Isiah's captor felt his pockets. After a moment he pulled it out. "Found it."

Enrik took it from the man. He turned the artefact over in his hands. "That wasn't so hard, was it?"

Isiah forced himself to stand tall. He fought the welling hopelessness. Enrik pocketed the artefact and walked away.

"Put him with Tessa," he said. "And make sure they can't escape me again. I won't have anyone else get in my way."

Oasis

ISIAH'S CAPTOR DRAGGED HIM TO THE EXCAVATION SITE. Piles of earth and rock lay piled around a deep pit. Wooden platforms and winches leaned over it, coils of rope dangling from them.

"In there," the Raider ordered. Isiah stumbled as the man pushed him. "Watch your step. Enrik won't help you if you break a leg."

Isiah grabbed one of the ropes and climbed into the pit. At the bottom, a jagged hole revealed a large cavity—the cavern he and Tessa had climbed out of. Raiders scurried back and forth, yelling orders and securing the ropes. Isiah eyed his surroundings for some kind of escape.

"No you don't," his captor snapped. He drew his sabre and prodded him. "Keep moving."

Isiah climbed to the bottom of the pit. Loose dirt covered the floor, and the walls were scarred with pickaxe-holes. Another rope led from the bottom of the pit into the cavern below. He grabbed it and descended.

Cool shadows washed over him. A few crates were piled against one side of the cavern. The acrid smell of explosives hung thick in the air. Several Raiders stood guard. Isiah reached the bottom of the cavern and one of them tied his hands behind his back. He eyed the tunnels leading further into the ruin.

"Nothing awaits you down there except death," his captor said. He grinned, exposing a few missing teeth. "The gorgons are hungry."

The Raiders finished binding Isiah, then shoved him in the direction of the crates. Tessa sat among them. When she saw him, she straightened up.

"Isiah," she said. She struggled against her binds.

Isiah slumped next to her. His captor bound his ankles, then waved a sabre in his face.

"Don't try anything stupid," the man said. "Or we'll throw you headfirst into the gorgons' den."

The Raiders marched away, leaving them alone. Isiah cursed under his breath. *Enrik is right.* He shouldn't have tried to play the hero.

"Why are you here?" Tessa asked. "Did Enrik find you?"

"I came to help you," he said. He looked down at his binds. "At least, I tried."

"Where's Lazaro? Did you see him?"

"I broke him out of the prison," he replied. He told her about their escape from Alcabaza—and how he bonded with the dragon.

Tessa's face fell. "You were right. They won't find us here."

A sand vortex spilled into the cavern. Enrik materialized and walked to the stone door. He produced the artefact from his pocket.

"I thought you ought to see it," he said to Isiah. He turned the artefact over in his hand. "So much suffering for such a simple object."

Enrik slotted the artefact into the hole next to the door. A plume of dust erupted from its edges as he pushed it open. The light from their torches rippled across the cave within, reflecting off the swirling water.

"The oasis," Tessa whispered.

"So it is," Enrik replied. He motioned to his Raiders. "Load it up."

Pulleys squealed as the Raiders yanked on ropes. Isiah watched as they began passing large ceramic jugs into the cavern. A Raider dragged one to the door and started filling it from the oasis.

"Wait," Isiah said. "What are you doing?"

"Such a valuable treasure doesn't belong in the hands of any passing traveller who stumbles upon it," Enrik replied. "There are more than a few people who would pay a fine price for *this* magic."

Tessa glared at him. "You're stealing it?"

Enrik shrugged. "Isn't that what you would do? You're no different than us, Tess."

Her nose shrivelled. "Don't call me that."

The Raiders filled the first jug and then dragged it to the hole. They secured the ropes around its handles and carefully lifted it into the light beyond.

"I never thought the oasis existed," Enrik said. "Like the rest of you, I thought it was simply a rumour, until some interested buyers appeared with a very enticing offer." He paced back and forth in front of them. "Ever since some of the nobles in Paradon fell sick, they flew into a panic."

Isiah remembered Ward's argument with the noble about his father. "My father was ill. That's why they held my Ceremony early."

"The nobles are paranoid at the best of times," Enrik said. "Losing such a high-ranking member sent them into a frenzy . . . and panicked buyers offer the highest prices."

"You're selling it to them?" Tessa spat.

"Don't act like it was such an easy decision," Enrik replied, feigning offence. "I refused at first—until they opened their treasury doors. Besides," he added, "I didn't even know where to begin looking for this oasis until they showed me the way." He produced a crumpled piece of paper. Isiah's stomach dropped as he realized what it was.

"Their archives contained a rough guide," Enrik explained. "Somebody had left it out. They gave it to me, and it showed me that the oasis was right on our doorstep." He paused. "Of course, I didn't know where, and all the old ruins have been looted, so the nobles gave me explosives to start looking."

"The earthquakes . . ." Isiah said.

"My explosives upset the fault lines, revealing the ruin entrance." Enrik scowled. "But Lazaro had to get in my way. I warned you to stay out of it, but of course, you didn't listen. His hot-headedness would never let him turn an opportunity down to spite me." Enrik knelt in front of Tessa. "Which is why I have to kill him. If you hadn't escaped, I'd be rich already."

Tessa glared at him. "You're a traitor."

Enrik chuckled. "Please. You're friends with *him*." He thrust a finger at Isiah. "He's one of them too." He turned to Isiah. "Tell me, boy, why *did* you want the oasis? It's for your Mark, isn't it?" He chuckled. "You're just as selfish as I am."

Isiah met the man's gaze. He refused to speak.

"What would you have done after you'd cured it?" Enrik asked. "Once the dragons no longer hated you? When your people would accept you again? You'd go running back to them, wouldn't you?"

"That's not true," Tessa said.

"Nonsense," Enrik snapped. "Tell her, boy. You know the Raiders will kill you."

"Isiah." Tessa looked at him. "You weren't going to run away, were you?"

Isiah shifted his weight.

"See?" Enrik said. "He's only here because he wants the cure. Then it's back to his filthy Paradon to pretend all this never happened."

Behind him, the Raiders continued filling the jugs. Isiah watched as they lifted each one out of the cavern.

"Someone will find out what happened," Tessa said. "Once the other Raiders hear you sold our magic to Paradon—"

"Not once I pay them their weight in gold," Enrik replied. "Their lips are sealed. As for Lazaro, he's a wanted man." He laughed. "Who would have thought making so many enemies would come back to haunt him?"

Tessa narrowed her eyes. "Is it worth breaking the Raider's Oath?"

Enrik's smile faded. "I wouldn't have needed to break the Oath if you hadn't got involved."

He turned and marched away. Isiah racked his brains for a plan. He wished he hadn't thrown his knife away. When he looked over at Tessa, she refused to make eye contact with him.

One of the Raiders broke away from the group. "That's the first batch done," she said.

"Good. Load up my eagle. I'll take the water myself." Enrik winked at Isiah. "I didn't just buy those crystals for *you*, boy. There's no harm in having a plan in case Paradon decide to re-negotiate."

Excavation

"KEEP GOING!" A RAIDER CALLED. "Enrik wants this oasis drained by mid-day."

Isiah sat in the shadows, slumped against a crate. The Raiders stood in a line, passing jugs between them. Each one was almost as tall as Isiah was. He strained his neck to see how much water was left in the oasis, but from his position, it was impossible.

The Raiders looped ropes around the jugs' handles and lifted them out of sight. Enrik wandered about, watching the operation. Half-way out of the cavern, one of the jugs lurched.

"Watch out," a Raider yelled.

The ropes came loose. He made a grab for the jug, but it broke free and dropped to the cavern floor. It landed with a crash and shattered, spilling its contents.

Enrik swore. "Be careful. Every jug we lose will cost us dearly."

"Relax," a one-eyed Raider said. "We have more than enough."

"This water is liquid gold, Iris," he replied. He scowled at a few pools that had collected in dips in the rock. "Every drop spilled is lost forever."

Isiah let the Raiders and their bickering fade to the edge of his awareness. He tugged at his binds, trying to work them loose. Away from the Raiders and their torches, darkness offered him some precious concealment. He glanced at Tessa. She hadn't spoken to him since their confrontation with Enrik.

"I—I'm sorry I lied to you," Isiah said.

"Not the time," she replied.

The minutes ticked past. Isiah lost track of time. The Raiders began using cups to collect the last of the oasis water.

"Nearly there," Iris said.

Enrik smiled. "Good work. We'll be rich by sundown."

A few of the Raiders whooped and high-fived. As they were distracted, a shape darted to Isiah's side.

"Isiah," Aron hissed. "Tessa."

Isiah sat up. "Aron?"

"Shh." Aron held a finger to his lips. "I can get you out of here, but you have to be quiet."

Aron began hurriedly untying Isiah's ankle binds. As he worked, the boy's hands shook. "Go into the ruin," he said. "It's your only chance." He finished untying Isiah's ankles and moved onto Tessa.

"Thank you," Tessa said.

Aron opened his mouth to reply, but a pained gasp escaped him. Isiah's blood ran cold as he looked down to see a sabre protruding from Aron's middle.

"Got you," Enrik snarled. He yanked the sabre free and Aron collapsed onto his side. "Get them up."

A few Raiders dragged Isiah and Tessa to their feet. Aron clutched a hand to his middle, groaning in pain. A pair of Raiders lifted him by the arms.

"I suspected someone had helped Isiah before," Enrik said. "I knew he couldn't have escaped my hideout on his own." He grabbed Aron's hair and lifted his head. Aron's face was contorted in pain. "If you're so willing to betray me for their sake, you can join them."

The Raiders dragged Isiah and his friends over to the oasis. The pool sat empty, its rocks bone-dry.

Tessa struggled against them. "What are you doing?"

"I can't have anyone spreading word about what happened here," Enrik replied. "I'll have to get rid of you."

The Raiders cut Isiah and Tessa's binds, then threw the trio into the empty pit of the oasis. Isiah rubbed his wrists as the bloodflow returned.

"I won't break the Raider's Oath again," Enrik said. "Suffocation will do my job for me."

Isiah's face paled as he realized what was happening. The Raiders filed out of the cave. "You can't do this—"

Enrik ignored him. "But I'll show you some mercy." He nodded to Aron, who lay curled up on the floor. "He has a sabre. I'll let you decide which one of you wants to use it first."

Enrik produced the artefact and dumped it inside the cave with them. He then grabbed a pickaxe and raised it above his head. With a grunt of effort, he brought it down on the artefact.

The artefact shattered. The door began to grind closed.

"I have a few spare explosives," Enrik called through the narrowing gap. "Soon there'll be no evidence this place ever existed."

Isiah pulled himself to his feet and threw himself at the door, but it slammed shut and plunged them into darkness. The faint sound of the Raiders laughing wafted through.

Silence descended. Isiah pounded on the door. "Let us out!" Each strike sent bolts of pain through his hands, but he didn't care.

He whirled away from the door, scanning for some kind of escape. Darkness enveloped him. His lungs strained at the dust-filled air. Each breath felt heavier than the last. He could almost feel himself running out of air.

Snap out of it. He forced himself to focus.

A faint light caught his eye. The shards of the artefact were still glowing. He knelt and turned it over in his hand. It cast just enough light to illuminate the ground around him. Tessa's shallow breathing came from his right. Further away, Aron groaned.

"Tessa," Isiah said. He crawled in her direction. She sat with her arms wrapped around herself.

"It's getting harder to breathe," she said. She sucked at the air. "We're going to suffocate!"

"T—try to calm down." Isiah felt like an idiot saying it.

"They're going to set off the explosives." Tessa's voice grew higher. "We'll be buried alive!" Her breathing grew faster. "I can't breathe."

Isiah grabbed her shoulders. "You've got to slow down." He racked his brains. "Trust me."

"Trust you!" Tessa whirled on him. "You lied to me. How long have you been planning to run away? You used us."

Isiah winced at the venom in her voice. "I didn't want you to get involved," he started.

"I stole from Lazaro for you. I never do that!"

"I'm sorry," Isiah said. "I couldn't tell you my plan. I *have* to run away. The Raiders would never accept me."

Tessa sniffed. "I did."

The faint sounds from outside ceased. Isiah knew they didn't have much time left.

"We're going to get out of here," he said. "But first you have to stop panicking."

Tessa hesitated. Slowly, her breathing began to return to normal. She swallowed. "Okay."

Isiah turned to the broken pieces of the artefact. "Help me put these together. There must be a way to unlock the door from the inside."

"What about Aron?" she asked.

Isiah crawled to the boy. Aron had shifted into a sitting position, pressing a hand against his middle. Blood oozed between his fingers. Isiah wrung his hands. "I don't know."

They went to work piecing together the artefact. Enrik's pickaxe had broken it into several large shards. Isiah tried to force the bits together in his hands. Tessa worked alongside him. Her warm breath tickled his ear.

"There," she said. "I think we've got it."

Isiah held the pieces together, the inspected the door. Another hole, the same size and shape as the one on the outside, was cut into the rock. Praying it would work, he slotted the broken artefact inside.

Nothing happened for a moment, then the door gave a clunk. Isiah pushed it with all of his weight. Tessa joined him. Faint light spilled through a widening crack. They forced it wide enough to slip through and piled into the cavern on the other side.

The crates were stacked in the centre of the cavern. A fuse snaked up the hole in the ceiling and out of sight. The hiss of sparks met his ears.

"You get Aron," Isiah said to Tessa. He sprinted toward the explosives. A spark crept along the fuse, winding toward the crates. Isiah collapsed to his knees and tried to pull the fuse free. It didn't budge. He redoubled his efforts, but it held fast.

The sparks inched closer. Isiah leapt to his feet and tried stomping it out. The sparks stung his leg, but it refused to die.

He looked around and a rock caught his attention. A sharp edge lined its side from where it had been torn away from the wall by a prior explosive. Isiah grabbed it, then rushed over to the fuse and brought it down. The fuse began to fray. With the sparks closing in, he did it again, then a third time.

Tessa pulled Aron through the door. She saw the sparks and her eyes widened. "Hurry up!"

Isiah raised the rock above his head and brought it down with all his strength. The fuse split. He grabbed the lit fuse and threw it aside. The sparks reached the end and fizzled out. Isiah sighed and collapsed on the ground.

"Aron needs help," Tessa said. He heard the worry in her voice. "He's really hurt."

Aron leaned against her, one arm over her shoulders. Blood stained his clothes from the wound. She carefully lowered him to the floor. "I don't think he can climb out."

Isiah inspected the wound. Enrik's sabre had left a hole through Aron's middle. Aron wheezed with each breath. Isiah fought the bile climbing his throat.

"We don't have any bandages." Isiah looked around the cavern. "Maybe the Raiders left something behind."

His eyes came to rest on the shattered jug. Some of the water from the oasis pooled in depressions in the rock. His Mark itched, but he shoved the sensation away. "Help me carry him over there."

Tessa obeyed. They carried Aron to the smashed jug and set him down. Isiah cupped the oasis water in his hands while Tessa peeled Aron's hand away from his wound.

"I hope this works," Isiah said.

He carefully let the water pour into Aron's injury. The boy gasped and tensed, then his breathing became stronger. Tessa watched with wide eyes as the wound began to close. Flesh stitched together and bloodstains faded.

"The pain is going," Aron murmured. A cold sweat covered his forehead, but the colour began slowly returning to his cheeks. "I can't believe it's real."

Isiah straightened up. "Enrik has taken the rest."

Aron grabbed his sabre. "Take this." He awkwardly pulled the sheath from his belt and handed it to Isiah. "You'll need it if you're going after him."

"What about you?" Tessa asked.

"I'll only slow you down," Aron said. "You go. I'll be fine staying here."

Isiah stuck the sheath through his waistband. "Then we need a way to fly."

* * *

Isiah's muscles burned as he hauled himself up the rope. Tessa climbed after him, her face set in determination.

He reached the daylight and clambered into the pit the Raiders had excavated. More ropes and pulleys dangled above them, but the sides were jagged enough to offer handholds. Isiah ignored the pain in his muscles and clambered out of the pit.

A voice reached his ears from above. "The explosion should have gone off by now. Maybe the fuse went out."

"And if it hasn't?" a voice replied. "It'll blow you to smithereens."

Isiah reached the top of the pit and crouched, peering over piles of earth. A couple of Raiders stood guard in the remnants of the camp.

"Suppose Enrik doesn't come back for us," the first one said. "How do we know he won't take the money and ditch us?"

Tessa scurried out of the pit and ran to the cover of a tent. Keeping low to the ground, Isiah went after her. He spied the dragon hunched in the far side of the ravine. A third Raider kept it at bay with one of the crystals.

"We'll go after him," the second Raider said. "As soon as those three are buried, we go. That's what Enrik told us."

"And what about the dragon?"

The man shrugged. "We'll leave it for the other Raiders to deal with."

Isiah drew his sabre. The two Raiders stood on the other side of the tent, facing the dragon. He hesitated. Tessa made a chopping motion to her neck. Isiah grimaced.

He leapt from cover and lashed out at the nearest Raider. His sabre bit into the man's neck and he dropped with a yell of pain. The other Raider whirled around. Isiah jumped over the writhing man and landed a blow to the Raider's sword arm. He staggered away with a curse, clutching it to his chest.

Tessa rushed past Isiah and drew the fallen Raider's sabre. She thrust it in the man's direction. "Try to fight and we'll kill you."

The Raider recovered himself. "You'll never catch him in time," he said. "He'll be across the Tablelands before you know it. The Royal Guards will kill you on sight."

Isiah puffed up his chest. "Not with a dragon, they won't."

From the far side of the ravine, the dragon let out a bellow. Upon seeing them, the guard with the crystal faltered. Isiah broke into a run toward him.

The guard abandoned his post and bolted. The dragon lumbered over with a hiss of recognition.

Isiah sheath his sabre and raised his hands to slow the beast. "Woah." He shakily put his hand on the dragon's snout. It replied with a blast of hot breath.

Tessa hung back. She eyed the dragon nervously.

"You have to trust us," Isiah said.

She wrapped her arms around herself. "You know I don't like dragons."

The dragon let out a deep grumble. Tessa flinched and took a step away.

"What if you stole one of the Raiders' eagles?" he asked.

"It doesn't work like that," she replied. "You have to bond with them first."

"Then this is our only chance of catching Enrik." Isiah took her hand. "You can do this, Tessa."

Tessa hesitated, then took a deep breath. Isiah guided her forward and placed her hand on the dragon's snout. "It won't hurt you, see?"

Tessa's muscles tensed as her fingers met the dragon's scales. Her breath escaped her in a rush. "Are you sure?"

"I know it." He let go of her hand and she remained in place.

"How do you fly with no reins?" she asked.

"I don't know yet," Isiah admitted. "It just kind of works—Ward said it's something about the magic they use when they bond."

"But you're Marked," she said.

"I know." Isiah knew he should be dead. He moved to the dragon's wing and climbed atop its shoulders. "Maybe we needed each other's help."

Tessa hurried around and climbed up after him. Isiah gripped the dragon's neck and it burst into motion. It lumbered along the length of the ravine and launched itself into the air with powerful wingbeats. The twin overhangs rushed to meet them, then fell away as the dragon broke through and soared into the open air.

"Which direction did Enrik go?" Isiah asked.

Tessa thrust a finger past him. "There." A group of silhouettes hovered in the distance, flying away. "There are at least a dozen eagles," she said. "Are you sure we can do this?"

Isiah urged the dragon forward. It lowered its head and fell into pursuit. "We have to."

Mesa

THE DRAGON RACED ABOVE THE BADLANDS. Its wingbeats echoed in Isiah's eardrums, rising above the pounding of his own heart. His sabre rattled against his side, and Tessa's breath tickled the back of his neck.

The shape of Enrik and the Raiders grew larger. They were flying in a straight line away from the lakebed—toward the distant border. Isiah made out the jugs hanging from a harness draped across the back of Enrik's eagle.

"What do we do once we reach them?" Tessa asked. Her arms were wrapped tightly around Isiah's middle.

"We stop him," Isiah replied.

The dragon roared in reply, making his bones tremble. Ahead, one of the Raiders spotted them. His eagle gave a screech of alarm.

Enrik twisted around. Even from so far away, Isiah made out the hatred on the man's face. Enrik motioned to his Raiders and they fell away.

"What are they doing?" Isiah asked.

Tessa drew her sabre. "Attacking."

The eagles fanned out to try and surround the dragon. The beast hissed in warning. Orange light welled in its chest. This time Isiah didn't stop it.

An eagle attacked. Isiah tightened his grip as the dragon lurched away, claws flashing. The bird struck its underside and bounced away. The other eagles closed in.

Death by a thousand cuts. Isiah remembered what Reuben had told him. He gritted his teeth. "Not this time."

The dragon unleashed its fire. Eagles screamed in terror and pulled away as a fireball scorched the air. It struck one across the back and flames raced across its Raider. The dragon descended on a second eagle with a flurry of wingbeats. It connected with the bird and tore at the exposed Raider on its back.

Iris swore. "What are you waiting for? Get in there and fight!"

The Raiders recovered themselves. They circled the dragon, waiting for their chance to strike. Tessa twisted around and brandished her sabre.

"They're trying to attack us from behind," she said. An eagle flew above them, talons twitching in anticipation.

Isiah pressed his legs into the dragon's flanks. "Come on," he urged. "Keep flying."

Plumes of hot breath erupted from the dragon's nostrils. It kept its eyes fixed on Enrik, but his large eagle kept pace ahead of them. Tessa let out a cry as Iris attacked.

The dragon folded its wings and twisted in the air. The eagle flashed past. Iris swung her sabre, but it glanced harmlessly off the dragon's scaly flank.

271

Another fireball welled in the dragon's chest. It grabbed a nearby eagle in its talons. The bird tried to twist away, but the dragon blasted it with fire. Tessa winced as the eagle dropped like a ball of screeching flames.

"Three down," Isiah said. He looked around to take stock of who remained.

A shadow passed over his head. He yelped and ducked as an eagle swooped over, talons clicking. The dragon cried in alarm and erupted upwards, snapping at the bird with its massive jaws. The eagle escaped unharmed—its rider wasn't as lucky. His screams were cut short and his lifeless body dropped.

"It's only one dragon," Iris yelled. "Knock it from the sky!"

The other Raiders faltered. Some tugged uselessly at the reins as their birds broke away in panic. The dragon bellowed and closed in. Another fireball split the sky. Iris's eagle twisted away, but the flames swept across its tail feathers and sent it reeling away with a terrified shriek.

"The Raiders are fleeing," Tessa said. "I knew they were cowards."

Enrik's eagle drew steadily closer. The shadow of their dragon fell over it. Isiah made out the twin harnesses that hung from the bird's flanks, each one filled with a dozen ceramic jugs.

Enrik drew his sabre and glanced over his shoulder at them. "All the more riches for me," he snapped. "The oasis is *mine*."

A spark flickered in the dragon's chest, then died. Its sides heaved as it gave chase. A smile crept across Enrik's face.

"It's tiring," he said. "Give up now before I drop you from the sky."

Isiah narrowed his eyes. He willed the dragon to fly faster. The massive creature bore down on Enrik. Its jaws were almost within reach of him . . .

Enrik's eagle dropped out of range. Enrik ducked beneath the dragon's head and swung at its neck. The dragon roared and jerked away.

"I'm too agile," Enrik yelled. His eagle dipped below the dragon and came up on their right. "You can't keep up."

The dragon twisted around to attack him, but the eagle dodged again. They began to descend in altitude, toward a towering mesa that loomed above the surrounding land. Isiah tugged on the dragon's neck, but it failed to climb higher.

"You can't keep up," Enrik said. He flew above them, leaning over the side of his eagle. "You're going to crash."

Desperation welled inside Isiah. He willed the dragon to keep going. *Come on!*

The dragon gave a sudden burst of energy. Enrik's eyes widened as it powered itself toward them and collided with the eagle in a mass of slashing talons. The bird shrieked in alarm. Material shredded and buckles snapped. Half of the harness came loose.

"No!" Isiah made a grab for it, but the broken half slipped free and plummeted through the air. Isiah watched as it struck the ground far below and shattered, spraying its contents.

"Isiah!" Enrik yelled. The lopsided eagle careened toward the mesa. It hit the ground and stumbled, dragging the remaining half of its harness behind it. Enrik jumped from his eagle's back. "You'll regret that," he snarled.

The dragon landed with a jolt. It snarled at Enrik, but he pulled something from his eagle's harness—another crystal. The dragon hissed and backed away.

"It won't help you now," Enrik said. "Come and face me, Isiah. It's time I got rid of you."

The weakened dragon shied away from Enrik. Isiah eyed the remaining oasis water.

"You want it?" Enrik said. "Then what are you waiting for?" He darted forward and swung the crystal. The dragon hissed. Its back legs met the edge of the mesa and it scrambled for purchase. Enrik's hand began to dissolve into sand. "Or I'll come up there myself."

Isiah jumped from the dragon's back. He hit the ground and forced himself to stand tall. "You killed Ward."

"No," Enrik replied. "You were the one who attacked the lakebed. *You* caused his death."

Tessa landed beside Isiah. "You broke the Oath."

Enrik took a fighting stance. "And I'll do it again."

Enrik charged at them. Isiah raised his sabre to parry the blow. Enrik tried to strike again, but an attack from Tessa forced him away.

"Two against one?" he said. "Where's your sense of honour?"

He lashed out at Tessa, who dodged the blow. Isiah readjusted his grip on his sabre as the clash of steel rang out. Enrik repelled Tessa and whirled on him. Isiah parried the blow and stumbled away. Enrik closed in.

"Nobody cares about you, boy," he spat. "You'll die and not a single person will mourn you."

Isiah blocked again. His dragon bellowed, but the glow of Enrik's crystal kept it at bay. Isiah's heels met the crumbling edge of the mesa. He fought to keep his balance.

Tessa yelled and swung her sabre. Enrik wheeled away as it struck the armour on his shoulder and glanced off. His expression darkened. "Attacking me from behind? I always knew Lazaro had raised a brat."

Enrik dissolved into a vortex. Tessa shielded her eyes as sand whipped past her.

"Look out!" Isiah cried.

Tessa spun around as Enrik materialized. Sparks flew as their blades collided. Enrik planted his foot against her stomach and kicked her. She gasped in pain as she hit the ground and slid off the edge.

"Tessa!" Isiah ran to where she had disappeared.

Enrik charged after him. "I'm not done with you yet."

Isiah reached the edge. Tessa clung to a jutting ledge. Her feet dangled over empty air. She looked up at him with wide, panic-stricken eyes.

"Now you can join her." Enrik launched a kick. Isiah twisted away in time and retreated to solid ground. His lungs heaved, and his sabre felt heavier with every passing second.

Enrik wiped a hand across his reddening forehead. "Give it up, boy."

Isiah scanned for some way to reach Tessa. Enrik stood between them like an immovable wall. The man raised his sabre and closed in.

275

"You can't beat me," he mocked. "I've been fighting since birth."

Enrik swung again. Isiah parried once, then a second time—slower. With each movement, he felt the strength leeching from his body. Soon Enrik would hit his mark.

Enrik lunged forward. He collided with Isiah and threw him to the ground. A stinging pain seized Isiah's arm where Enrik's blade had caught him. His dragon bellowed again, tugging as if on an invisible leash.

"It ends here," Enrik said. He aimed a cut at Isiah's throat.

Isiah clenched his fist. He lobbed a handful of dirt and sand into Enrik's face. The man staggered back with a grunt of pain. Isiah scrambled to his feet and, ignoring the blood seeping from the cut on his arm, closed in.

Enrik stumbled away with a string of curses. He lashed out at Isiah blindly. Isiah dodged the blow and struck his free arm. Enrik dropped the crystal and hissed in pain. He made a grab for it, but it bounced off the edge of the mesa. Isiah's dragon roared, clawing at the ground.

"Isiah!" Tessa called.

Isiah tore himself away from Enrik and ran to her voice. Enrik scrambled onto his eagle and spurred the bird into the air. A voice screamed at Isiah to give chase, but he shoved it away. *Not without Tessa.*

He collapsed to his knees on the edge of the mesa. Tessa clung to the ledge, one hand gripping the rock, the other wrapped around a scraggly bush. Her knuckles were white, and her face was red from the effort. Her feet dislodged showers of rocks as she fought for purchase.

Isiah carefully lowered himself onto the ledge. Every muscle urged him to go faster, but he knew if he did, he'd slip and fall himself. He reached the ledge and grabbed hold of Tessa's arms. He dragged her to safety and she collapsed on top of him.

She panted. "I thought I was going to fall."

"No." Isiah forced himself to speak. The adrenaline began to fade, leaving him weak and trembling. "I've got you."

Tessa grabbed the rockface. "Where's Enrik?"

"He took off," Isiah replied. "He's getting away."

A roar from above cut them off. The dragon's head appeared over the edge. Tessa spurred into motion. "Then let's go after him."

Isiah reached the top of the mesa and climbed onto the tired dragon's back. They took off in the direction Enrik had gone.

"This time, I'm gonna get him," she said.

"Be careful," Isiah replied. He braced, waiting for her usual rebuke.

"I've got you to look out for me, haven't I?"

"Yeah." Isiah nodded to himself. "You have."

They left the mesa behind and flew into rockier terrain. Towering spires and craggy buttes pitted the landscape, broken by deep ravines with thin rivers snaking through the bottom. Isiah kept his hand on his sabre hilt, studying the way ahead for Enrik. The dragon powered on with steady wing beats, but Isiah knew it didn't have much left in it.

"Enrik can't have gone far," he said.

"His eagle must be tired by now," Tessa said. "He can't outrun us." She narrowed her eyes. "So what's his plan?"

A deathly silence descended on the landscape. Isiah studied the narrow crack of sky ahead. Beyond, in the distance, the border sat as an orange-green smudge.

An explosion of wingbeats sounded to their right. Isiah's eyes widened as a shape fell over them with a piercing shriek. Enrik let out a battle cry as his eagle descended on them.

Isiah ducked and the eagle's beak snapped the air where his head had been. Tessa cried out as the bird's talons locked around her arms and she was wrenched from the dragon's back.

"Isiah!" she yelled.

The dragon roared in alarm and twisted around. Enrik's eagle was too slow this time. The dragon's jaws flashed through the air and clamped down on its wing. The bird screeched in pain, fighting to remain airborne. Enrik's expression melted as the dragon grabbed the eagle and sank its talons into the bird's flesh.

The eagle writhed beneath the dragon's grip. The damaged harness creaked in protest. As the two massive creatures wheeled through the air, the buckles snapped. The harness came loose and the jugs plummeted.

Tessa screamed. Isiah's blood ran cold as she slipped from the eagle's grip.

"No!" Isiah yelled. Adrenaline flooded his veins. Time seemed to slow. With every fibre in his body, Isiah wrenched his eyes away from the jugs and spurred the dragon toward Tessa.

The dragon went into a dive, its head lowered and wings folded flat against its body. It caught up to Tessa and grabbed her with its talons. The blood rushed to Isiah's head as it exited the dive and soared over the ravine. The jugs hit the bottom and shattered, spilling their contents. Enrik's eagle spiralled out of view, a trail of bloodied feathers floating behind it.

Isiah leaned over the dragon's flank. "Are you alright?" he called.

Tessa gripped the dragon's leg. She looked up at him with wide eyes. "Isiah," she gasped. "How—"

"I said I've got you," he replied. "I couldn't let you fall."

The dragon began to slow. Each breath came heavier than the last. Isiah guided the dragon toward a jutting ledge. It set Tessa down, then hit the ground and stumbled a few steps. As the last of its strength left it, Isiah climbed from its back and ran to Tessa's side.

"Isiah." Tessa stumbled over to him. Dust coated her clothes, and her cloak was ripped from the eagle's talons. "What happened to Enrik?"

"He crashed," Isiah replied. "I saw him go down." He studied her. "You're bleeding."

"It's fine," she said. Blood stained her shoulders from where the eagle had grabbed her. "I'll live." She hesitated. "The oasis water . . ."

Isiah swallowed. "I know." As the emotions from the fight began to wear off, a hollowness replaced it. He felt like he was about to pass out.

Isiah studied the ravine. Enrik and his eagle had dropped out of sight somewhere far below.

"What now?" Tessa asked.

Isiah's gaze drifted to the horizon. The border of the Badlands seemed to beckon him, orange mesas giving way to grassy plains. A voice urged him to keep flying toward it.

"We'll let the dragon catch its breath." He paused. "And catch our own, too."

Tessa wiped the dust from her face. A few strands of sweat-soaked hair clung to her forehead. "Then what?"

Isiah took one last look at the border, then faced back the way they had come.

"Then we go find Lazaro."

Aftermath

THE DRAGON REACHED THE MESA ABOVE THE lakebed and went to land. It hit the ground and lowered its body so Isiah could climb off. A few scratches, covered in dried blood, marked its side, but the creature seemed unharmed.

"Where did you leave Lazaro?" Tessa asked. "He'll be looking for me."

Isiah raised a hand to his forehead. A few dark shapes were closing in. As they drew closer, Isiah made out the figure in the lead.

"Isiah!" a voice yelled. Isiah craned his neck to the sky as a group of eagles approached. They fanned out and circled the dragon. Lazaro brandished his sabre, his face twisted in a snarl.

Tessa ran forward and raised her arms. "Stop!"

The eagles descended. Lazaro jumped off the second his bird touched the ground and stormed over. "What did you think you were doing?" he snapped. "That dragon could have killed us all!"

Isiah raised his hands to shield himself. The fight with Enrik had robbed his muscles of the last of their strength. Lazaro seemed to tower over him. His face shone an angry red, and a vein bulged in his neck.

"How dare you get in my way," he spat. "I told you I had a plan! I don't know what stupid idea was going through your head—"

Tessa stepped between them. "Enough!"

Lazaro faltered. "What did Enrik do to you, Tess? Are you hurt? I swear if Isiah let you—"

"He saved me." She puffed herself up. "He killed Enrik, too." Her voice took on a softer tone. "He chose me over the cure."

Lazaro scowled. "There *is* no cure for being Marked."

"There was," Tessa said quietly.

The other Raiders gathered around. Darla eyed the dragon warily. She wrapped Tessa in a hug. "I'm glad you're safe, Tessa."

Lazaro looked between Tessa and Isiah, fumbling for the words. He threw up his hands. "Fine. If you trust him more than your own brother, I'll leave you to it." He stomped off. Helen and Antony went after him.

Isiah plonked himself on a boulder and looked across the Badlands. His breath escaped him in a rush. A minute later, Tessa joined him. They sat together in silence.

"Thanks for saving me," Tessa said at last.

Isiah shrugged. "You would have done the same for me, right?"

Tessa glanced at the other Raiders. "I would." She paused. "I'm sorry about what happened to the oasis."

Isiah dropped his gaze to his lap. The weight of losing the water began to sink in. He imagined it seeping into the soil, gone forever.

"You won't find a cure now, will you?" Tessa asked.

He shook his head. "It was my only hope."

The dragon hissed and shook its neck. The eagles eyed it warily. Isiah met the beast's gaze. "But maybe Ward was wrong."

"What, about your people?" she said. "You can't go back to them, can you?"

"No." Isiah sighed. "The nobles will never accept me."

Tessa shifted closer. "Well, maybe you don't need to go back."

Far below, a line of merchants wandered through the Badlands, pack animals in their wake. The twin suns blazed above, warming Isiah's skin. He raised a hand and touched his Mark. "I've got nowhere else to go now."

"You can stay with me," Tessa replied.

"But the Raiders—"

"I'll figure something out," she said quickly. "Or we'll leave Alcabaza." She glanced away. "Raiders are supposed to look after one another, remember?"

"Yeah." Isiah smiled. "I guess we are."

His face fell as Lazaro marched into view.

"Isiah." The man came to stop in front of them. The other Raiders flanked him. Isiah tensed, waiting for another fight. "Thanks for keeping Tessa safe," Lazaro said.

Isiah faltered. "What?"

"You heard me," he replied. "You brought her back in one piece. Thank you for that."

Isiah shifted his weight. He searched for something to say.

"The others and I were talking." Lazaro cleared his throat. "They want to take you back as a Scavenger. You've shown yourself as more than capable."

"I will," Isiah said before the man had a chance to change his mind. "But I'm still Marked."

"Maybe I acted too hastily," Lazaro admitted, "when I threw you out, an' all." He looked at the others. Antony nodded at him. "I'm sorry I treated you the way I did."

Isiah stood. He tentatively shook the man's hand. "And I'm sorry about what happened to your house."

"Tess is safe," Lazaro said. "That's all that matters to me. I guess I can trust you now to help look out for her."

Tessa folded her arms. "I don't need looking after, you know."

Lazaro smiled and clapped her on the shoulder. "There's my sister."

Tessa sidled up to Isiah. "But maybe I do need you guys sometimes."

Lazaro straightened up and raised a hand to his forehead. Isiah followed his gaze. A figure hobbled across the mesa.

"It's Aron!" Tessa cried.

As the figure came closer, Isiah made out Aron's features. They both broke away from Lazaro and sprinted over.

"Are you alright?" Isiah asked when they reached him.

"It still hurts a bit," Aron replied, still holding his side. "But I'm not dead."

"How did you get out?" Tessa asked.

"I climbed," he replied. "Up the trail. I hoped I'd find someone out here." He cocked his head. "What happened to Enrik?"

Isiah hurriedly told him the story of their fight—and Tessa's fall in the ravine.

"So he's dead?" Aron asked. "There goes my job." He laughed, then grimaced. "What are you planning on doing now?"

"I don't know," Tessa admitted. "The Raiders in Alcabaza still think we broke the Oath. Our house is ruined."

"I can tell them what happened," Aron said. "I'll let them know the truth."

"Will it really work?" Isiah asked. "What if they don't listen to you?"

"I'm friends with all the Scavengers," he replied. "They trust me. I'll get the word out about what Enrik was doing in that lakebed, and his plan for the oasis. It will clear your name, I promise."

Isiah and Tessa helped Aron hobble to Lazaro and the others, where he told the Raiders his plan.

Lazaro scratched his short-cropped hair. "It might just work," he said. "But what about Isiah's Mark? The Raiders know the truth."

"None of the others have seen Isiah," Aron replied. "After that dragon broke out, what's to say Lazaro's Marked Scavenger didn't high-tail it back to Paradon, never to be seen again?" He nudged Isiah. "As long as you keep your head down, they'll be none the wiser."

"Some of Enrik's Raiders escaped," Isiah replied. "What if they come back?"

"And risk being killed for breaking the Oath?" Aron said. "None of the others take too kindly to those who work with Paradon. Anyone associated with Enrik will skip town if they have any sense." His face fell. "I'm sorry about your cure."

Isiah took Tessa's hand, and she smiled at him. "Don't be," he said. "It's okay."

The dragon perched on the edge of the mesa, watching the land below like a guard standing to attention. A thin wisp of smoke curled from its closed jaws.

"What are you gonna do about that?" Aron asked. "Not even *I* can convince the Raiders to let a dragon live with you."

Isiah mulled it over. "I think I have a plan."

Epilogue

THE DRAGON SOARED ACROSS THE BADLANDS, its iridescent scales reflecting the bright sunlight. Isiah clung to its back, his cloak rippling behind him. Tessa's arms were wrapped around his middle, and her hair blew in the breeze. Further away, Lazaro flew on his eagle, ready to carry them back to Alcabaza.

The Badlands rushed past below, a jumble of dusty rock and painted cliffs. With a flick of its tail, the dragon adjusted its course, steering them towards a cluster of tall buttes and spires.

"This is the place," Isiah said. He had to shout over the wind. The dragon's wingbeats swirled in his ears, deep and rhythmic. The scar over its neck had begun to heal, and its eyes shone with renewed vigour.

A cave materialized ahead. The dragon glided into the shadow of the spires and landed, making loose stones clatter to the ground far below. Isiah swung a leg off and dismounted.

Tessa brushed her hands together and looked around. "This is where we found it."

"Her," Isiah corrected her.

Tessa raised an eyebrow.

"Ward told me," Isiah replied. "In the arena." He walked to the ledge. Far below, a dusty trail snaked past a shallow pool—the same one he'd found after first entering the Badlands. "She should be safe here," he explained. "The spires will protect her, and we're close to the border where the Royal Guards fly."

Tessa's nose crinkled. "Tell me about it."

The dragon slithered into the cave. Its nostrils flared as it sniffed, taking in the environment.

"There's water nearby," Isiah continued, "and she can hunt on the border for animals and stuff."

Lazaro landed on a spire nearby. He squinted against the sunlight. "Few Raiders pass here," he called. "Your dragon should be able to slip by unnoticed . . . provided it doesn't start harassing us."

"She won't," Isiah said. "She was wild before—but we've bonded."

"And I can fly you here with Vyrro," Tessa added. She stroked the dragon's flank. "I'm starting to warm to them."

Isiah smiled. "I guess we're not so bad, huh?"

"Don't push your luck," Tessa teased. After a second, she grew more serious. "What are you going to name her?"

"Huh," he said, "I hadn't thought about that."

"How about Aegon?" she suggested.

Isiah raised an eyebrow. "How did you come up with that?"

Tessa looked at her feet. "It was the name of my mother's eagle."

"Aegon," Isiah repeated. He nodded to himself. "I like the sound of that."

He turned to the dragon. She watched him with a knowing gaze. "And I think she likes it too."

Tessa slipped her hand around Isiah's. "Come on. Let's take Vyrro back to the city."

Isiah lingered for a moment. His gaze flitted in the direction of Paradon, then he turned away.

"Alcabaza it is."

Get a Free Book!

He dreamed of killing a dragon. Now he has to save one.

A single dragon pelt could buy Cole a life outside the slums—but when he joins a band of outlaws to seek his fortune, the hunt doesn't go the way he thought.

Because dragons aren't the monsters he believed... and the moment he refuses to kill it, he becomes the prey.

Stuck with a wounded dragon and with rival hunters closing in, Cole has one chance at survival:

Keep it alive long enough to escape the wilds.

Grab your copy now at: www.morganclasperauthor.com

Acknowledgements

I hope you enjoyed the first book in the *Chronicles of Alcabaza*. Writing this book was a blast, and I'm glad I had the opportunity to bring this world and its characters to life. I hope you enjoyed reading about Isiah's adventures, and I also whole-heartedly hope that you'll stick around to discover what happens next.

There are many people I'd like to thank for bringing this book to life. I'd like to thank my long-time editor Darcy Werkman for this thoughtful insights and feedback. His input really helped this story shine, and he brought my view to life in ways I couldn't have done on my own.

I'd also like to extend my thanks to my cover designer Fabrice Bertolotto for his incredible work on the cover. His artwork never fails to bring each book I write to life. I'd also like to thank my illustrator Marina Baskakova for her beautiful ink illustrations. Writing a book always brings you into contact with such talented people, and this is no exception.

I owe my parents a great deal for their tireless support, as well as my Nanny and Grandad for their encouragement and commitment to reading everything that I write! I'd also like to bring attention to HEMA and the historical martial arts community, who first infused me with a deep appreciation for sabres and the art of historical combat.

And of course, I'd like to thank you, the reader, for picking up this book in the first place. I hope to see you again soon.

- Morgan

About the Author

Morgan Lee Clasper is a fantasy author and freelance copywriter who has over seven years of experience in the publishing industry. As a copywriter, he's worked with New York Times, Wall Street Journal, and USA Today bestselling authors to craft beautiful book blurbs, engaging author bios, and eye-catching sales copy.

Morgan is the author of the YA fantasy series The Frostwing Quadrilogy and the Chronicles of Alcabaza. When not writing, he enjoys studying philosophy, existential psychology, and Christian and Orthodox theology. For more information (and a free book!) visit: www.morganclasperauthor.com